Wood's Reach

A Mac Travis Adventure

Steven Becker

* * *

Join my mailing list

and get a free copy of Wood's Ledge

http://mactravisbooks.com

Chapter 1

The scream of line pouring off the reel startled Mac awake. Swinging his feet down from the console, he jumped from the seat at the helm of the twenty-foot center-console, stumbling before he found his feet. The fish on the line was a surprise. He had hoped to get off the island and rest for a while before resuming his work. It was just in his nature to throw a bait out when he was on the water, so before getting comfortable, he had put a small lobster head on a lightweight trolling rig.

Line continued to disappear and he saw an indistinct shape jump on the horizon, its splash confirming it was a large fish. Wide awake now, he gently lifted the rod from the holder mounted on the gunwale and took a deep breath. With the rod tip high, he slowly tightened the drag. His calmness hid the adrenaline that was rushing through him, his years of experience warning him this was a critical time in the fight. With a large fish, it was all about the relationship between the hook and the fish's mouth. Tighten the drag too much and the hook would pull; too loose and the contact would break.

With the first run over, Mac tried to guess what was on the other end of the line. It was behaving oddly for a backcountry fish. Aside from the tarpon, which were seldom found in open water, the jumpers were typically on the Atlantic side, past the reef in the deep waters of the Gulf Stream, but that didn't preclude big fish from the Gulf side. Taking his first turn of the reel to get a sense of the drag, he was rewarded by a few inches of line coming in. But the fish must have sensed the pressure and taken off again. Not expecting anything this large, he wasn't equipped for the battle, and the small reel was running low. He had to consider his options. The sportsman in him wouldn't allow him to cut the line, and the conservationist was not willing to allow hundreds of yards of monofilament to be lost to the sea.

It was either tighten the drag and fight, which would increase the risk of losing it, or pull the anchor and run towards it. He looked around, observing the shallows surrounding him, and decided he had to fight. The center-console had three feet of draft. Adequate for most areas, but the backcountry of the Keys was famous for its flats and shoals, many covered by only inches of water. Being pulled onto the mudflats was not appealing, especially as it was high tide and would only get worse as the waters receded.

With the rod braced just below his groin and his left hand on the reinforcement above the reel, he gently tightened the star-shaped wheel that controlled the drag. The fish pulled again, but after two long runs, Mac sensed it was running out of gas. Gently he turned the wheel until he could feel the tension increase, and in one motion he brought the rod tip high in the air and pulled the fish toward him. Quickly dropping the tip, he reeled as fast as he could. He repeated the process until a long grey shadow appeared in the water.

His heart dropped when he saw the distinct shape of the shark. It looked to be over six feet and probably weighed two hundred pounds. Without a large freezer, though, the meat would spoil, and the only way to make the tough bull shark meat palatable was with a deep fryer—neither of which he had. Still cautious of his adversary, he continued to reel the exhausted fish to the transom, and when the swivel attaching the leader to the line hit the rod tip, he reached into his pocket, removed a knife, and cut the line. The hook would rust out of the fish's mouth, and losing the short piece of heavy leader material was better than risking his hand to the shark. Mac stood there and watched the shark swim away before he motored back to the island.

Rising several feet from the high tide line, the half-acre island was mostly scrub and mangroves, similar to many of the surrounding keys, but if you looked carefully, you could see evidence of man's presence—both the good and bad. Wood, Mac's mentor, had originally built a small house and workshop on the island in the early '90s after accepting the property from the Navy in exchange for some off-the-books work. He had retired and lived here for almost twenty years before getting killed in the process of saving a presidential candidate and maybe the country. Mac still felt guilty about getting him mixed up in that affair.

It was now on him to rebuild the house after it had been virtually destroyed by a fire set by a rogue CIA agent out for vengeance. The only thing that had saved it was the two five-hundred-gallon water tanks on its roof. He had spent the last few months rebuilding and repairing the structure, both to rid himself of the guilt that it was his fault, and to try and lure Wood's daughter, Mel, back to the Keys. He shook his head as the blowback from his bad decisions and adventures replayed in his mind.

Trying to shake off the melancholy, he went forward to pull the anchor but found it bound in the sandy bottom. Back at the helm, he started the single 250-hp engine and bumped the boat forward enough to take the slack out of the anchor line. He ran to the helm before the current could reverse the momentum and pulled the slack from the rode. Finally, after a tug-of-war, the hook released and he was able to haul it in. Before bringing the anchor aboard, he dunked it several times in the water to free the sand and mud before hauling it on board and lashing it down.

He motored slowly toward the island, less than a half mile from the deep cut where he had anchored, thinking about the next phase in the project as he drove. A heron reminded him of the shallow rock that stood sentinel to the channel that Wood had dredged years ago, and he cut the wheel hard to starboard, rounding the rock and coasting to a stop before reaching the beach. Tossing the line over the lone pile, one of the only visible signs of life here, he tied the boat off and hopped into the knee-deep water. Wood had devised an ingenious system of hiding his boats, using skids buried in the sand and a winch hidden in a clearing concealed by brush. He would open a handwoven mangrove gate that was also virtually invisible and crank his old skiff into the clearing. Once the gate was returned, it would take a very good eye to discover his ruse.

Mac had no need or desire to go through the trouble and simply left the boat tied off. He entered the clearing through the open gate, now lying on its side in need of repair, adding that to the list of things that needed attention. Following the well-worn path, he entered another clearing, this one much larger, which held the house and workshop.

The land around the house was barren now. The palms that had shaded the two-story home and the brush that had grown around it were all now charred stumps. Wood, an engineer who had built or retrofitted many of the bridges connecting the Keys, had built the house to survive the devastating hurricanes that plowed through the chain of islands. The concrete piers, which had already survived several surges brought by the storms, were unharmed by the fire, though smoke damaged. The structure resting on them was a different matter. The roof, covered in galvanized metal sheets, was largely intact, but all that was left of the structure underneath were the heavy posts and beams. The exterior walls, whose windows were once covered by lovingly handmade Bahamas shutters, were gone. It stood open to the weather, not a good thing in this climate.

The sun was four fingers from the horizon, and Mac looked around to see what he could accomplish in the hour of remaining light. Climbing the ladder, he reached the main floor and resumed gutting the interior. Sitting on an upside-down bucket with a stack of wood studs in front, he started to pull nails from the old wood. Anything he could do to reuse the material was well worth his time, the alternative being to haul the debris and dump it at the landfill in Marathon. He would then have to buy and transport the new supplies back to the island. A few hours pulling nails would save considerably more than the cost of the wood.

He was halfway through the pile when the sound of an outboard distracted him. The high whine of the motor told him it was either a local running full speed back from a favorite flat or a tourist gambling on his chart plotter to guide him through the maze of keys and shoals the area was famous for. Hoping it was the former and he wouldn't have to pull an arrogant tourist off a flat, he climbed the ladder to the roof.

The stairs leading to a small widow's walk were gone, but the platform that had held the two water tanks that had saved what was left of the house still remained. The heat from the fire had melted the black plastic tanks, dumping a thousand gallons of water on the building and saving what remained of it. He stood there, shielding his eyes from the setting sun, and quickly located the boat. From the course it was taking and the profile of the boat, he guessed it was a tourist rather than a local in some kind of trouble, something far from a rarity here. The Keys, especially the backcountry between Big Pine and Key West, were famous hiding spots for pirates and smugglers. It was far too often that a local fisherman, faced with hard times and with no other way to save his boat, was forced to run contraband. He started the internal argument he always lost if they should ground. He climbed down to get the towline ready for the inevitable.

It was a tourist for sure, he thought now. He could see the deep V of the hull and the rooster tails of the twin outboards flaring behind it as it cruised close to the shallow water to the east of Harbor Channel. It was running close to full speed, its trail evident in the disturbed sand kicked up in its wake. The other boat was about a quarter mile back, and even from this distance Mac knew it wouldn't catch its prey. The low lines of the flats boat were just breaking the plane of the water when it cut across the flat and headed on a course to intercept the larger boat. Drafting less than a foot, the flats boat screamed by close enough for Mac to see the driver. That was when he heard the first gunshot.

Jesse McDermitt was as close to a neighbor as one got out here. The retired Marine lived several miles away on another small island in the Content Keys. Mac wasted no time in descending the ladder and running to the center-console. He knew Jesse would be there for him, and if Jesse was after someone, Mac would be there to offer whatever help he could. Shots were fired from the lead boat, but the motion of the boat threw off the shooter's aim, and he could see them splash into the calm water a hundred yards short of the flats boat. Racing to his boat, he jumped aboard, released the single line, went to the helm, and started the engine. With a quick look back at the two boats, he backed out of the narrow cut and pushed down the throttle.

What he needed was a way to contact Jesse and coordinate their efforts. Cell phone reception was sketchy at best this far from land. The only means of communication was the VHF radio. He turned on the unit and unclipped the mic, but hesitated before calling. The standard hailing frequency was channel 16, but that was monitored by the Coast Guard and local law enforcement. There were rumors that Jesse had some government ties, but the relationship wasn't clear and he didn't want to step on his toes.

Instead he put the mic down and steered to the east, away from the flats. He had a plan now and could only hope Jesse would figure out what he was doing.

Chapter 2

Mac exited the narrow dredged cut from the small key and entered Harbor Channel. Both boats were running northwest toward Marathon, and Mac quickly cut across the channel and entered Cutoe Banks, a dangerous and unmarked area between Harbor Channel and Spanish Key. The high tide had brought several feet of water with it, but the extra depth, although allowing more area for the lead boat to cross, also concealed the shoals, some hidden by less than six inches of water.

Skirting the submerged hazards, Mac steered to the outside of the banks, allowing the escaping boat the deeper water of the channel, and with Jesse running the flats on the inside, they worked together to corral their prey. Both men knew these waters like the backs of their hands, and the boats slowly converged, forcing their prey into the shallows between Cutoe Key and the banks.

The sound of the escaping outboards changed—a high whine drifting back to him on the wind. Mac was watching intently, but he could have closed his eyes and known the other boat had grounded. Dropping speed, he waited for Jesse to make the first move, figuring he would know the adversary they faced. Mac pulled to the edge of the flat and saw the two men on the grounded boat, wondering if they were locals and he should intervene. After a quick look, neither man registered in his database, and the man behind the wheel would be hard to forget. It looked like his round head was stuck on his body without a neck, and Mac filed him away as Ironhead. The other man was smaller and looked more like a lawyer.

Ironhead drew a pistol and pointed it at him. Slamming the throttles in reverse, Mac spun the wheel and sped out of range. Once he felt secure, he ducked behind the console and watched. Bullets splashed the water a hundred yards short and then their aim changed. After realizing they were not shooting at him, he remained where he was and chanced a look. Jesse was returning fire, but the shots were wide. Jesse was a retired Marine sniper, so Mac knew he was firing to pin them down, not to hit them. Both weapons were at the limits of their range, and with the light chop on the water, their aim would be thrown off, but Mac knew Jesse, and if he wanted them dead, they would be facedown on the deck.

Another sound caused him to look up, and he saw an unmarked helicopter speeding toward them. It approached and circled, dropping altitude as it evaluated the threat. Mac could see Jesse on his radio and assumed he was talking to the pilot. The helicopter continued to circle but remained high enough to avoid the gunshots fired from below. Soon the sound of another boat came from the northwest. The sheriff's boat approached, expertly avoiding the shallows as it coasted to a stop at the edge of the deep water and hailed the stranded boat.

"Drop your weapons and prepare to be boarded," a man's voice boomed loudly from the exterior speakers.

Mac turned to the boat and saw the two men drop their weapons overboard. Carefully he marked the spot in his mind to try and retrieve them later. No point letting them sit there for a lobster diver to wander across. The men had their hands over their heads, and the helicopter dropped altitude to cover the approach of the sheriff's boat. Mac was caught off guard by the blast from an approaching helicopter, and he looked in Jesse's direction. The flats boat had turned and was angling away from the action. Following his lead, Mac pulled the throttle back and followed

Jesse into Harbor Channel.

The two boats bobbed side by side, both men quiet, neither the type who needed to talk everything through. They watched the men climb off the stranded boat under the drawn guns of the deputies. They waded to the sheriff's boat, climbed aboard, and were handcuffed to a railing. With the prisoners secured, the boat took off in the direction of the mainland. The helicopter turned back and suddenly the scene was silent. The only sound now was the idling of Jesse and Mac's well-tuned engines, and the waves slapping gently against the hulls as the two men worked with the current to keep their boats in the channel.

"Beer?" Mac asked.

"Sure. I can swing by your place. Want to see what you're up to," Jesse responded.

Mac led the flats boat up Harbor Channel and into the cut leading to the single piling where he tied off. Jesse utilized the Maverick's shallower draft and edged almost to the beach, where he raised the engine and dropped the power pole. Mac waded in and the two men clapped each other on the back.

"Good to see you, man," Mac said and led Jesse to the main clearing.

"You too. Thanks for the help there," Jesse responded.

Mac knew he had it handled without him, but let it go. They walked to the clearing, and he went to a small propane refrigerator, where he pulled out two bottles of beer, shook off the moisture and handed one to Jesse. "Can I ask what those guys did?"

Jesse took a sip and tipped the bottle to Mac. "You know how it is," he said. Mac understood and the two men drank together in silence. It was an interesting friendship, both men naturally reclusive and quiet, but having developed a respect for each other over the years.

Jesse broke the silence. "You've got quite the project going here. I didn't know the damage was this bad."

"It's just work," Mac said and drank again. "Something to do so I don't have to think about business and Mel. If you think this is bad, you ought to see my old house."

Jesse left it alone and finished his beer. "What's that buddy of yours, Tru, up to? Isn't it about time he stirred up another hornet's nest?"

Mac shook his head solemnly. "You have no idea. Last I heard, he was in Key West working a parasailing gig."

They both laughed at the thought, finished their beers, and walked back to the beach together. Mac stood there as Jesse backed out of the cut, watching him enter the channel, then cut the wheel to starboard and speed away. When the white running light from the flats boat faded into the distance, Mac picked his way back to the clearing, fighting the mosquitos as he went.

He pulled a large lobster tail and a beer from the refrigerator by the shed and went to the grill. Using a match, he lit the burner, the ignitor long lost to the salt and moisture in the air. Solar electric and propane were his energy sources, but the photovoltaic panels had been damaged in the fire, leaving him with only gas appliances. For the time being, the only electrical power came from a small generator used to operate the tools he needed to rebuild the house. Rain barrels were the water department, and along with the refrigerator, the water heater and grill comprised his utilities. When completed, the house would use the roof for both solar panels and water collection, greatly increasing the capacity of the island.

While the grill heated, he grabbed another beer and moved into the shed to avoid the mosquitos. The small room was overloaded but organized. On the right was a sheet of plywood where the solar equipment would be mounted. Against the back wall, gear and tools were piled on steel shelves. The left-hand side had a workbench with shelves overhead for more tools and hardware. The space was cluttered, but somehow it reassured him. He lit a kerosene lamp and sat on a barstool pulled up to the bench. Once the light had evened out, he pulled out a manila envelope, opened it, and took another sip of beer, steeling himself for the latest bad news.

His livelihood, a converted forty-five-foot lobster boat, had been confiscated when Trufante, his wayward friend and deckhand, had been talked into a quick score. He had finally gotten it back, but the feds had not taken care of it while it was in their care, and one of the twin diesels had seized. Removing the invoice from the envelope, he placed it on the counter, deciding another beer was in order before he got the bad news. After putting the lobster on the grill and grabbing a fresh bottle, he sat down and reviewed the carefully itemized bill.

Not as bad as he'd thought, but it was considerably more than his meager cash on hand. He might have gotten his boat back from the feds, but his commercial fishing license was still suspended after Trufante's illegal plundering of the lobster casitas. Mac had earned a good deal of money working with Wood and salvaging when he could, but the cost of rebuilding the house on the island and his boat at the same time was beyond his means. Now without the fishing income, he was living on his small nest egg. He thought back to the lost stash of gold he had cached on the reef, again realizing how foolish he had been to trust his treasure to the sea. One stray anchor had dispersed the contents over the seafloor—probably never to be found again.

He reached up for the thumb drive on the shelf and turned it in his hand. The images on the drive contained what he thought were the clues to a mystery—one that might have a large payday attached to it. Over the years he had tried to figure out the mysterious tattoos, suspecting they led to a treasure, but had hit a dead end. He'd never had the right eyes to analyze the images, and the mystery had remained unsolved.

The smell of the lobster cooking brought him back to reality, and he went outside to check the grill. The tail was ready. Taking it from the grate, he sat down and ate in silence, his thoughts drifting to his other enigma—Mel.

* * *

"You freakin' morons," Hawk berated the two men sitting in the Mercedes with him. "How the...?" He stopped short, knowing his breath was wasted on the men, one a thug hired for his muscle, the other a disbarred lawyer employed for his brains. He stared at them, then turned away and started the car. Pulling out of the sheriff's station, he turned onto US-1 and headed north. After a silent mile, he turned right into a driveway. "We'll talk on the boat." It had taken a long call to the sheriff filled with promises of future favors to persuade him to drop the weapons charges. That was the easy part. It was ICE and the antiquities trafficking charges that worried him—the federal agency was known to act quickly.

He parked under the house, built ten feet above the ground, and walked down the gravel path to the boat, unable to take his eyes off the red labels stuck to the doors. His house had been confiscated within hours of the men's arrest and the discovery of the antiquities they were carrying. Fortunately, the sixty-five-foot steel-hulled trawler he had just boarded was held in a shell corporation and shielded from the authorities. He would have to move it tonight, probably to his ex's house—the end to a wonderful day.

The men sat across from him in the salon. "Who leaked the information?" he asked.

"I don't know, but that dude out there got wind of it somehow and was all over us. We made the transfer like you said, but they were on us in seconds. All we could do was run," the lawyer said.

"Run right into the sheriff is where you ran. Now you cost me twenty grand cash to bail your asses out."

"We'll take care of it," the muscle-bound man with no neck said. "I want a piece of that guy."

Hawk rubbed the little hair on his balding head. "Let it go. We've got bigger fish to fry."

Chapter 3

"We gotta talk," the man said as he walked up to Trufante.

The lanky Cajun continued to hose off the parasail boat, ignoring the request. The man went to the spigot and turned off the water. "Now."

Trufante turned to face him.

"You can't be doing that."

"Doing what?" Trufante asked.

Both men wore khaki shorts and matching polo shirts with the name of a water sports rental company embroidered on the front. Trufante, however, looked ragged and, aside from wearing the clothes, was breaking most of the dress code rules.

"Come on, dude," the other man said. "It's one thing to be helping the girls into the harness, another to be feeling them up. You got to keep your hands to yourself."

"Shoot. Ladies love me," Trufante said, his Cajun accent getting deeper as he went on the defensive.

"Well, that was the last complaint. One of these women is going to sue us."

"Y'all got insurance for that, don't you?" Trufante asked.

"I gotta let you go, man. You're a blast to work with, but this is going to end badly," the man said and turned away.

Trufante dropped the hose and kicked the transom of the boat. Losing the job was not the end of the world. It was temporary and wasn't really his thing, though the contact with the women tourists was kind of nice. All told, though, he'd rather be fishing, but it had been a dismal lobster season and the dolphin hadn't started to run yet. Most years, stone crabs bridged the gaps between seasons, but they had been down as well, forcing him to seek another line of work, at least until something better came up. Mac kept saying he'd get his commercial license back before too long, but he spent all his time rebuilding Wood's place. With no options in Marathon, Trufante hopped on his bike and relocated sixty miles to Key West to take advantage of the influx of spring break tourists.

He looked down the dock, trying to see if Shelly was still in the office. Might as well get his last paycheck and blow this town, he thought. Without a reason to stay, he figured he'd head back to Marathon and try to talk Mac into doing something that made some money. He walked toward the office and tried the knob, but the door was locked. He banged a few times, then shielded his face and peered in. There was no one there. Moving into the shade, he reached into his pocket and pulled out the tip money he had earned today. He counted out fifty dollars in wadded-up fives—not bad for not doing much, but nowhere like the cash he and Mac used to make.

Walking over to Front Street, he decided to take a detour to Mallory Square and watch the tourists gape at the sideshows and the sunset. After that, maybe go to the Turtle and have a few beers. His bike was parked at a friend's apartment on the other side of Duval Street, and he rationalized it was all on the way. The crowd thickened as he approached the square. With spring break came the families, an entirely different crowd than he was looking for, and he thought about shining it and just getting a beer when he saw her.

It was more a dance than a walk. Almost as tall as his six-foot frame, she looked lost, wandering in circles with a purple suitcase in tow. Her frizzy hair partially covered her face, allowing only a glimpse of a proud nose and full lips, then fell halfway down her back. Loose clothes concealed her body, but her shorts showed off legs that were long and lean. Wanting to see her eyes, he moved at an angle towards her and commenced the patented Trufante courtship dance. He liked what he saw.

She was still bopping her head, and he looked for the telltale earbuds, but her hair concealed her ears and there was no sign of a cord. She started to circle back like she was lost, and he decided to make his move.

"Y'all lookin' like you could use a little help, or maybe a tour guide?" he started, lighting up his thousand-dollar smile that was said to resemble the grille of a Cadillac.

She ignored him, still listening to whatever song was playing in her head. He followed her to Caroline Street, where she turned left. Closing the gap, he walked next to her. "If you're lost, I can help."

"Huh?" She looked at him. "Just wastin' away in Margaritaville," she sang softly, whispering the words.

He froze when he saw her deep green eyes. All he could do was stare.

"Cat got your tongue?" she asked.

He shook his head, trying to regain his composure. It wasn't often that a woman had this effect on him. "Shoot. I was only asking if you needed some help. You've been walking in a circle."

"Can't find my way home," she sang—the old Blind Faith tune.

"But are you wasted?" he asked, referencing the beginning of the line. She smiled and his knees almost gave out. "Where ya headed?"

"Damn boyfriend and I split up, and I think the jerk-off took the car. I've been walkin' these streets all afternoon." She stopped at the corner of Whitehead and looked both ways, as if the car would magically appear.

Trufante shook his head in sympathy. "Yeah, sometimes it's better to just have a beer and chill. Things seem to solve themselves."

She sat on the suitcase and put her head in her hands. "Name's Pamela," she said, looking up.

"Pajama Bama," he said and she laughed. "Come on. Old Tru will make it all better. Promise. I'll even buy," he offered, fingering the cash in his pocket.

"Money's not the problem. I'm just kind of bummed is all," she said.

Now this was his kind of woman. "Let's go, then. No strings. We can just hang out." He held his hand out for her.

It felt like a jolt of current had just gone through his body. She rose and looked him in the eye. There weren't many women who could eyeball him, and he found himself staring at her—he was hooked.

"Well?" She shook her head, trying to break the spell.

"Yeah, I got that too." He took the handle of the bag and started toward Duval. "Turtle's right up here. Local's kind of place." He led the way across Duval, dodging the tourists and vendors. Scooters, bikes, rickshaws, car and foot traffic all blended together into a mass of partiers heading toward the bars now that the sun had set and the Mallory Square show was over for another night. Taking her hand, he led her past the main drag and onto a quiet side street.

His eyes opened, alerted by the sun streaming through the flimsy curtains. Like every morning for the previous week, he turned his head and saw her there next to him. Somewhere he knew this was too good to be true, like every other windfall in his life had been starting back in Louisiana. In the decade before Katrina had hit, he had lucked into the Army Corps of Engineers concrete contracts to reinforce the jetties. It was all good until it wasn't, and it had all gone to hell after the storm, and his work failed. With only an old fishing boat to his name, he had port-hopped along the Gulf coast, picking up whatever work he could before finally landing in Marathon.

She stirred, rolled over, and smiled at him. "Just another day in paradise," he said and kissed her.

"Right on. How 'bout a cheeseburger, then?" she said, using her unique dialect of song lyrics.

He grabbed her butt and leaned in to kiss her again, but she rebuffed him. Not the first time, but he hoped paradise wasn't wearing thin. "Shoot. I'm all about breakfast. Let's go get some grub."

They dressed and walked down the exterior stairs of his second-floor apartment. His bike fired up and they both hopped on. Loving the freedom of Florida's no-helmet law, Trufante turned onto US-1 and headed south. He pulled into a breakfast-and-lunch place a few miles down the road. If there was any tension or doubts on his part, it was always about this time of the day, when it was time to decide what to do until you could justify the first beer and things got easier. They had already done a lot of the tourist stuff: kayaking, fishing from the bridges, and hanging out on Sombrero Beach. He'd even let her talk him into renting Jet Skis for an afternoon. He'd had a blast, but was constantly looking out of the corner of his eye to make sure that Mac or one of his other buddies didn't see him on what they regarded as the curse of the Keys.

While she sipped her coffee, he looked around and grabbed a *Keynoter* newspaper off an adjacent table. Always curious about the local gossip, he opened the paper and started reading.

"Hey. We ought to check that out," she said.

He put down the paper. "What?"

She grabbed the paper from him and pointed at the headline. *Confiscated Goods Auction Today*. "Maybe we can score a better living arrangement."

"You're not liking the Hotel Trufante?"

She reached for his hand. "No offense, babe, but I'm used to something a bit more upscale."

He looked into her eyes, wondering again where she came from. She had spoken little of her past or her circumstances, but the word "job" had never been mentioned, nor had her credit card been refused. *Whatever*, he thought. *If this is a ride, it's a good one. Might as well see how it ends.* "So, you'd buy something?"

"I've heard they sell really cool stuff for pennies on the dollar at those things," she said.

The stump of his finger started itching at the mention of confiscated goods which, down here, usually meant drug dealers; he'd lost the rest of the digit in a grinder at the expense of one. "You don't want to get messed up in that," he cautioned.

"No harm in looking." She read the article. "Starts at eleven. Just enough time to finish breakfast and head over."

With an awkward silence between them, the first of their budding relationship, they finished breakfast, she paid, and they left the restaurant. They rode south to the Marriott, where he turned in and parked the bike under the canopy. Looking at her, he thought she appeared different entering the hotel. This must be Pamela for real, he thought, not her alter ego, Pajama Bama, that he had spent the last week with.

They entered the ballroom, or the large room that sufficed for one in the small town of Marathon. Chairs were set up in rows with a center aisle leading to a podium. The setting reminded him of a church—another omen. At the entrance was a long rectangular table manned by a half dozen law enforcement officers.

"Why don't you look around? I'll register," she said and approached the table.

He didn't mind moving away from the uniforms and took himself on a tour of the room. Around the perimeter were cases of jewelry and watches, most too gaudy for anyone besides a rapper or dealer. Between the cases were easels with poster board displays of the larger objects: boats, cars, and houses. She joined him, and he felt like a married couple as they walked around the room together; he more interested in the boats, she in the houses.

"That's the one." She stood in front of a display.

"Shoot. Betcha that sucker is over a million," he said, peering sideways at the waterfront house.

"I've heard you can get them way below market at these auctions. That's the one I want," she said and fanned herself with the placard used for bidding. An announcement was made and the crowd went for their seats. "Come on, they're getting started."

He followed her to a pair of empty chairs near the front, far from the back row, where he would have felt comfortable. The bidding started, and he nodded off until an elbow jabbed him awake. Opening his eyes, he groaned inwardly as he saw her hand raised high above her head, waving the placard back and forth. He sat up and started paying attention as the bidding went back and forth. He was shocked at how low the numbers were, but they were slowly climbing. Eventually most of the bidders backed out, leaving only Pamela and a man in a suit. He was sweating, the suit too thick for the climate, and Trufante was surprised when he turned to the man next to him, obviously hired muscle. Trufante got a bad feeling when he turned to stare at them and pulled her hand down.

"This is some bad shit," he said in a whisper.

"Oh, come on. Have some fun." She smiled like a little girl and shot to her feet, raising the bid.

Defeated, the man sat down, but Trufante would remember his face and his look toward them as he conceded.

"Going once … going twice … sold," the auctioneer yelled and smashed the gavel down.

"Woo-hoo," she sighed. "My island in the sun."

She got up to leave, but Trufante pulled her down. "At least wait this out and blend in with the crowd on the way out. Those guys are creeping me out."

Chapter 4

Dawn was not quite ready to make an appearance when Mac woke. He'd spent plenty of nights sleeping outside, but mainly on boats. The clearing Wood's house was built in may have concealed the house, but it also provided a barrier to the sea breeze. With no air moving through it, mosquitoes invaded at dusk and the clearing was thick with dew in the mornings. He'd tried sleeping under a net but found that more annoying than the pests it was to supposed to protect him from. In contrast, Wood's house had been well thought out, positioned to catch the predominantly southeasterly breeze; the living quarters, rising ten feet above the ground, were comfortable and bug-free. Once he paid off the repairs for his boat, he intended to bring it out to Wood's island and live aboard, but for now, he was stuck on the ground.

He walked down the path to the beach and pulled an old kayak out of the brush. It was too dark to work, but the fishing was generally good at dawn. Gathering the paddle and two rods lying beside it, he pulled the boat into the water and maneuvered it between his legs, grimacing when his butt met the dewy seat. He settled into the small boat and paddled along the flats flanking Harbor Channel, watching the eastern sky for the first hint of daylight. Turning to the left at the end of the invisible bank, he coasted by a lone egret standing on one leg and watching the water intently, undisturbed by the small craft. With an easy cadence, he stayed in the center of an unmarked narrow slot that held seven feet of water running between foot-deep flats on each side. There were no markers here, the channel known only to locals, and not many of those. It was one of a thousand well-guarded spots in the maze of the backcountry, known only to a few locals and not appearing on any hot spot maps or charts. He coasted to a stop ten minutes later when he reached the end of the channel.

With deep water surrounding him, he used one blade of the paddle as a rudder, turning the kayak and allowing the incoming tide to grab the plastic hull. After a few adjustments, he was satisfied with the drift and deployed the two rods, one on each side of the kayak. With the butts set in their holders, he sat back, letting the current take the boat and dipping the paddle in the water whenever he needed a course correction. The first pass yielded nothing, and he reversed course and paddled back to his starting point. Starting to doubt himself, he checked the lines and started his second drift. The sun was just above the horizon now and he knew his window was shrinking. Years ago, when Wood had dredged the small channel to his island, he had dumped the rubble here, making the bottom a prime spot for snapper and grouper, but so far it had yielded nothing.

As the sky brightened, he finished the second drift and set up for the third and last pass, more concerned about his plans for the day than about catching anything now. The work on the house was rather mundane at this point—just demolition—and his mind kept drifting back to the repair bill for his boat. He really wanted to get it back, but piecing together the money to pay the bill would be a challenge. He thought of every option open to him, drawing blanks on most. The last was a man he would use only as a last resort. Hawk, often said to be a descendant of the original wreckers of Vaca Key, was notorious throughout the area for his larger-than-life personality as well as the treasure he pulled from the sea.

Mac had done enough salvage to know that the divers and captains got most of the glory, but it was the moneymen, often in the background, that enriched themselves. Before steamships, the predominant trade route of the treasure-laden wooden ships ran just offshore of here—between the Keys and the Bahama Bank. The square-rigged ships relied on the Gulf Stream's powerful current to propel themselves back to Europe, but they were hard to maneuver and often collided with the shallow reefs just offshore. This area still held more than its share of the gold, silver, and jewels that had been lost over the centuries as the treasures of the Americas was shipped to finance the wars of Europe. Hawk had a reputation for skirting the law and reaping the bounties from long-lost wrecks most didn't know existed, as well as having his competitors mysteriously disappear.

The thumb drive supposedly held the answer to a riddle that had plagued Mac for years, and he knew Hawk would pay for it. Mac and Wood had discovered a section of an old Mayan wreck while rebuilding the No Name Key Bridge twenty-odd years ago. Circumstances and a sibling feud between the remaining twin chiefs of an indigenous tribe had put the project on the back burner. The brother was dead, but the sister remained at large and still claimed the rights to the site. Salvage around any historic site was a bureaucratic nightmare, but without ties to the original inhabitants of the islands, it had been impossible to get a permit for the search. Hawk had offered many times to buy the information they had, but first Wood, and now Mac, refused to sell. Maybe it was time to consider it.

Without even a bite, he finished the drift, reeled in the lines and paddled back to the island, still wondering what to do. He reached the beach and pulled the kayak back to its resting place, but instead of leaving the two rods there, he carried them back to the clearing and set them against the shed to be rerigged. When you don't catch fish, you have to change things up. Before his next attempt, he would tie on fluorocarbon leaders and new lures.

Still unsure what to do about his boat and the thumb drive, he climbed the ladder and started taking his frustration out on the charred wood studs remaining at the back of the house. The heat came with the sun, and sweat poured off him as he worked. After tearing out the last wall, he stacked the studs and stared out at the open expanse of water. Flats boats were moving toward the bonefish and permit grounds. Several larger vessels were heading into the deeper waters of the Gulf, after the grouper and snapper that were more abundant there. He was about to turn away when one of the boats turned out of the channel and approached the island.

He waited until the boat committed, and immediately saw the Monroe County Sheriff's insignia on its side. A uniformed man was behind the wheel, but Mac didn't recognize him or the other man, who was dressed in khaki pants and a button-down shirt. He figured they just wanted a statement about the chase yesterday, but he was still uneasy. The law coming all the way out here probably wasn't good news. He climbed down the ladder and walked quickly to the clearing.

The deputy had done a good job navigating the narrow cut and had already tied a line to the aft cleat on Mac's center-console by the time he reached the beach.

"You Mac Travis?" the man next to him called out.

"That's me. What can I do for you?" He tried to stay calm and polite.

"Mind if we come ashore and talk to you?"

Mac couldn't see any harm, and with the deputy there, he didn't think it would do any good if he protested. "Fine by me, but you'll have to get your feet wet."

The man took a step to the gunwale and looked over the side into the calf-deep water. "This won't take long. We can just talk here."

Mac would have laughed except for the official nature of the visit. "I've got work to do. Mind if we get right to it?"

"Word's gotten out that you're doing some construction out here."

Mac wasn't sure where this was going. "Just some repairs is all."

"Sorry. I'm the building inspector for the county," he said and held out a laminated card with his picture. "You're going to need a permit to rebuild that house in there." He paused. "There are some zoning issues that have come up as well."

"I'm just fixing what was here," Mac said. He balled his fists and took a step closer.

"No need for that," the inspector said. "Just come into the office and file for a permit."

Mac looked at both men. He had not meant to show aggression, but his natural disdain for bureaucrats had gotten the better of him. "I'll do that," he said.

"You're going to have to stop work pending approval," the man said, holding out a clipboard. "And the payment of the fines."

Mac looked at him, his first reaction was to make the man get out of the boat and present him with the paperwork, but he thought better of it and waded toward the sheriff's boat.

"Sign here, that you received this notice." The man offered the clipboard to him.

Mac wasn't about to read it. He had known he was screwed the minute the boat had pulled into the cut; he just hadn't known how badly. After scrawling his name on the bottom of the page, he handed it back to the inspector, who tore off a copy and returned it to him. The deputy wasted no time. He went forward and released the line, started the engine, and backed out of the cut. Mac stood there, knee-deep in the water with the paper in his hand, watching as the boat turned and sped for Marathon.

Finally he waded back to the beach and walked back to the clearing. He considered having a beer but thought better of it. In the shade of an undamaged palm tree, he sat and looked blankly at the notice. After a few minutes, the words started forming; the first thing he noticed was the box checked at the bottom indicating triple permit fees for starting work without a permit.

His tossed the paper aside and stared at the house, knowing he somehow owed it to Wood and Mel to finish it. Between the cost of repairing his boat and now this, he regretted what he had to do. There was always the chance that, if he was able to walk into the building department with the money this afternoon, they would waive the triple fee. It was worth a shot, no matter how unlikely. If that failed, he would need to see Hawk—and soon.

Behind the newly rebuilt shed, he stood under the spigot mounted above his head. One of his only concessions to comfort was hot water, and he winced as the water ran cold before the small on-demand heater kicked in and warmed it. When the house was rebuilt, he would set new water tanks on the roof, their dark color providing enough solar heat even during cloudy periods for the water to hold in the eighties. The small propane heater would then kick in and boost that easily to the hundred degrees he now enjoyed. Finished with his shower, he picked through his pile of clothes, not really sure what was clean or dirty, before selecting cargo pants and a worn T-shirt. After dressing, he went into the shed, grabbed the thumb drive from the shelf, and stuffed it into his pocket.

The center-console cut effortlessly through the glassy water. What little wind there had been this morning had died now. He passed the flat where the boat had grounded yesterday, noticing it was gone, and thirty minutes later he rounded the marker and entered the small lagoon for the Thirty-Third Street boat ramp and the Marathon Yacht Club. Tying the boat to the pier, he grabbed the keys and started walking.

Chapter 5

Mac figured he should check with the building department first; he already knew where he could find Hawk later. From the boat ramp, he walked the quarter mile to US-1 and turned to the right. He stayed to the edge of the sidewalk, dodging several bicycles and jogging strollers in the few blocks before he reached the government offices. Standing in front of the door, he waited a few long minutes, clutching the rolled-up paper in his hand, desperately wanting to avoid facing what lay inside.

Finally, he braved the entrance and was assaulted by the chill of the government-issued and taxpayer-paid air-conditioning. Shivering, he proceeded to the counter marked *Building* and waited. Fortunately there was no line, or he probably would have walked out. An auburn-haired woman saw him and approached. Immediately he smiled at her, recognizing the familiar face.

"Hey, Sheryl," he said.

"Mac," she replied. "What can I help you with?"

He wondered about the coldness of her greeting. She had never been a close friend, but they had known each other from his days with Wood, when they had come here regularly to pull permits for their bridge contracts.

"Thought you had moved," he said.

"Well, things don't always work out," she replied.

Word had gone out that she had moved up to Tampa with

Will Service, a local fly-fishing guide. There were rumors floating around that Will had gotten mixed up with a local poaching ring, but that was all he knew. His lack of interest in the news kept him off the coconut telegraph. That might explain her attitude, he thought. He unrolled the paper and laid it out facing her.

She glanced at it. "Let me see what I can do for you," she said and left him standing alone.

His stomach churning, he watched her walk away. While he waited, a harried clerk came out to help a local couple who had come in just after him. He listened to their laundry list of complaints, sympathizing with them as they just shook their heads when every request they made was met with a no.

"Mac, why don't you come back here?" Sheryl said, opening the drop-down access built into the counter.

He entered the back area, almost laughing that the government had gone so far off the rails that they needed physical barriers between them and the people they were supposed to serve. Sheryl led him to a line of offices and knocked lightly on an open door. The man sitting behind the desk motioned them in and Mac reluctantly sat.

"Good luck, Mac," she said and walked out the door.

He wanted her to stay. There was something about her manner that reassured him things might not be as bad as he expected. "Can't you stay?"

"Got to go. You know where to find me if you want to catch up," she said and left.

Mac watched her until she rounded the corner. He turned to the man at the desk. "Well?" he asked impatiently. If they had bad news, he wanted it over quickly.

"Mr. Travis," he started.

This was not going well. "Just Mac is fine."

"Mr. Travis. We need to talk about the project you are working on."

Mac glared at him, waiting for him to continue.

"It seems there was no permit for the original structure, septic system, or cisterns."

Mac lowered his head. He had expected bad, but this was worse. "And...?"

"Back when Woodson built it"—he cleared his throat—"things were a little looser around here, but these days, to rebuild a structure that we don't acknowledge as existing is no easy matter—especially out there."

Mac knew where this was going. The federal and state governments had become stricter through the years about the backcountry—restricting access, creating marine sanctuaries, and limiting building. "It was his land."

"Well, that's the other thing. His daughter owns it now, through his estate. If you want to go through the process of rebuilding whatever he had out there, you better start with getting approval from her."

Mac had enough. "Can you write down the procedure for me?" He felt the blood pounding in his ears and knew he needed to get out of here. The man reached into a drawer and pulled out a form.

"These are the steps. You need to get Ms. Woodson's notarized signature allowing you to do the work and submit the package with eight sets of signed and sealed plans," he stuttered again. "And we'll be sending Ms. Woodson a copy of the notice as well."

Mac took the paper and looked at the agencies involved. From the Army Corps of Engineers to Fish and Game, the list was daunting if not impossible. Just getting the plans and engineering done would cost him thousands. Then he looked at the bottom and saw a list of fees. After a quick calculation, he realized the permit alone would be close to thirty thousand dollars.

He dropped the form on the man's desk and rose to leave.

"There are severe consequences if you continue construction without a permit."

Mac glared at him and left. He retraced his steps to the counter and caught Sheryl's sympathetic eye as he opened the gate. Head down, he walked quickly, not caring about the looks he received from the people sitting in the uncomfortable stack chairs, waiting their turn. He left the building and walked back to the highway, wanting a drink as badly as he ever had.

He passed by Thirty-Third Street, almost turning to go back to the boat ramp, but decided that would be running away from his problems. Fingering the thumb drive in his pocket, he crossed the street and continued north, turning left on Thirty-Fifth. He walked to the end of the street, past stacks of lobster traps on the left and the parking lot for Keys Fisheries on the right, before climbing the steps to the second-floor tiki bar.

The Rusty Anchor would have been his first choice and even worth the walk to see Rusty, but Hawk would not be found there. The bar was a mix of tourists and locals, mostly associated with the charter fishing boats moored below in a small harbor.

He looked around and saw Hawk sitting at a table in back, carefully picking oysters off their shells with a small fork. Before he could approach, he heard a familiar voice.

"Yo, Mac."

He immediately recognized the Cajun accent and looked to the bar, where he saw Trufante. Moving through the crowd, he headed toward his mate. At least he might steel himself with a drink and have a few laughs to break the tension before he had to deal with Hawk. He joined him at the bar and looked out past the narrow work area for the bartenders at the view of the water below the rolled-up plastic used on rainy days. Thankful for the breeze that cleansed the air, taking the cigarette smoke with it, he slid into an empty spot.

"How you been, Tru?" he asked.

"Damn fine, Mac. Key West didn't work out too well, except for meeting this one." He turned to the woman on the other side of him, pecking away at her phone. "This here's Pamela, but I call her

Pajama Bama. Say hey to Mac Travis, babe," he said.

She looked up, and Mac's first thought was to wonder what she was doing with Trufante, but the Cajun was a charmer, and Mac never doubted his ability to date over his head.

"Hello, Mac Travis," she said. "How 'bout a five o'clock somewhere?"

Mac was amused when she started humming the melody of the Jimmy Buffett song. "Beer'd be good," he said, not trusting the scotch on the shelf behind the bar.

"Get him a shot too," Trufante said.

"Yah. One bourbon, one shot, and one beer," she called out to the bartender.

Mac smiled for the first time today. The bartender brought over the shot and beer and he toasted his friend. Whatever it was went down hard and he took a long swig of the beer to chase it. Turning away from the bar to hide his expression, he saw two men enter the room—the same men from the grounded speedboat yesterday. He watched as they walked to Hawk's table, where they stood for a minute before sitting.

"Hey," he whispered to Trufante. "You know those dudes with Hawk?"

"What are you worried about Hawk for? Hey, is that what you're doing here? I wondered when you walked in the door why you were here instead of at Rusty's."

"I could ask you the same question," Mac said, already suspecting that Trufante either owed Rusty money or was looking for work here. "Anyway, have a look."

Trufante turned to Pamela and looked over her shoulder. "Hmm. Babe, have a look there. Those the dudes you bid against?"

They were all looking at the table now, but before Mac could change his stance, he saw the man he had nicknamed Ironhead stare straight at him, or was it past him? Trufante stood several inches above him and right behind.

"Tell me a story, and give me the short version," Mac told the Cajun, wondering if he would be dragged into another of his messes.

"Well, ya see... " Trufante started.

He stopped short when Hawk rose and started toward them. Ironhead was about to get up to follow, but with a hand gesture, Hawk ordered him back in his chair. "Take her and get out of here," he whispered to Trufante. "I'll catch up to you later."

Trufante turned to Pamela, saying something Mac didn't hear. They finished their drinks in one sip and were past Mac on the way out the door. The moment they moved for the exit, Hawk signaled the man in the suit to go after them.

"Travis," he said. "What brings you to these parts?"

Mac fingered the drive in his pocket and hesitated. As much as he needed the money, he didn't want to deal with this man. "Just checking on Trufante," he said.

"I'd say that's a load of crap. No one that's not looking for trouble seeks out Trufante." He gave Mac a sideways look. "You looking for trouble, Travis?"

Mac didn't answer.

"That's a bit of a pickle you're in with the building department," he said, grinning.

Mac had suspected he'd been set up, and now he knew who did it. There was no way the building inspector would have known he was rebuilding Wood's place—unless someone had told him.

"Maybe you are here looking for me? Maybe needing some cash to pay for permits?"

Mac reached in his pocket and pulled out the drive, knowing it was a mistake the minute he did it. Hawk took a step closer, close enough that Mac could smell the cheap scotch on his breath. He put the drive back in his pocket, changing his mind. Nothing was worth dealing with this psychopath.

"I'll find it some other way," he said and turned to the bar.

"As they say, we can make this easy or we can make this hard," Hawk said and motioned for Ironhead, who was immediately on his feet, covering the distance between them in several large strides. Standing a close, but respectful distance away so that Hawk could talk, he crossed his arms and blocked the exit.

"Now, maybe you give me that drive and all your problems will go away. The repairs on your boat, the permit," Hawk said.

Mac felt trapped. There was no way he was going to give the drive to Hawk now. He pocketed it and looked around for a way out. Ironhead noticed and moved a step closer. "Let me think about it," he said, trying to buy some time and space.

"I think not. Let's have it." Hawk extended his hand, palm open.

Mac saw the only way out, and without hesitating, he took a step back, vaulted the bar, and jumped over the back bar and off the deck. Flying through the air with his hands windmilling, he braced himself. Just before he hit the water, he straightened his legs to lessen the impact on his almost-fifty-year-old body. Remaining underwater, he swam to the seawall and carefully lifted himself to see above it. As he looked around, he heard a commotion by the stairs. Ironhead was coming toward him, barreling through a group of tourists, tossing them aside as he descended.

Mac exchanged glances with a tattooed woman standing by the railing and screaming into her phone. She winked at him. Celia was another one of those Keys associates; though not a friend, she was someone he might have at one time or another done a favor for. She now repaid him and moved to the stairs to block Ironhead. Using the cover of one of the boats, Mac pulled himself from the water, turned, and ran toward the mangroves.

Once he reached the cover of the brush, he chanced a look back and heard Celia screaming at Ironhead, blocking his path with her intimidating body, her loose sarong swaying as she moved. Mac didn't miss the irony that her payback was sport for her.

He turned and followed the edge of the mangroves, carefully avoiding their roots until he emerged at the parking lot for the boat ramp. The center-console was where he'd left it, and he reached into his pocket for the keys, checking that the thumb drive was still there before crossing the asphalt to the boat.

Chapter 6

Trufante led Pamela from the bar. He looked back at the crowd around the stairs but didn't hesitate, knowing that when trouble was near, he was a bullseye. Pushing her in front of him, he hustled her to his bike. Minutes later, they were cruising toward the Seven Mile Bridge, where he slowed and pulled into the parking lot used by walkers and joggers for the old section of the bridge that ended at Pigeon Key.

At this hour, the lot was empty, and he pulled to the side, where they could not be seen from the street. He knew this area was frequently patrolled at night for vagrants, but he wasn't planning on doing the two-mile tourist walk.

"You've got some interesting friends," Pamela said.

"Shoot. Me and old Mac go way back," he said, not bothering to deny it. "What'd you want to do?" he asked to change the subject.

"I'd really like to check out the house. Can we go cruise by?" she asked with a smile she obviously knew he wouldn't say no to.

He thought for a minute. After seeing the two men that had bid against her at the auction hanging around Hawk, he was suspicious. She rubbed against him, and his better judgment, which he often pushed aside, again retreated. "Why not?" he said and hopped back on the bike. Hopefully the men would be tied up chasing Mac and have no interest in them.

"Mind if we stop by a liquor store first?" she asked, climbing on behind him.

"Now you're talking." He gave her the best version of his smile, kicked the starter, and revved the bike. They pulled to the edge of the lot, and he felt her arms circle tightly around him and her body rub against his while they waited for the traffic. It was a long wait, but he didn't mind, barely noticing the empty tractor-trailers heading back after dropping their loads in Key West, or the trucks towing boats, clogging the narrow artery. Finally there was an opening. He kicked the bike into gear, accelerated, and turned left.

Pamela motioned him into a parking lot with a sign for what looked like an expensive deli and liquor store. He complied, and after picking up a bottle of champagne, they headed back onto the highway, traveling another mile before turning right onto Sombrero Beach Road. He slowed as they approached the high school and continued until the road ended in a cul-de-sac by the beach. Out of real estate, he had to stop and have her check her phone for directions. They backtracked and took a left.

"Hot damn," Trufante said as they got off the bike. The house was as nice as any he'd ever been in, and for a minute he forgot the circumstances she had bought it under.

"See? I told you," she beamed.

He stashed the bike behind some bushes and followed her to the front door. She tried the knob, but it was locked, and she turned to him with an impish grin. He knew that look and smiled back. "Guess you don't want to wait until Friday to get the keys. Old Tru can take care of that."

She smiled back. "The bank wire will go through tomorrow, and I'll have the keys the day after." He circled the house, checking all the windows and doors, with her following close behind, clutching the bottle of champagne. "Can't you get us in?"

He sat on a chair by the pool. "I know I seen something on

sliding glass doors. You know, on the Internet."

"YouTube," she said and pulled her phone out.

He watched her navigate to a screen and type in something he couldn't read without glasses. A minute later, she sat next to him and held the small phone between them.

"Can't believe this shit's on the Internet?" he exclaimed after watching the thirty-second video of a man breaking into a sliding glass door. "I got this."

He rose and went up the stairs to the screened-in patio overlooking the backyard and canal. Facing the door, he started lifting one of the panels. Nothing happened. "Gotta be a trick to this," he said.

"Here, watch it again." She held the phone out and replayed the video.

"I got it now. Lift and jerk." He went back to the door, and in ten seconds it was open. "That Internet shit ought to be illegal," he said as he entered the large living area. "Damn, furnished and all. Let's hit the couch and pop that cork." He dove onto the leather sectional.

"I want to check it out first," she said, activating the flash from her phone.

"Hey. Don't be doing that. People'll see the light. I'm betting that on a street like this, there are some nosy-ass neighbors."

She turned off the light and came toward him. "I guess it'll wait a few days," she said and held out the bottle for him to open.

"Why don't you come here first?" He reached for her.

* * *

Mac was about a mile offshore when he saw the boat coming after him. He pulled back on the throttle, turning hard to starboard, and steered an easterly course, away from Wood's. If it was Hawk who had tipped off the building department, that meant he knew Mac was living at Wood's and would look for him there. He had lost his house after the insurance company had refused to pay for the damages caused by the same CIA agent who had set fire to Wood's. They had claimed it was terrorist activity and declined to pay, and Mac, unable to afford the repairs himself, had let the bank have the house. Now, although he hadn't been by to see it, he had heard they had demolished the structure.

Hawk would surely check the island first, thinking that was where Mac was headed. With few boats on the water, he decided to run dark. Without the aid of navigation lights or even the GPS, he cruised over the familiar waters, fingering the thumb drive as he followed the shoreline a safe distance offshore to avoid the shoals and flats invisible in the dark.

He needed to do something with the data. The hours he had spent staring at the pictures on the drive over the years had revealed nothing to him, and he knew he needed another set of eyes. Someone he could trust and who had the skills to solve the puzzle. Alicia was the answer, and he was surprised he had not thought of her before. The former CIA agent was a legend with data. Now working on contract and living in Key Largo with her boyfriend TJ, she was the one person he could trust to figure out the puzzle of the tattoos on the drive. Reputedly, the puzzle dated back to the Mayans; the answer, he was sure, was passed down through the generations by their body art.

Between the cost of the fuel and the dangers of navigating the waters of the Keys at night, he tried to figure the easiest way to get the data to her. Although far from a computer guy, he knew the Internet was faster than a boat—he just needed to get access to a computer.

A glance over his shoulder confirmed that the boat with Hawk's men was still on course to Wood's island, apparently unaware that he had turned away. He changed course and headed toward land, where he pulled into a small cove and turned back to watch the stretch of water north of the Seven Mile Bridge. The boat was still visible, the LED running lights like neon signs on a gas station in the desert. He watched it until it was over the horizon before pulling out of the small harbor. Trufante's apartment was only another mile up the coast.

* * *

Hawk was just able to catch his drink before it spilled when he felt the wake hit his trawler. He cursed the unknown boater running too fast through the canal. Buried back in the narrow channels behind the Sombrero Golf course, his sixty-five-foot steel-hulled trawler was tied off by a small house—his ex's. It was the only deal he could cut after his house had been confiscated and sold in record time by ICE. He enjoyed the small cabin, just forward and down a few steps from the wheelhouse, that he used for an office. Sitting in an easy chair in the corner, where he could look at the bookcase that held a record of his finds, he drank. It was his own personal showcase, containing one piece from each of the treasures he had found. One single piece that he had held on to after selling the rest.

"What'd you mean he's not there? Where else would he have gone?" Hawk screamed into the satellite phone. "Have a look around and see if he's been doing anything out there besides rebuilding the hermit's house, and then get your ass back here."

"What am I looking for?" the voice came through the receiver.

He pulled it away from his ear and gave the device a look meant for the man on the other end.

"You'll know it if you see it." He hung up, knowing the man wouldn't. Good muscle seldom meant brains, and Mike didn't disappoint. He kept the men paired for a reason: one had the brawn and the other had the brains. But they were separated now, with Mike going after Travis, and Wallace, who had already lost the Cajun, on his way back now. Once Mike returned from the island, he had another job for them.

His paranoia had grown over the past few days. First, he'd had to bail his employees out of jail after they had run aground and lost a shipment of artifacts. The government had made it too difficult to sell anything legally. Everything he found was classified as an antiquity or deemed to hold historical or archaeological value, and they wanted it for themselves. All his goods were now discreetly sent to Miami, where they were shipped offshore. In order to make a living in his line of work anymore, you had to sell abroad.

And then, it was troubling about the auction. He hadn't anticipated losing the house to another bidder. Most everyone in town knew the two men represented him, and most knew better than to bid against him. But Trufante didn't represent any kind of majority, and the girl was a wild card. She was on his list.

Something remained in the house the woman had bought. After the property had been confiscated, there had been too many eyes on it to go back, but now that the woman had bought it, it might be off the government's radar.

The phone buzzed, and he grunted at Mike to get back to Marathon. He wanted the unfinished business taken care of tonight.

* * *

With nowhere else to go, Mac changed course and turned towards land. Not sure if Trufante had a computer, or even if he could figure out how to use it to send the data to Alicia, he steered to the Cajun's apartment. Mac's relationship with electronics was similar to his ups and downs with women. They had to have a direct purpose and be easy to understand, the prerequisite eliminating most devices besides a GPS and just about every woman he met. Mel was an exception, but Wood's daughter was in Virginia, swearing she would never come back to the Keys. He thought about calling her to let her know about the notice, but he rarely used his cell phone and in fact wasn't sure where it was.

Mac navigated the mangrove-lined creek that led to Trufante's apartment. His navigation lights and electronics as well as the beam of a strong searchlight were on now, the risk of being seen minimized by the thick brush closing in on either side of him. In reality, this close to land, he was less obvious lit up like a Christmas tree than running dark. The channel opened and he found himself in a small basin. As he turned to the right, it opened further. He spun the boat, skillfully backing it into an empty slip at the seawall servicing a small two-story apartment building. Tying off the boat, he jumped onto the dock, now well above the gunwales with the low tide. Passing the run-down craft next to him, he left the dock and followed the path to the stairs. Trufante's apartment was on the second floor, and Mac climbed the back stairs, turning when he reached the landing to check on his boat. The Keys were the only place this level of housing would have a dock as an amenity, and it was well used, crowded with boats in all states of disrepair. He checked the dock, not trusting the residents with his boat.

Trufante was legendary for his open-door policy, and he was surprised when he found it locked. He reached underneath the moldy mat and pulled the key out, unlocked the door and put it in his pocket. If he was going to use the apartment, security needed to be improved.

The place was cleaner than normal, and Mac noticed several feminine items around. No wonder the door was locked, he thought; she just didn't know about the key. In the kitchen, he poured himself a glass of water and picked up the old landline phone. Remembering the old days, before the Internet and cell phones, he dialed 411, wondering if it still worked. He was surprised when the call was picked up but grimaced when he heard the computerized voice. He got the number for TJ's dive shop and dialed, doubting anyone would answer this late.

It rang half a dozen times, and the recorder came on. He was about to hang up, but with nothing to lose, he started to leave a message. Suddenly he heard a live voice on the other end.

"Yo, Mac. Wait a minute, and I'll turn that thing off," TJ said. There was a moment of silence, and he was back. "Charter's slow this time of year, so I get the calls up here just in case. Can't afford to be losing business."

Mac had been to his place and knew "up here" meant his apartment above the shop. "Hey, man, I'm looking for Alicia," he said.

"No worries. Here she is," he said.

"Mac?"

He heard her distinctive voice and smiled. The once-timid former desk agent had become one of his most trusted friends—and there weren't many. "Hey, girl. How goes it?"

"All good, but I know if Mac Travis is calling, it's not to say hello. What've you got?" she asked.

"You're right. I could be a bit more social. There's some data on a thumb drive I've had for years. I thought it would be a good time to figure out what it means."

"Broke?"

She had figured him out already. "I've had some interesting developments. Any chance you can have a look at it?" he asked.

"Sure, just email it over."

"That's a little beyond my reach right now," he said.

The line was quiet for a few minutes, and he could hear her talking to TJ in the background. "We've got nothing tomorrow. How about we come down that way?"

Chapter 7

Trufante woke with a start. He looked around the dark room, disoriented. It was quiet in the house, not like when no one was home, but deadly quiet—missing were all those background noises that blend together, only evident when the power is off. He raised himself an inch at a time. Moving Pamela to the side, he raised his head above the couch like an animal, sniffing for a predator.

Someone was outside, by the door he had broken into. He heard it slide and lowered himself when the beam of a flashlight played across the room. With a hand over Pamela's mouth, he rolled them both silently off the couch and onto the floor, where he pulled the ottoman against them. Locking eyes with her, he tried to reassure her.

"You know where he stashed it?" a rough voice asked.

Trufante was on full alert now.

"Said it was in the back bedroom. Under the bed, there's a plywood lid with a space below," another voice said.

Keeping his eyes on hers, he removed his hand from her mouth and put a finger to his lips. She obeyed the command. It sounded like the men were moving toward the bedrooms.

"What's going on?" she whispered.

"It told you this was a bad idea," he whispered back, instantly regretting it. "It's okay." He gave her a reassuring look.

The sound of furniture being moved came from the back of

the house, and then the whine of a cordless drill. He suspected they had found the stash.

"Is that freakin' silver?" he heard one man exclaim.

"It ain't candy," the other man said. "Give me a hand, will ya?"

Trufante knew the accent was from up North; maybe New Jersey, he thought.

"You got it all?" New Jersey asked.

"Yeah, Wallace. Let's get out of here," the other man said.

Trufante pulled Pamela closer when he heard the man approach.

"I'm gonna call the boss and let him know we're good. He was more than a little pissed about what happened earlier," Wallace said.

Trufante felt the men moving toward them and tried to shrink, but it was too late. He could feel the couch sink as the man sat. If he swung his feet around, they would be discovered. There was nothing he could do but hope for some luck, something that regularly eluded him.

"Hey, boss," the man said. There was silence for a minute while he listened. "Yeah, we got it. Be over there shortly."

He thought they were in the clear until Wallace kicked the ottoman away. "We gotta go," he said and stood up.

The man's foot landed squarely on Trufante's calf, causing instant and intense pain. He bit his tongue to prevent any sound from escaping. The man must have felt something unusual and kicked again. Fighting the pain, Trufante managed to remain quiet, but it didn't matter—the beam of a flashlight caught him square in the eyes.

"Well, look here, Mike. We got that Cajun lover boy and his girlfriend. Must have been having a nice housewarming. Champagne and all." He picked up the bottle. "Perrier-Jouët, very nice. Must be the girl that picked that out. Your sorry ass wouldn't know that from warm PBR."

Looking up at them, Trufante realized they were Hawk's men. The same men from the auction and the bar.

"Get on your feet, you damn Cajun," the man with the New Jersey accent said.

Trufante looked from man to man, then to the door behind them, wondering if there was any way out. Pamela was fidgeting beside him. He tried to hold her down, but she struggled to her feet. There was no stopping her.

"This is my house now. What are you guys doing here?" she said.

"Let me handle the bitch," the larger man, the one Mac had called Ironhead, said.

"We got to get back to the boss. Take them in the back. I'll try and find something to tie them up with," Wallace said.

"Too bad they won't fit in the hole in the floor," Ironhead said, waving the cordless drill at him and pulling the trigger.

As the men debated his fate, Trufante looked for a way out. The open patio door was only feet away. He could probably get past them and jump to the ground, but he looked at Pamela next to him, clearly scared after they had rebuffed her claim of ownership.

Wallace was looking at them strangely. "Might work. Good idea." He turned back to them. "Let's go."

"Serve them right for buying the house from under us," Ironhead said and pushed Trufante toward the hall.

They were in the back bedroom. The bed was pushed to the corner, and the carpet was rolled up halfway across the room.

"I thought I told you to put everything back," Wallace scolded the bigger man.

"Ain't no matter now," he said and pushed Trufante to the floor. "He might be a little long, might have to cut off another appendage."

Trufante shot him the finger with his stub. He looked in the square space in the floor. It was about a foot high, the width of the joists, and three or four feet square.

"The Cajun first. I'm thinking we take the girl back to the boss. Let him have a go at her, you know, for buying the house," Wallace said.

"I'd like a go at that," Ironhead said and pushed Trufante toward the hole.

"Don't," Pamela pleaded.

"Come on, lover boy, get in," Ironhead said and kicked him.

Trufante looked up at Pamela, pleading with his eyes. "Find Mac," he said and put his body in the space. It was a tight fit, but he coiled up his lanky frame and complied.

"He'll die in there," Pamela said. "You can have your damned house. Just let us go."

Ironhead was placing the plywood piece over the opening. What little light the streetlights cast into the room was gone, and Trufante found himself enveloped in darkness. He heard footsteps above him, and the whine of the drill as Ironhead secured the lid. The carpet was rolled out, and he heard the feet of the bed frame slide over him. He waited until he heard their car start before rubbing his butt against the wood. The phone was still in his pocket, but reaching it was another matter.

He felt around the dark space with his hands. The joists surrounding him were solid—at least an inch and a half thick. The plywood below him was encased in stucco, making up the ceiling of the open space below. The only way out was above. He had only counted four screws, but the lid didn't budge when he tried to push his body against the cover. Lying on his side with his knees in his chest, there was no way he could generate the force required to pull the screws from their hold in the joists.

He was sweating now, the small space heating up quickly from his efforts. The air seemed stale as well, and he started to worry if there were enough cracks between the wood to allow air to circulate. The phone was his only way out, and he struggled to reach it. Contorting his body, he tried to roll onto his back, without success. He lay back panting, feeling light-headed, drinking in the last of the air.

* * *

Mac sat back on the couch, holding the thumb drive in his hand. He thought about staying here, but figured once Hawk realized he had disappeared, he would connect the dots and have Trufante's apartment checked. There were not that many options open, his antisocial behavior having made him more enemies than friends. He thought about hitching a ride to Key Largo instead of waiting until tomorrow for Alicia and TJ to come to him, but the Keys were different now than when he'd thumbed his way down here twenty years ago. There was a better chance of landing in jail than getting a ride.

He got up and started pacing the living room. Feeling claustrophobic, he put the thumb drive in his pocket and left the apartment. There was a slight breeze coming from the southeast, probably less than ten knots, and he thought about protected anchorages. Not sure if Hawk would send his thugs by land or sea, he went downstairs to the center-console, released the lines, and started the engines.

He pulled straight out of the slip and retraced his route through the harbor. At the beginning of the mangrove channel, he cut the engines and drifted, checking for the sound of an approaching boat. He heard the whine of an engine, but it quickly passed, the sound dying with it, and he waited another minute before starting the engines and running the channel.

He exited the lagoon unchallenged and steered toward deeper water. Dropping the hook on the Gulf side, even with its small coves and lagoons, was not an option. The protected spots weren't on his list of acceptable anchorages; houses surrounded them, and he feared a homeowner might call the police. The open water, although it provided good holding, was too exposed for his liking. Even with his white anchor light on the T-top lit, it wasn't elevated enough to be visible from a distance, and he feared a casual boater or hungover fisherman would run into him.

Boot Key Harbor was too close to his old house, and crowded with liveaboards. The best solution was Sister Creek. The mangrove-lined shores of the inner channel were either deserted or government-owned, housing the radio towers that still broadcast propaganda to Cuba. Accelerating, he headed a quarter mile out before cutting the wheel to port and turning west to allow him enough clearance from the shoals to leave his electronics off. The navigation lights were dark as well, but his finger rested by the switch in case a boat approached.

Mac cruised west, roughly following the coast until the lights of the cars and trucks on the Seven Mile Bridge became visible. Leaving the protected waters of the Gulf side, he headed for the gap between the second and third piling of the old bridge, about a hundred yards from land, pushing the throttle down to make sure he had enough horsepower to avoid the strong, swirling currents channeling through the concrete abutments. He cleared the bridge, and away from its protection, the waves grew and the wind hit his face. He had a decision to make. Slowing, he evaluated the conditions before choosing the outside passage. He cruised past the entrance to Boot Key Harbor, not regretting his choice even when the first wave crashed into the bow, sending spray across the boat. It was better to be wet than to be seen.

Once clear of the small group of boats moored in a cove on the outside of the markers, he rounded Knights Key and headed offshore enough to pass a small unmarked island surrounded by shoals that guarded the entrance to the creek. He saw the light of the first marker, steered a wide path around it, and entered the channel. When he reached the second marker, he obeyed the sign posted below it and cut his speed. Using the lights from the houses on the right to guide him, he stayed towards starboard until he was clear of the shallows, now impassable with the low tide. The radio towers were in front of him now, and he turned to port, slowing to drop anchor, when he changed his mind and reversed course. He would sleep a lot better if he knew what Hawk was up to.

The entrance to the network of canals servicing Flamingo Island lay dead ahead, and he steered through the maze of man-made channels, careful to keep his speed down. No reason to anger one of the residents and get the police involved. He idled by the round house on the right that guarded the entrance, and turned to port at the first opening. This was no place to be if you didn't know your way, and although it was one of his favorite mullet grounds and he knew these canals well, he turned on the navigation lights and chart plotter. He would look more out of place running dark here as well.

He followed the canals around until he hit the last turn, and Hawk's ship loomed large in front of him. Larger than the surrounding boats, its tower rose to the height of many of the sailboats' masts. Killing the lights, he dropped speed again and coasted toward the boat. As he approached, he saw the lights on in one of the cabins. It was quiet, and he wondered what he expected to find here. Hawk was home, but there was no sign of his henchmen. Just as he was about to turn, a car pulled into the driveway of the small house by the dock and cut its lights.

Mac let the current take him to the other side of the canal, where he grasped for the rail of one of the boats docked there. Doors slammed, and he heard a woman's voice. He couldn't make out what she was saying, but she was clearly not happy. Moving to the bow to get a better look, he saw Ironhead and the Weasel dragging a woman down the path to the boat. She looked familiar, and he cursed under his breath when he saw it was the same woman Trufante had been with at the bar.

Chapter 8

The woman struggled as they pushed her across the short walkway from the dock to the deck. Hawk yelled something to Ironhead, who finally lifted her off her feet and carried her aboard. A minute later, the screams were almost inaudible, muffled by the steel bulkheads of the cabin.

Grasping the bow rails and cleats of the docked boats, Mac pulled himself closer to the steel-hulled trawler. It was not like the fiberglass pleasure boats the name might bring to mind, but a heavy research vessel. The shiny paint job, deep green with yellow accents, concealed the heavy workhorse that it was. Though not fast, it was built for heavy work in big seas. The flared bow, designed to cut through big waves, towered over the low freeboard of the much smaller center-console, and he was able to use it to conceal himself as he moved to the edge of the neighbor's dock and pulled the boat underneath the shadow of the bow. The center-console sat much lower in the water, but if he decided to board, he could reach the deck of the larger ship by climbing on the T-top. He was about to make his move when he heard the cabin door open and saw the shadow of a man on the deck.

Climbing onto the neighbor's dock to get a better look, he moved behind the cover of a large mangrove branch. From here he could see Ironhead walk back to the dock and cross to the path. He lost sight of him there, but the opening and closing of a car door told him where he was. A minute later, he emerged again, carrying several bags. He handed them off to Wallace, who waited on deck and returned to the car for another load.

The cabin was quiet now, and Mac wanted a better look. Quietly, he slid back onto the boat and climbed the stainless tubing supporting the T-top. He slid onto the fiberglass cover, carefully avoiding the GPS and VHF antennae. Mac reached out for the railing of the larger boat, missing by only a few inches. Using one of the mangrove branches, he pulled the small boat closer, gaining the height he needed, then released the branch, ducking when it snapped back. The boats started to separate again, the strain of their lines pulling them back to their original positions. Mac didn't waste any time. He rose and vaulted the rail, then flattened himself on the deck, waiting. He looked around at the foredeck. The only forward-facing windows of the wheelhouse were dark, making him confident he had not been observed. Slowly he rose to his knees and crawled around the structure until he could see into the large rectangular cabin windows.

He was about to move closer for a better look when he froze. The cabin door opened, and he heard activity on deck. Slowly, he moved past the dark windows and saw three men standing with their backs to him on the starboard side. There was a large bundle between them, and Mac expected the worst.

"Bring the boom over," Hawk ordered in a low voice. "Quietly."

That's odd, Mac thought. *Why would they need a boom to dump the body?*

"Gear up, Mike," he said.

Ironhead pulled a scuba tank, buoyancy compensator, and regulator from a locker by the transom and expertly set up the gear. He slid into the straps of the vest and waited while Wallace sprayed the mask with defogger, rinsed it, and handed it to him. His experience showed again when he silently moved to the transom and rolled into the water with a small enough splash that it would have given an Olympic diver a top score.

He heard a motor whir and looked toward the boom, where Hawk was at the controls lowering the cable. Wallace wrapped the heavy wire around the package, snapping the hook around the standing line. Mac crept a step closer, almost to no-man's-land, to get a better look when he saw a glint of silver just before Wallace sealed the bags with duct tape. Curious now, he watched as the boom lifted the package from the deck. Hawk manipulated the controls, moving the arm past the gunwale to extend over the water and then lowering the package into the canal.

They had done this before, Mac thought. They were too organized and quiet for this to be the first time, and he wondered what else was down there. The narrow canals were somewhat of an illusion. As wide as a street, they were deeper than one would expect. Years ago, before it was made illegal, the contractors had dynamited them and excavated huge trenches, using the rubble as fill for the houses now sitting adjacent to the water.

Over the years, Mac had dove in many of the canals to construct and repair the bridges connecting the small islands. He knew there could be fifteen or twenty feet below the waterline — plenty of depth for a well-concealed cache.

An unfamiliar noise came from inside the cabin, bringing his attention back to more important matters—the woman. He moved back behind the structure, watching as Hawk and Wallace repeated the process three more times. The boom was back in place, and Ironhead was aboard, stripping and storing the gear. A few minutes later, the men were dismissed, and Mac waited for the car to start, following its lights as it backed out, and turn onto the small bridge ahead of them that led to the mainland.

It was just the three of them now, at least as far as he knew. This might be the only chance he had to save the girl. He needed a distraction to get Hawk back on deck. He saw the control box for the boom and slowly crept to the edge of the wheelhouse, slithering onto the rear deck. Lights were on in the cabin, but he was able to stay below the level of the windows, pausing when he reached the solid door to listen for any activity before crossing to the starboard rail and grabbing the control box. It was mounted on the boom, with about ten feet of electrical cable connecting the controls to the motors and hydraulic pump.

Studying the box in the low light, he found the toggle to raise the cable and flipped the switch. The motor whirred and slowly reeled in the loose wire. Once the slack was out of the line, the hydraulics emitted a high-pitched whine that turned into a screech as the mechanism struggled against the tension of the line. As he expected, the ship went dark when the power surge overloaded the motor and blew the main breaker.

It was time. Mac dropped the box and went to the port side, hiding behind the hinged side of the door. The beam from a flashlight could be seen in the cabin, and he readied himself. Looking around for a weapon, he found nothing—he would have to rely on surprise and subterfuge. The beam became more focused, and suddenly the lights came back on. Hawk had reset the main breaker. Now, Mac hoped he would investigate what had happened. Sensing the door opening before the hinges moved, he crouched down.

Hawk emerged from the cabin, his shadow visible on the deck before his body. Although Mac would rather have smashed his head in, he waited patiently for him to start across the deck. The minute Hawk moved to the rail to check the boom, Mac slid around the opened door and quietly closed it. Turning the lock, he inhaled deeply and started searching the cabin.

He found her bound and gagged in the forward stateroom locker, but before he could untie her, he heard Hawk struggling with the cabin door. She was scared and trying to yell through the gag. Mac put a finger to his mouth to try and quiet her. He heard voices outside and moved to the cabin door. Hawk was outside on his cell phone, screaming at someone. Time was running out, and he went back to her, not concerned about noise now. Fumbling with the knots on her ties, he finally released her, but it had taken longer than he wanted. Next, he pulled the tape from around her mouth, releasing the wadded washcloth they had used to gag her.

"What the hell is wrong with these people?" she started.

"Where's Tru?" Mac asked.

"Back at the house. Bastards locked him up."

"Okay. We'll get him, but first we need to get out of here. I'm pretty sure Hawk's called his muscle back," Mac said, looking around the cabin for another exit besides the door leading to the deck. He saw the hatch above and jumped on the bed. It would be a tight fit, but he thought they could make it.

"Are you ready? Follow me, and don't ask questions." Hoping she could follow orders, he cranked the lever on the hatch and watched it rise. Seeing that it was going to be too small, he pulled the screen out, reached through the opening, and yanked the plastic cover off its hinges.

Scraping his sides against the frame, he hauled himself through the opening and paused to see if Hawk had heard him. From the corner of his eye, he saw the headlights of a car turn into the driveway, and he knew it didn't matter.

"Hurry. They're on the bow, getting away," Hawk yelled at the men running toward the boat.

"Come on." Mac reached down through the hole and pulled Pamela onto the deck. Without a word, he moved forward to the bow and jumped across to the T-top of the center-console. The fiberglass T-top roof wobbled under his weight, but he ignored it and turned back to help her. She was already in midair. Landing in a crouch, she followed him down the rungs of the stainless tubing.

The engine started, and he risked a look up at the bow of Hawk's ship. There were two men standing above him. From this angle, they were shielded by the flare of the bow, but the second he moved away from the dock, they would be exposed. With no choice, he went back to the helm and pulled the throttle back into reverse. Wincing as the engine cowling slammed into the dock, he pushed the handles down. The boat moved forward while he cut the wheel hard to the left, smashing the cowling against the other piling. Gunshots were fired, and he ducked behind the console, pulling the woman with him.

He was moving away from Hawk's trawler now, staying close to the boats docked on his port side, using them for cover as he followed the slight bend in the canal. They were almost clear when he heard the sound of an outboard coming toward them. By the volume alone, he could tell it was moving faster than the posted no-wake speed limit. Thinking back, he realized he had only seen Wallace on the boat with Hawk. Ironhead must be in another boat, trying to trap them. Just as he thought it, a cabin cruiser turned the corner, and he could see the unique shape of Ironhead's torso at the helm, silhouetted in the moonlight.

The boat was bigger than the center-console, and Mac tried to judge its height off the water. It would be close, but it just might work if they could get past Hawk without getting shot. He pushed down on the throttles and slammed the wheel to the right, hoping the hull could make the hundred-and-eighty-degree turn without smashing another boat. A large sportfisher encroached into the canal, forcing him to waste precious time reversing and then straightening the boat for a better angle before proceeding.

"Hold on. This is going to be tight," he said. Looking at her tall figure, he added, "And you better duck." Without enough room to accelerate to full speed, he did what he could and slammed the throttle to its stops. The motor revved, and the boat jerked forward. Gunshots hit around him, but he ignored them, pushing the "bow down" buttons on the trim tab controls as hard as he could and hoping the boat would go on plane before it hit.

There was a loud smash as they cleared the bridge. He didn't dare look back, but he knew at a minimum the electronics on the roof were gone. Disregarding the speed limit, he continued past the low bridge and turned right into another canal, hoping Ironhead would take the bait. There was only one exit from the maze of canals, and if this didn't work, they could easily be trapped.

The reassuring sound of metal on concrete carried over the night air.

Chapter 9

Mac pulled back on the throttle, knowing the chase was over before it started. He looked up and saw stars shining where the T-top once would have shielded them. The stainless steel tubing remained, but the fiberglass cover and the antennae for all the electronics were gone. The boat would surely be noticed if he didn't get out of here, but he needed to find Trufante first.

"It's only rock 'n' roll, Mac Travis." Pamela grinned at him. "But I like it."

She was bopping to another song in her head, and now he saw what connected her and Trufante—the need for trouble. "You know where that house of yours is from the water?"

"Barely from the street," she said. "Had to use the maps app on my phone to find it. Tru thought he knew where it was, but he-"

Mac cut her off. "Pull it up," he ordered.

"You can't always get what you want. But if you try sometime—you get what you need," she continued on her Rolling Stones tribute, handing him the phone.

Mac looked at the dark screen and handed it back to her. "Can you help out here?"

She took it back and swiped her finger across the bottom, and the screen lit up. After she pressed several buttons, the map appeared. "It's here."

He glanced over. "Can you zoom out so I can see the canals?"

She manipulated the screen until he saw a blue dot in the large turning basin they had just entered. The red dot, indicating the location of the house, was in one of the side canals not far from where they were.

"Got it," he said. "Keep an eye out for anything you recognize." He turned right into another unmarked canal.

She was humming "Can't Find My Way Home" now.

The houses and boats passed by as they navigated the waterway. Glancing down at the phone sitting between them on the leaning post, he watched the dots converge until they were right on top of each other. "Anything look familiar?"

"That one. See? That's Tru's bike behind those bushes," she said, pointing to a dark house.

Mac turned to port and coasted to a stop along the dock. He looked at her, about to ask for help with the lines, when he saw the fear in her eyes. "Hey. It's all right. Tru always lands on his feet," he said, moving forward to tie off the boat before the current could get a hold of it.

"It's all my fault. He warned me about buying the house from the auction."

He turned to comfort her but saw a pair of headlights turn onto the street. "We gotta get Tru first. Then we'll talk," he tried to reassure her. The lights went past the house, and he shut off the engine. "Come on."

He hopped onto the dock and extended a hand for her. She looked scared, but she took his hand, her long legs making easy work of the transition. They climbed the back stairs to the house and found the patio door open. He jumped when she turned on the flashlight on the phone and went ahead of him to the bedroom.

"He's under the bed."

Mac peered underneath, expecting to find him bound there, but it was empty.

"No. We have to move it. There's a compartment in the floor."

Together they moved the bed, and she showed him where they had taken the carpet up. A minute later, they were staring at the outline of the plywood cover. "I'll be right back. Gotta find a screwdriver."

As he walked away, he heard her singing something, probably to Trufante. The woman was an enigma, but he would expect nothing less from Trufante. For now, all he could do was get the Cajun out of here and find somewhere safe to figure things out. Sending them to TJ's now, instead of waiting until the morning for them to come down, might be the best course of action. He suspected that Hawk might take some time to lick his wounds, but he'd be back.

Bounding down the steps two at time, he reached the patio and glanced toward the quiet street, wondering where the car had gone. Curious, he risked a glance around the concrete pilings supporting the house and saw it parked down the block. There were no lights on, but he thought he saw the outline of a head in the driver's seat.

Thinking he'd deal with him after Trufante was free, he went to the boat and retrieved the toolbox. Back upstairs, he returned to the bedroom and looked at Pamela's face in the glow of the phone, rocking softly to some tune in her head. Ignoring her, he set the plastic box beside the panel, opened it, and removed a screwdriver. Using all his force against the handle to prevent the tips from stripping, he extracted the screws one by one and finally lifted the lid.

Trufante was curled up in a ball, his frame barely fitting inside the cache. A lifeless eye looked up at Mac, who exhaled sharply when he realized his friend was still alive. Pamela appeared next to him, and together they lifted him out of the hole. "You good?"

"Damn headache is all—champagne will do that to ya every time," he said, shaking his head.

"Come on," Mac said. He noticed something between one of

the joists and the plywood below it. "Can you shine the light in there?" he asked Pamela.

She was on her knees, fussing over Trufante, who sat on the floor with his feet in the compartment. Together they examined the interior of the space. The light hit something. At first, Mac thought it was a discarded screw or nail left over from the construction, but when he moved closer, he realized it was a coin. Taking a flathead screwdriver from the box, he carefully dug it out of the tight space it was lodged in and held it up for them to see.

"Hot damn," Trufante said. "They pulled a bunch of whatever that is out of there."

Mac almost told them he had seen where it was now stored, but thought better of it. Though he trusted the Cajun, this information was better held close. "I'll check it out later. We better get out of here."

They left the house and were standing together on the back patio when Mac remembered the car parked out front. "Follow me." He led them downstairs and to the dock, trying to remain in plain view of the street. Talking loudly, he told them they could stay out at Wood's tonight and made a show of helping them into the boat. The engine fired, and he leaned over to Trufante.

"Take this," he said, reaching into his pocket for the thumb drive, and after pausing for a second, he grasped the coin too. He handed them both to Trufante. "Stay low in the stern. When I back out, and the mangroves block the view from the street, you two hop off. I think one of his henchmen is waiting in a car a few houses down. If he thinks we're all together on the boat, my guess is he'll go and report back to Hawk. Once he's gone, take the bike and head to Key Largo. Alicia's expecting you tomorrow, but I think it's better to get you two out of town tonight."

Trufante nodded. "What about you?" he asked and leaned over to tell Pamela the plan. She nodded her head and moved to sit on the transom.

"Don't worry about me," Mac said softly, then called out

loudly for Tru to get the lines.

Trufante went to the bow and released the forward line, then went aft to the transom where he untied the stern line. "Okay," he called over the noise of the engine.

Mac looked back at them, and they nodded they were ready. Slowly he reversed, cutting the wheel to swing the bow away from the dock as if he were merely pulling away, but he let it go a few seconds too long, allowing the stern to fall back into the mangroves. The boat shifted when the couple jumped to the seawall, and he calmly pushed the throttle forward and started moving away from the dock.

* * *

Hawk sat on the deck of his trawler watching the headlights from the police car recede from the driveway. What had started as a contentious discussion with the deputies quickly became friendly after Hawk placed a call to the sheriff's private line. The deputies had been warned to back off the antiquities dealer and focus on Travis. Hawk went below and glanced at Ironhead, lying on the couch with an ice pack on his head. Passing by him without a word, he grabbed the bottle of scotch and went for the cabin door, the sight of the man turning his stomach.

"I could use a swig for the pain," Ironhead moaned.

Hawk turned on him. "The only pain here is the one in my buttocks from you. That was my boat you wrecked, and now I have to have it pulled out of the canal before my ex finds out."

"What about dropping me by the hospital? I'm pretty sure something's broke."

Taunting him, Hawk took a swig of the amber liquid directly from the bottle. "I'll give you some aspirin and a glass of water. That's all you'll get from me. Go ahead, they're in the drawer by the sink."

Hawk's gut feeling was confirmed when Ironhead, belying

his alleged injuries, jumped off the settee and went for the bathroom. Jiggling the pill bottles he had already removed and stuffed in his pockets, Hawk smiled to himself and went out on deck.

He heard cursing, and drawers being slammed through the open door, but he ignored it. Mike had a history, one he knew well. He'd already caught him pilfering pills and had removed everything except the generic aspirin from the bathroom.

"I can't find shit in there," Ironhead said, standing in the doorway. "I'm out of here."

"Do what you must, but I'll have no part in it," Hawk said.

"Whatever." Ironhead walked to the walkway.

* * *

His head throbbed in rhythm with every step he took. There was nothing Hawk was going to do for him. Cursing himself as he walked, he hoped he hadn't screwed up the relationship. The guy wasn't fun, but the work was interesting—and it paid. Where else could he go and be allowed to dive as well as break heads? All bosses were assholes; the only real problem was the pills—and he needed some now.

He looked straight ahead as he crossed over the bridge he had just smashed the boat into, not wanting to see the damage, or the condescending look he knew would come from Hawk, who was sitting on the deck of the trawler. He followed the golf course around a bend, passing a row of boats moored against the seawall, then a resort, an apartment building, and an empty marina. Reaching the first cross street, he continued straight for another block until it dead-ended into Sombrero Beach Road, where he turned left. On his right was the small strip mall that held the Brass Monkey. If there were pills to be found on this blasted island, they would be here.

He crossed the street and entered through the blacked-out

door. Music greeted him, and although there were laws against smoking in bars, the place reeked of it. Searching through the sea of bobbing heads and loud voices, he saw an empty seat on the far side of the bar. He worked his way around the room, dodging bodies until he reached the vacant stool.

"Hey, Mike, you're not looking so hot," the bartender said.

"I got trouble. You got something that can help?"

The bartender shook his head. "You know you got some credit issues."

Ironhead reached into his pocket and pulled out two twenties. It was all he had left, and he wondered if payday would even come this week after he'd wrecked the boat. He placed the bills on the bar.

The bartender eyed the bills before grabbing them from the scarred copper bar top. "Should leave enough for a chaser. Want a beer?" A minute later he placed a beer on a cocktail napkin and with a practiced hand slid two pills underneath it.

Ironhead grabbed the bottle and took a long swig. With his other hand, he snagged the napkin and extracted the pills. Feeling better at the sight of them, he slammed the oxycodone in his mouth and finished the beer. That would take care of things tonight, but tomorrow morning the ordeal that had become his life would resume.

He saw Wallace coming towards him and put his head down. It was one thing to be reprimanded by Hawk, but he was not about to take any crap from the failed and disbarred lawyer. It was bad enough he was forced to spend most of his days with him.

"Thought I'd find you here. Boss is pissed," Wallace said.

"Whatever," Ironhead said, hoping the pills would take effect quickly.

"If you don't have any other offers, I'd be thinking about making amends," Wallace said.

The bartender made a move toward them, but Ironhead waved him away. He turned to Wallace. "What do you have in mind?" He hated groveling.

"They thought they were slick, but I watched them," Wallace said.

"You want a pat on the back or what?"

"Travis got the girl, and they went back to the house where we had the Cajun in the floor."

Ironhead was focused on him now. "And?"

"I saw the three of them get back on the boat and start to pull away. It was then I noticed the bike."

"What bike?" Ironhead asked.

"Remember, we never saw a car, you know, how they got to the house in the first place."

Ironhead realized he was right. That was how this whole mess had started. If they'd known the couple was in the house, they would never have broken in—at least not then. "So, what of it?"

"I pulled out, you know, to give them the slip. Then I saw the Cajun and the girl jump off the boat and make a run for the bike. I followed them back to his apartment," Wallace said with a big grin.

Chapter 10

Mac's first priority was the boat. There were probably more twenty-foot center-consoles in the Keys than Toyota Corollas, but there was only one with a torn-off T-top. If he wanted to stay invisible, he needed to get rid of the now worthless stainless structure that had supported the old top and would catch the eye of anyone who saw it.

Mac had spent a sleepless night anchored on a shallow mudflat in Boot Key Harbor. Trusting the tides, he had risked the shallows and grounded the boat in two feet of water, using several nearby wrecks to provide some cover. It would be morning before the tide came back in and floated him off. Until then he was stuck.

The only hassle he had encountered was the mosquitoes that kept him awake. They were gone with the dawn and, like clockwork, just after the sun rose, the boat lifted and he was free. After pulling the anchor, he motored across to the main channel and turned to the west, following the markers past the gas docks and turning into a small canal before the harbor entrance. He idled to a dock on the left that serviced the boatyard and tied off the boat.

While he walked to the office, he looked around the work area for his boat and found it sitting on supports near the back of the yard, buried behind several other boats that were currently being worked on. It didn't look like it was going anywhere soon.

Head down, he entered the small office.

"Hey, Mac," the man behind the counter said. "I'd shake your hand, but... " He continued to clean his hands with a rag.

"Bill," Mac replied. He stood there, staring at the coffeemaker.

"Go ahead. First one's on the house," he said. "Come to take care of that invoice? Just need to get paid and put a few finishing touches on her and she's ready to go."

Mac poured a cup and sat down on a barstool by the counter. "That's going to have to wait. I see you've got her in the back anyway. Just add on the storage charges."

"So, what brings you by?" Bill asked.

"Got into a bit of a scrape last night. I was wondering if you can pull the tower from my boat?"

"Sure. No big deal. What am I doing with it?" Bill asked.

"Store it until I can find a new top," Mac said.

Bill put down the rag and went to the door. Mac grabbed the coffee and followed him out. Together they stared at the center-console.

"You got a story to go along with that?"

"If I told you Tru was involved, would that suffice?" Mac answered.

"Probably. I'll keep an eye on the *Keynoter* for the official account."

"You do that. I just can't be running around like this," Mac said.

An hour later, the tower was unbolted, and a forklift lifted it off the boat. Mac watched the operator set it next to his fishing boat, then climbed back aboard the center-console. "I'll cover that next week," he said and fired the engine. Mac untied the lines, waved a thank-you to Bill, and waited for the flooding tide to push the boat away from the dock. When the boat was in the center of the canal, he eased down on the throttles and idled out of the canal.

He steered through the last pair of markers and accelerated, surprised by the additional speed the 250-hp engine provided without the weight of the tower. The only drawback was that without the antennae, the electronics were worthless, but this was his backyard, and he steered back to Wood's by memory.

After tying off, he climbed down and walked back to the house. He found his phone on the workbench, the battery dead. Starting the generator, he set the phone to charge and left the shed. Sitting on a stump, he thought about what he needed to do next. He wasn't a gun guy and had nothing more powerful than a twenty-two, a small-gauge shotgun, and some spearguns, but thinking there might be a need now, he remembered Ironhead and Wallace dropping theirs into the water when the sheriff arrived.

* * *

The sun hit Trufante in his eyes and he rolled over, smiling when he found Pamela was next to him. Day eight. A few ups and downs yesterday, but the streak was still alive. He brushed the hair covering her face aside and watched her eyes move as the light hit them.

Finally she opened them. "Hey. We gotta go," he said.

"We were supposed to go last night," she said, rubbing the sleep from her eyes and propping herself up on an elbow.

The sheet fell from her body, and Trufante did all he could to pull himself away. "Needed to chill for a bit after that near-death experience. Anyway, old Alicia'd get her fangs out if we came barging in there at two a.m." What he didn't say was that he needed a drink after being sealed in the compartment in the floor. He looked at what little remained in the bottle next to the bed. *Maybe more than one*, he thought.

"It wasn't like you were in a rush either." The words came out meaner than he had meant and he quickly countered, "You and Mac had your hands full too."

"Me and Mac Travis. Ought to be a song."

He ignored the line, getting up and going for the shower. With his head under the water, he started to think about how to apologize, something he wasn't very good at, when he felt a body rub against him.

They were out of the apartment half an hour later, heading toward Miami. They cruised through the Upper Keys, passing stacks of lobster traps and strip malls with small businesses and tourist shops huddled on small spits of land between the bridges that spanned miles of clear blue water. Trufante pulled over at a small restaurant in Islamorada and they went in for breakfast, failing to notice the white sedan that skidded to a stop and pulled in next door.

* * *

"You're supposed to be watching them," Wallace scolded the man in the passenger seat.

Ironhead set down his phone, resisting the urge to swat the smaller man like a fly. Instead he tried to control his breath and watched as Trufante and the woman entered the restaurant. "It'd be a piece of cake to just take it from him."

"Boss said no. If he's right, they're heading to see this woman that's supposed to have ninja skills. Let the expert figure it out—then we take them both," Wallace said.

"True that," Ironhead said. He needed to watch himself now, his experience telling him that the next few hours would be bad. The drugs he had bought at the bar last night had worn off and his pockets were empty. That thought took over his mind and he picked up his phone.

"What're you doing? Updating your Facebook status?" Wallace laughed at himself.

Ironhead gave him a look and turned away so the other man couldn't see the screen. His stubby fingers had a hard time with the keyboard, but he finally entered his search phrase. A minute later, the screen showed a plain building with a blue metal awning in front. The sign said Department of Veterans Affairs, and the address put them only a mile away.

He tapped the wheel, trying to subdue his urge to drive there now. The scam had worked more than once. But Wallace would surely report him to Hawk. He would have to suck it up and wait. Finally, the restaurant door opened and the couple walked out, mounted the bike, and headed out of the lot. Ironhead and Wallace followed a respectable distance behind, easily blending in with the late-morning traffic. US-1 opened to two lanes in Key Largo, making it easier to tail them provided he made it through all the lights. The plain white car blended in with the line of traffic following the only route to the mainland. There would be no reason for them to suspect a tail.

The motorcycle braked and turned right onto a small side street, jarring Ironhead back into the present. He slowed just in time to see the bike turn into a small parking lot adjacent to a two-story building backed up to a dock. A big red flag with a white stripe running diagonally across it stated its business.

"What the heck? They going diving?"

Wallace didn't answer for a long moment. "Be patient."

The couple entered the shop based on the first floor and a few minutes later followed a heavyset man with short dreadlocks sticking straight out of his head around the back.

"What do we do if they get on a boat?" Ironhead asked. The fact that there were no pharmacies on the water didn't escape him.

Wallace was on the phone and held up a finger. He gave the address and name of the shop to whoever was on the other end and waited.

* * *

"Alicia Phon!" Trufante hugged the woman. "Goddamn if you ain't lookin' good. See that? I hook you up with TJ and—

damn, look at you." He released her and turned to Pamela. "Hey, babe, this here's Alicia. We go way back."

"Yeah, way back to last summer," Alicia said, and they shared a laugh. "Mac said you had something for me to take a look at?"

Trufante dug in his pocket for the thumb drive and handed it to her. He paused and reached back in, extracting the coin. "He told you about the drive, but he wanted you to have a look at this too."

She spun the coin in the light. "Interesting. Which first?"

"I'd do the coin myself, but Mac wants you to look at the drive," he said.

"Okay, I'll get on it," she said and turned to the man with the dreadlocks. "Can you do without me on the afternoon charter? I'd really like to get into this now."

"Shoot. I'll fill in for you," Trufante said before he could answer. "Me and TJ got this for you."

"What about me?" Pamela asked.

"You ain't been to the Keys until you snorkeled the reef. Hold on to your hat, babe, this is going to be awesome."

She smiled and they walked downstairs. TJ asked them to stay by the boat while he rounded up the passengers and brought them around back. Trufante helped the eager tourists onto the boat and loaded gear while TJ gave the safety briefing. He looked over at Pamela, sitting with the other tourists, and wondered what her real story was. She looked like she belonged more with them than with him.

* * *

"Well, what now?" Ironhead asked as the boat pulled away from the dock.

Wallace stared after the boat. "Keep an eye out, I'm going to check out the upstairs."

"Like hell. You watch the damn place," Ironhead said. If there was a search to be done, he was going to do it. The upstairs looked like an apartment—and apartments had medicine cabinets. He didn't wait for an answer.

He climbed the stairs two at a time and arrived on the landing, where he opened the door to the apartment. The kitchen was on his left, and he quickly crossed to the bar-height counter, where he scanned the papers and keys strewn across it. Not finding the drive, he moved to the living room, which held nothing either. The bathroom caught his eye, and he crossed the room, passing a pair of doors that he assumed were for a closet on his way to the hallway. A bedroom was to either side, but they could wait. His first stop was the medicine cabinet, which revealed little other than a man and a woman's toiletries. Getting anxious, he pulled the vanity drawers out one at a time, rifling the contents in the process. In the right-side drawer, he found what he was after.

Two prescription bottles stared at him, and he picked the largest up first. The drug was foreign to him, obviously not one of the opiate family he knew by heart. He set it down and lifted the other: industrial-grade Tylenol. He took half a dozen of the large white pills, hoping the horse-sized dose might help him through a rough spot, and looked at the container. The name meant nothing, but he memorized it anyway, repeating it over and over in his head as he checked the bedrooms and left the apartment.

"Alicia Phon—with a P-H," Wallace repeated the name. "Maybe we ought to let the boss know. See if that rings a bell anywhere," he said, hoping the name would salvage the mission.

Chapter 11

Alicia plugged the thumb drive into an empty USB slot in her computer and waited for the files to load. One at a time, they populated the screen. She browsed through the pictures, trying to sort through the different angles, finally settling on four that represented the group. Pursing her lips, she applied some filters to even out the images. The photography was amateurish, even though she knew it had been done quickly under less-than-ideal conditions.

Next she cropped the pictures, placed them side by side on one of the large screens mounted on the wall in front of her, and stared at them. Ensconced in TJ's war room, she studied the patterns. What had once been the gamer's paradise was now their joint command center. His half of the room, with a captain's chair in the center, resembled the flight deck of the USS *Enterprise*. Her side was more utilitarian. The black-painted walls and grey ceiling lent a theater-like atmosphere. The small ductless air conditioner kicked on, providing a gentle stream of cool air on the back of her neck, but she hardly noticed. The low hum of the other electronics in the room was just background noise as well.

She stared at the photos, trying to follow the intricate patterns that were rumored to hold the secret location of a treasure cached somewhere in the Middle Keys. The tattoos passed down from generation to generation of the local Indians somehow held the key to the riddle—if only someone could decipher them. Like so many other treasures, each generation knew less and less, and now, they couldn't put the clues together. On the thumb drive were the only images of the deceased Teqea and Diego's bodies. Mac had almost lost his life inadvertently putting the collection together and had spent hour upon hour trying to figure out their meaning, but had run into a wall every time.

A thought occurred to her as she sipped from her water bottle. The patterns were unique—much like fingerprints. If she could find a database to run them against, the images might match something, somewhere. Opening another window, she opened the portal to the FBI and, using a friend's credentials, logged in. The original images on the left remained static while those on the right whirled past, seeking some kind of match.

Her concentration was broken by a noise from the living room. TJ was out on the charter and not expected back for another hour or so. If someone from the shop wanted her, they would text. With her heart pounding in her chest, she listened and heard it again—the footfalls of a large man. Leaving the program running, she got up, went to the door, and placed her ear against it. She held her breath and listened, but there was nothing now. Carefully she cracked the door and peered out. Squinting as the bright light hit her, she scanned the room, starting with the kitchen and moving through the dining room. Nothing was there, but a movement from the hallway by the bathroom caught her eye.

The man rifling through the drawers was frightening. She quickly shut the door and stood with her back against it, trying to calm herself down. A loud chime made her cringe and she glanced at the screen. The program had acquired a match.

She picked up the phone and hit the recent calls screen and then the top name, hoping he would answer.

* * *

"Where is she?" Hawk screamed into the phone. "That's why they're there—not for the snorkeling, you idiot. Travis had them take the drive to her." He set the coffee down on the table before he spilled it. It was hard to find good help down here, but these two guys took the cake. Mike could dive, and Wallace knew his way around the shadier side of the law, but even with their skills they were bumbling idiots. "Find her," he muttered and hung up.

Then the door to the house opened and Hawk's day went from bad to level nine in Hell. The house belonged to his ex, who, as his last resort when his house had been confiscated, had been open to a cash payment for letting him dock the boat here. He'd made a deal with the Devil when he did it, and he knew that, but there were no other options. After he'd been accused of selling Florida's history to China, most of his friends had shunned him, even before the latest incident. The commercial marinas spurned him, leaving her as the only one willing to accommodate him—for a price. But that didn't mean he had to like her.

"What the hell happened last night?" she screeched across the backyard.

"If you weren't in some kind of a wine-induced coma, you might have seen it. Some idiot came flying through here and crashed his boat into the bridge." He had no problem lying to her.

"And you had nothing to do with it?" she asked accusingly. "And you still owe me alimony."

He'd had enough of her bloodsucking bitterness and turned away, trying to think of who would fence enough of the coins he had stashed last night to give him some cash. He was cash-poor, but treasure-rich. The salvage business had always been a free-for-all, from the original wreckers in the eighteenth century to the first divers not too long ago. With the improvements in detection equipment and diving technology occurring at the same time, the long-lost Spanish wrecks had started to reappear. When the state had gotten involved in the '80s, the honeymoon was over. Now the government not only wanted a piece of the action, but insisted on sending archaeological experts to look over your shoulder. It had been speculative at best, even back then, but now with the state taking more than their fair share, it was impossible to even cover your costs.

He'd known when Wood and Mac had found the piece of the Mayan wreck back in the '90s that they were off the rails. The Mayans were known to have traveled much of the Caribbean and transported fortunes in gold. It had already been documented that they'd established trading routes through the Keys and up the southwest coast of Florida. But there was no need to haul along a fortune in gold to trade with the backwoods Florida Indians, or at least that's what he'd believed. The American indigenous people had a long history of being taken advantage of, and there was no reason the Mayans would part with their gold if they didn't need to.

No, he suspected that the notion of the tattoos of the old Toltec Indians containing some secret to an ancient treasure was wrong. But until Travis showed up with the drive, there was not enough evidence to figure out what the body art really meant.

The decision to send the men to follow Trufante to Key Largo had been an easy one after he'd checked Alicia Phon's background. A quick search had confirmed that the drive was heading to one of the top data analysts in the world. Alicia Phon—even her name sounded like a wonk, but if she could figure out the riddle, he needed her.

He picked up the phone and hit the button marked *Wallace*. The disbarred attorney answered on the second ring. "Get the girl and bring her and that damn drive back here."

"Got it, boss," Wallace said.

His blood was starting to boil at having to trust these two to do anything. "And don't screw it up," he screamed into the phone before disconnecting.

He cringed when the house door opened again. It had been just long enough for her to down another glass of wine. "Can you keep it down? I don't need the neighbors to know your dirty laundry," his ex yelled.

* * *

Startled by the ring, Mac grabbed the phone off the shelf. Surprised by the call, he disconnected the charging cord and looked at the display. To avoid the noise of the generator, he walked away from the shed.

"Hey," he said, not recognizing the number.

"I think we need to have a conversation," Hawk's voice came through the receiver.

Mac took the phone away from his ear and stared at it. Placing it back, he said, "You want me, you know where I live, and I don't know how much of a conversation it'll be." He was about to hang up when another call displayed. "Wait," he said.

He was ready to disconnect and pick up the other call when Hawk said, "Alicia Phon."

Not acknowledging, he cursed his lack of techno anything and pushed the button that said swap calls. "Alicia?" Mac asked, not trusting the display.

"Mac—wow, you answered. I think I found something," she said.

"Never mind that. Hide the data and get out of there," he said. "Where's Tru and TJ?"

"On a charter," she answered. "Out snorkeling. There was somebody up here snooping around. I don't think he saw me, though."

"Just go. Get somewhere safe and call me." He disconnected and tried to return to the other call, but the line was dead. He knew staying here was not going to help anyone. If she had found something, it could solve his problems, but if Hawk got to her first, they would multiply.

He ran to the beach and into the water. Untying the line, he pushed the bow forward to spin it and jumped over the gunwale. The engine started and he cruised out of the channel, pausing where the man-made excavation ended. The rock guarding the northern approach was exposed now that the tide was moving back out, and he looked down at the old cable lying in the water. Wood had rigged it to act as a boom, an old naval trick to stop boats from entering a harbor. When it was raised to just below the waterline, any approaching boat would either be holed or have its lower unit torn off.

With Hawk threatening him, he contemplated rerigging it. The equipment was still there, but he doubted that the cable was still in one piece after so many years in the salt water. Adding it to his list of things to do, he reversed into deeper water and pushed down the throttles.

The boat planed out quickly, and without the weight of the T-top, he didn't even need the trim tabs. The display on the fuel gauge was showing the consumption per hour was down as well. All things to consider before replacing it. He cruised past the flat where the boat had grounded and spun the wheel. It would only take a minute, and he knew if he waited, the guns would be lost to the shifting sands after a couple more tide changes. Slowly he approached the flat, easing the bow forward until he felt the slightest resistance. He cut the engine, checked the current, and decided that if he was quick, there would be no need to anchor.

Stripping off his shirt, he grabbed a mask from under one of the seats and hopped over the gunwale. Within a few minutes he located a Glock 9mm. The other gun was more elusive, and after a few passes, he gave up. Back aboard, he lay the pistol on the seat next to him and took off for Marathon.

* * *

Alicia shut down the screens and pocketed the drive, intending to put it in the dive shop's safe. She looked at her phone, knowing TJ wouldn't be back for at least an hour. There was no answer on his cell phone, but she knew the reception at the reef was hit-and-miss. Once downstairs, she could try to reach him from the VHF base station in the shop. Grabbing her purse from the kitchen counter, she went for the door, but it opened before she could reach it. The body in the frame blocked the light, and she recognized the man who had been prowling around earlier.

She screamed and he was on her. He was fast for his size, and right behind him came the other, smaller man. The larger man ratcheted her arm behind her back, forcing her to her feet by twisting her arm up. She tried to step on his foot and elbow him, but her blows were ineffective against his bulk. Unless she could somehow hit his groin, she had nowhere to go.

"Scream and you're done," the voice said, increasing the pressure on her arm.

She searched for a way out, but the dock was empty. The smaller man pulled a knife and showed her the blade. Calling out for help might only endanger the employees in the shop, and that was not an option. Mac knew they were after her. He would help. "Okay. I'll go," she said.

They escorted her to the sedan. The larger man pushed her into the backseat and crammed his bulk in next to her. She slid across to the other side, away from the man. The smaller man climbed in the driver's seat and backed out of the space. He pulled onto the road and followed it to the intersection with US-1, where he put on his left blinker. *At least he's heading the right way*, she thought.

The larger man was looking at his phone. "Pull over in two blocks. You should see a strip mall with a blue metal roof overhang."

"Hawk said to bring her right back," the driver said.

"This'll only take a second," he said, staring out the window at the passing buildings.

Alicia watched and waited. If there was unrest between the men, it might give her the chance she needed to make a break for it.

"There," the larger man called out, pointing his finger at the approaching building. "Yeah, that's the one."

"Department of Veterans Affairs? I didn't know you were a vet."

"Neither do they," the man said and opened the door just as the driver parked. "Keep her running."

Chapter 12

Alicia's mind ran wild. The only redeeming factor was that they were heading toward Marathon, though she had no idea if that would be the final destination. The large man was subdued now, almost smiling. She had to assume it was drugs after seeing him emerge from the VA clinic with a small bag, and his new attitude as much as confirmed it. Filing the information away for later, she thought about her present circumstances.

The pattern recognition program had pulled up a match, but of what she didn't know. It might reveal the significance of the tattoos or just add another layer of questions to the puzzle. Now, away from her lifeline, with no phone or Internet hookup, she was starting to panic.

They passed Islamorada and followed the chain of keys toward Key West. Marathon was only forty minutes away, and she needed some kind of a plan before they got there. A restroom stop and a run for it might work, but that would be her only chance, and the odds were thin at it succeeding. Assuming that they had weapons, and with flip-flops on her feet, it could end badly. Additionally, whatever trust she had gained by not resisting would evaporate.

Her training had taught her to observe and record if she was unable to take action, and she watched the two men, listening to their sporadic conversation. Bored, her mind started to drift back to the images on her computer screen at home. Mac had contacted her about the data on the drive, so it had to be important. Now, with these goons involved, whatever was revealed by the tattoos had a danger factor. She looked at her watch. Three o'clock—TJ should be getting back from the charter soon. He would see her phone lying on the desk and start to wonder. She was confident that with the help of Tru, he would try to contact Mac, but where did this leave her?

Marathon approached, and she returned to the present. They passed Key Colony Beach, and then the airport. After another mile, they turned left at the Kmart shopping center, and then right onto the first street. The road followed a golf course, where Wallace made a quick left after the clubhouse. A small bridge lay ahead with a group of boats working around it. They crossed and turned into the first driveway.

"Don't try nothing, you hear," Mike said to her, lifting his shirt and revealing the grip of a gun. He got out of the car, walked around to her door, and opened it, pulling her out. Together they walked through the carport underneath the house and followed the path to the dock. A large boat was sitting there with the engines running. It looked like a research ship and appeared out of place in the residential setting. Mike pushed her up the gangplank, where she found herself face-to-face with another man, obviously the boss from the way the two men acted. Though balding, he had not caved in and adopted the current style of shaving his head. His fashion taste was off as well for the T-shirt-and-board-short capital of the world; he wore a tailored button-down shirt, tucked into khaki pants, and looked like he should be on a cruise ship in Miami.

"Welcome, Ms. Phon. You will be our guest here. Act accordingly and you will be well treated. Otherwise, Mike here will instruct you."

He turned and walked through the cabin door. Mike pushed her forward. Her Agency training had taught her to observe things that didn't fit, and as she looked at the deck before entering the cabin, she made some quick deductions. This was clearly not a pleasure vessel; rather, from the rigging, the electronics tower, and the utilitarian deck, she determined it was a commercial ship of some kind. Inside, it took her a moment for her eyes to adjust, but when they did, she found herself in the main cabin. A large chart table was against one wall, and across from it was a desk with a built-in settee and several deck chairs off to the side. Ahead was the wheelhouse, where Wallace stood, working the electronics.

"Get the lines," Hawk called, moving forward to the wheelhouse and taking the wheel. Wallace and Mike ran fore and aft following his command, and she felt the boat move away from the dock.

* * *

TJ skillfully placed the forty-two-foot dive boat against the pilings and called to Trufante to get the lines. While he held the converted sportfisher in position, Trufante tossed the fenders over and tied the boat off. TJ cut the engines and climbed down from the helm. He brushed past the glowing group that, many of whom, including Pamela, had just experienced their first taste of the reef.

"Hey, man," Trufante called, but TJ was already racing up the stairs.

With the captain gone, the passengers looked to Trufante for direction. Although not technically crew, he had assisted many of them with their equipment and offered some technique instruction. "Hey, y'all," he called out. "Thanks for coming. Grab some brochures at the front desk and spread the word." He paused for a second and gave them his full smile. "And don't forget to take care of your crew."

He signaled to Pamela to wait for a second and jumped onto the dock. One at a time, the passengers disembarked. He helped each one like they were his grandmother and shook their hands, taking the proffered bills, which he skillfully placed in his pocket.

Pamela was last. "I've got a tip for you, but it'll have to wait for later." She smiled and took his hand.

Now this was getting back to normal, he thought. "Glad you enjoyed it," he said.

"Really, that was awesomeness. I'm going to check out the store."

Smiling back at her, he patted her butt as she walked away. "I'm gonna run upstairs and see what's up with TJ," he said, starting for the stairs.

"Okay. I'll do some shopping," she said.

His long stride allowed him to take the treads two at a time. The front door was open, and he entered. "TJ?" he called out. There was no answer, and he moved inside. "TJ," he called louder.

"Hey. In here."

Tru walked through the double doors and entered the war room. He had heard about it, but never been inside. TJ sat at a desk with his head in his hands. "What's up, dude?"

TJ looked up at him. "Alicia's gone. I knew something was wrong when she didn't answer her phone when we were coming in. I had one of the guys downstairs come up and knock on the door, but there was no answer. Her phone's on the counter, and the car's still here too. I got a bad vibe about this."

"Shoot," Trufante started.

TJ cut him off. "It's not like her," he said, holding her cell phone. "She'd never leave her phone."

"What are you thinking?" he asked, looking around the room. On the side-by-side screens were the pictures of the tattoos. "I know that one," he said, pointing to the image on the left screen.

"What of it?" TJ asked.

"That's what Mac wanted her to look at." He walked toward the screens for a better look.

"I can zoom that for you," TJ said.

"Ain't no need," he said, staring at the tattoos. "That there's from a dude named Diego. Don't know what the other one is, but it looks kinda the same."

"That doesn't help find Alicia," TJ said.

"I'll call Mac. Maybe he knows something," Trufante said,

pulling the phone from his pocket and pressing several buttons. He held it to his ear, but after a minute, he pushed another button and slid it back into his pants. "Gone straight to voice mail."

"That's not good," TJ said.

"Just the way he is. Thinks the boogeyman can find it if he keeps it on."

"So, what are we going to do?"

TJ was getting anxious. "All roads lead down the old US-1 to Marathon. We had a run-in with some bad dudes last night. This has got to be connected." Trufante rubbed the stubble on his chin, trying to connect the dots.

"Okay. Let's get going," TJ said. Trufante followed him out of the room, and TJ grabbed the car keys from the counter.

"Maybe we should take the boat. Won't take but another half hour or so this time of day, and I'm guessing it'll come in handy."

TJ nodded and dropped the car keys. "Hold on," Trufante said and went back to the war room. He went to the desk and grabbed the coin.

* * *

Mac had already pulled back on the throttles and was just about to round the piling marking the channel to the boat ramp when he saw the sheriff's boat tied up to the dock. Without thinking, he dropped into neutral and pulled back slightly on the lever, giving enough reverse thrust to counteract his momentum. The boat was empty, but he saw the deputy that had brought the building inspector out talking to a couple about to drop their boat into the water.

Not wanting a confrontation, and expecting that they might be looking for him for a statement about the incident at Hawk's last night, he pulled back further and cut the wheel to the left. There was no doubt that Hawk would have blamed the crash on him. The bow swung over, and he had open water in front of him. Slowly he pushed the throttle forward, and the boat started moving away. Risking a look back, his eyes met the deputy's, and he knew he had made the right decision. Not wanting to look guilty, he turned east, following the coast. He rounded a point and chanced another look behind when he saw the bow of the sheriff's boat pull out of the cut.

To his right was a narrow opening that led to the marina at Keys Fisheries. It was his best option. There was no way to outrun the more powerful boat, and doing so would likely land him in jail. Ducking into the marina was his safest bet. If the deputy saw him, so be it. If he didn't, he had dodged a bullet.

He entered the marina, where he saw several open slips usually occupied by charter boats. He pulled into one, running forward to grab the line looped on the pile and tie it off before the boat coasted to a stop.

"Mac Travis. Come back to say thank you?" Celia put down her cell phone and moved toward him.

He had meant to thank her for creating a diversion the other night, but before he could say anything, her gaze moved from him to the cut, and he knew the deputy was there. "Yeah," he muttered, wondering what to do.

"It's your lucky day. Old Celia'll help you out again. Got no love for that effin' bastard. You know, me and him dated in high school," she said.

Mac jumped onto the dock and looked at her. "I'm open to ideas."

She shook an angry finger at the sheriff's boat as if it would ward him off. "Hide behind the console on that boat and watch me." She pointed to a large open fishing boat.

"I owe you," Mac said and went for the deck of the adjacent boat. He ducked behind the gunwale and watched.

Celia stood with her hand on her hip, her body language daring the deputy to come any closer. He must have gotten her message and idled out into the center of the harbor, where he worked both throttles to keep the boat in place, obviously not wanting to get any closer.

"Where is he?" he shouted across the water.

"What's a matter, babe?" She swung her other hip out. "I won't bite."

"I'm just trying to do my job here. We just want to talk to him, that's all," he said.

Mac almost believed him, but then he remembered Hawk's friendship with the new sheriff. There was no love lost between Mac and the sheriff, and even if they did just want to talk, they would make him come in and give a statement.

"He ain't here," Celia called back.

"I seen him come in here, and that's his boat," the deputy pleaded.

"I don't know nothin' about that effin' boat or anyone coming in on it," she countered.

"You run this place. Nothing happens here that you don't know about."

"Well, Mr. Deputy. You calling me a liar?" A string of expletives followed.

Mac was almost laughing when the deputy spun the boat and moved away. He rose from the deck.

"I owe you for that," he said.

"That was sport, my friend. But, come on, tell ol' Celia what you're up to," she said.

"I gotta beg off. Got a friend in trouble," Mac said.

"Wait here," she said, walking away with a swagger that made her weight seem right.

She was back a minute later and handed him a single key attached to a piece of foam. "Maybe this'll help. Ever run a quad before?" She pointed to the thirty-foot center-console that dwarfed his old boat. Four gleaming engines hung from the transom.

"I owe ya, girl," he said. Taking the keys, he jumped onto the deck.

"Yes, you do, Mac Travis, yes, you do. Take care of my babies now."

Chapter 13

Mac turned the key and scanned the cluttered dashboard. The four engine controls alone took up a huge amount of real estate, stacked two over two on the left side of the wheel. The twin touchscreen chart plotters filled the space above, and a row of gauges was to the right side, with two rows of rocker switches below them. He'd figure out the controls once he was clear of the deputy. He wanted to be gone in case the man discovered his courage and came back.

He depressed the start buttons one at a time, and the engines roared to life. Mac tested the wheel and nodded to Celia, who tossed the lines. The boat jumped when he pulled back the throttles, but he gained control, realizing that with 1000 hp behind him, he would need to be careful. He cut the wheel and took a deep breath as the bow turned to face the open Gulf. Even with all his years of running boats, the power behind him was scary. Easing the throttles forward to get the feel for them, he felt the boat slide away from the dock.

He almost reversed when he saw the deputy sitting outside the harbor talking on his cell phone, but he turned his head to hide his face and waited to clear the last marker before pushing the throttles down hard. The boat was on plane before he knew it, and like a horse, he gave it its head to see what it could do. Amazed at the speed, he cruised to deeper water, not turning until he was well out of the deputy's line of sight.

Cruising at over fifty knots, he checked the gauges and calculated the fuel consumption in his head. It showed plenty of fuel, but the engines were thirsty, their current consumption on the display reading almost thirty gallons an hour. He slowed to a modest twenty-five knots and looked ahead to the point of land that hid the Vaca Key cut. Following the shore, he stayed in the deep water between Rachel Key and Rachel Bank, rounded the point at Stirrup Key, and passed Russell Key, where he cut the wheel, leaving the green number thirteen marker on his starboard side. Slowing to fifteen knots, he stayed in the narrow channel between the markers, emerging a minute later on the Atlantic side. The small houses of Key Colony Beach were to port as he increased speed and entered the deeper channel between the mainland and the reef, where he turned toward the west. He cruised at thirty knots, the deep V of the bow easily tossing aside the two-foot waves, and started the electronics.

The unit on the left was configured for the radar; the one on the right showed the boat's location and direction of travel superimposed over a nautical chart. He had thought about heading to Key Largo, but if Hawk had taken Alicia, she would be heading this way. On a whim, he turned on his cell phone, setting it on the bench next to him while it started up. He passed the private island just offshore of Sombrero Beach and took a wide turn to enter Sister Creek. On reaching the first green marker, he slowed and picked up the phone.

There weren't many numbers stored in its memory, and the *T*s came up quickly. He cut the rpms and picked up the phone.

Trufante answered immediately. "Mac. They got Alicia," he yelled over the roar of the sportfisher's engines.

"Can you go below so I can hear you?" Mac said, surprised by how quiet the four outboards behind him were.

"Can you hear me now?" Trufante asked.

"Yeah. I had a feeling Hawk was going to pull something

like this. I'm heading into Sister Creek to see if he's still there," Mac said, turning the wheel into the canal.

"Me and TJ are heading that way. We're just passing Islamorada. Should be there in an hour or so."

"I'll call you back in a few and figure out where to meet." He thought for a minute, figuring that if Trufante was involved, anything could happen. It would be better to assign a rendezvous now, and there was only one place nearby where that would work. Although it would kill a small part of him to see the vacant lot where his house had been, he picked up the phone and hit redial. "Meet me at my old house," he said and hung up.

Hawk wouldn't know the boat, but he would spot him at the wheel. With that in mind, Mac stopped in a wider portion of the canal, its shape dictated by the natural mangrove shoreline. He climbed the stainless steel rungs and took control of the boat from above. There were no electronics up here, just the basic controls, allowing the driver a better view of the open water. For fishing, it was essential for extending the horizon to spot birds and debris floating in the water or to peer into the transparent water to see the reefs. For his purposes, it would shield him from any eyeballs at ground level.

He made the last turn and entered the dead-end canal, immediately cutting the engines. Still worried that he would be seen, he stayed against the right shoreline, cutting the line of sight from Hawk's boat, but also taking him longer to realize that the trawler was gone.

* * *

"Plot a course to Key West," Hawk ordered the guy they called Mike.

She tensed when he turned and came toward her.

"Easy there, sweetheart. I've got no interest in hurting you. Just want what's in that brain of yours," he said and sat in the chair across from her.

She continued staring out the large rectangular window, watching the water as they cruised west. Trying to estimate their speed and distance to Key West not only kept her mind off her predicament, but would also let her know how much time she had to work with. She doubted he was in a big enough hurry to redline the engines and guessed they were probably going close to fifteen knots. That would put them four to five hours out of Key West, depending on currents and wind. Plenty of time to delay him and find a solution.

"What do you want from me?" she asked meekly. The Agency training had taught her not to be aggressive in this kind of situation. Better to let her captor feel in control.

He shifted the thumb drive from hand to hand. "Just want to know what's on this. You figure it out and I'll cut you in."

"Cut me in for what?" She was curious now. Not that she would take the deal, but she sensed that he knew more than she did and might provide some information to help her solve the mystery.

"Don't play that game with me. I know you know," he said.

The only thing she knew for certain was that there were images of tattoos, and her program had found some kind of match. But she had been abducted before she could cross-reference what she'd found and discover the meaning. "I'll need some equipment to continue my research."

"I've got a laptop here. Get me the location and I'll make you a wealthy woman." He pushed forward the computer that sat between them.

The offer didn't appeal to her at all. If she'd wanted wealth, she would have stayed in Silicon Valley. "That toy? I can barely check my Facebook feed on that. I'll need more power."

"Please don't make this more difficult. I did my own research and know what you are capable of." He pushed the laptop the remaining inches to the edge of the table.

There was no harm, she thought. This could buy her some time. "I'll need a lot of broadband."

"Not a problem. Full Wi-Fi aboard," he said. "I'll leave you to it." He got up and walked forward to the wheelhouse.

It was a gamble using the remote access portal, but she had a failsafe and quickly loaded a cloaking program from the Internet. After it finished loading, she assigned a hot key combination that when activated would destroy anything recorded on the drive in an instant. A data expert could retrieve it, but that would mean time, and she figured Hawk was running on a tight schedule. Once it was installed, she breathed a sigh of relief.

With the program running in the background, she opened a browser window and entered an address. A peer-to-peer site opened and she entered her password. A minute later, the screen showed her computer in Key Largo. This would enable her to do some research, and, on the off chance that TJ was there, she could communicate with him. It was cumbersome switching screens back and forth, but she navigated to the match the database had pulled up and pushed Mac's drive into the USB port.

The image that her recognition program showed on the screen surprised her. It wasn't another tattoo at all, but an old chart. Forgetting her circumstances, her analytical brain took over, and she became totally absorbed in the work. Switching windows and opening databases was cumbersome on the single screen, but she now knew that Mac had been right. There was some kind of a map embedded in the tattoos. Now she just needed to figure it out. The knowledge might be the bargaining chip that could save them.

* * *

Working the throttles for the outside engines, Mac spun the boat and reversed his course. He had no idea when Hawk's boat had left, but with Celia's children purring behind him, he could make up the miles fast. While he steered the canals leading back to the inlet from memory, he waited for the screen on the left to power up. The radar display soon became visible, showing concentric five-mile circles centered on the boat. It was jumbled this close to shore, with too many boats and houses nearby. Patiently he navigated the channel, holding his speed down until he was clear of the last marker. He knew a boat like this, especially one owned by Celia, would be a target for the half dozen law enforcement agencies that patrolled these waters.

Clear of the inlet, he pushed down the throttle. Despite himself, he smiled as the boat went up on plane and hit fifty-five knots. Within minutes he was past Sombrero Light, the red steel structure standing sentinel over the reef five miles from shore. He kept going for another few minutes and slowed. Working the controls on the screen, he adjusted the radar and studied the screen, starting with the marks east and west of his location. The Bahamas were to the south, and he doubted Hawk had reason to cross into international waters, especially with a hostage aboard, and Marathon was to the north. If he was there, the radar would be useless.

Several large blips showed on the screen, and he looked out to sea trying to get a visual on the closest. It was a tanker, moving west, probably motoring just inside the Gulf Stream to save fuel. Using the size of the ship and relating it to the mark on the screen, he was able to narrow the search to boats the size of Hawk's. There were several, and he studied their courses, trying to guess which one held Alicia.

Three were headed toward Key West, and unable to make any further distinctions, he took a wild guess and headed after them. Two were in Hawks Channel, the inside passage, and the third was working at an oblique angle that looked like it was heading to the Cay Sal Banks, a shallow area in Bahamian waters that was coveted by fishermen. The only way to get confirmation was to follow them.

The blips on the screen became closer every minute. He soon ruled one out as probably a sailboat, and minutes later his guess was confirmed as he passed a ketch rig moving west. That left only one boat underway, and he pushed the throttles to their limits. At over sixty knots, he was moving about four times faster than the boat on the screen, and he soon saw a dot on the horizon that turned into a thin line and then took on the shape of a ship. He didn't need to get any closer to confirm it was Hawk.

Chapter 14

Mac knew he was outnumbered and outgunned. In his rush to escape the deputy, he had left the Glock aboard the center-console. The only weapon he had was speed. There was no way he could rescue Alicia by himself, and he didn't want to let Hawk know he had been discovered. Turning back, he pushed the boat to its limits, not surprised when the speed hit sixty-five knots. The faster he met TJ and Tru, the sooner they could be in pursuit. He locked onto the radar signature of Hawk's ship and set the most direct course for Boot Key Harbor.

Less than a half hour later, he entered the channel. Passing the gas docks on his port side, he idled past City Marina and turned left into one of the side canals. TJ's sportfisher was already docked, blocking the view of his old house—one that he didn't want to see anyway. The dock was too short for both boats, and not wanting to use his neighbor's empty section, he called to the men and pulled up alongside the larger boat. He eyed the house next door, wanting to get out of here before he was seen. Mac was responsible for the loss of his sailboat—the reason his dock was empty.

"Hot damn, Mac, nice wheels," Trufante said.

"We can thank Celia," he said. "I just spotted Hawk's boat heading toward Key West. Hop in, we can catch them."

TJ looked warily at him. "I don't know, Mac, better to have

my own boat."

Mac understood and explained, "We got to head them off. With the radar, we can race offshore, beat them down there, and get Alicia back."

"Take 'em by surprise," Trufante chimed in. "Come on, I gotta see how fast that sucker'll run."

Pamela appeared from the cabin and followed Trufante, both their faces lit up by the four engines on the transom like this was some kind of pleasure cruise. TJ nodded, locked the cabin behind her, and reluctantly stepped aboard. Mac gave orders to the men and tried not to frown at Pamela. He had no qualms taking a woman along; she was just unproven. He knew what he could expect from the two men, but so far she had a stronger magnet than Trufante for attracting trouble.

"Long, strange trip, Mac Travis," she said as she passed him, moving to the padded seat by the transom.

He ignored her and signaled to Trufante to release the lines, and minutes later they were past the last marker, picking up speed and heading southwest. The afternoon was beautiful. Under other circumstances, he would have enjoyed the light catching the ripples on the calm water and the feel of a well-built boat below him, cutting through the water. But his teeth ground together, and he was focused on only one thing.

"I think that's them," Mac said, pointing to a blip on the screen. It had been less than an hour since he'd had eyes on it, and he was glad the signal was still there. The boat should have made another fifteen miles, putting them off Sugarloaf Key.

All three men were leaning against the rocket launcher, hands firmly clenching the grab bars as they stared at the electronic display. They watched as the range narrowed; Hawk's ship was now inside the ten-mile ring. At this rate they would catch him soon. Mac needed a plan.

"He's got to be heading for Key West. We can cut outside and beat him there, then anchor in the channel behind old Tank

Island. They'll have to run past us to reach one of the marinas."

Both men nodded. He fine-tuned the throttles, synchronizing the engines at 4400 rpm, and watched the GPS. They were going over fifty knots now, and he looked over at the men. Trufante had a huge smile on his face. TJ was the opposite, clearly worried about Alicia. A glance back at Pamela confirmed that she was out in her own world. He added another 400 rpm, and the boat jumped forward and hit sixty knots.

Mac was used to navigating IFR, or "instrument flying required," as pilots called it. He'd been setting lobster pots and diving in all kinds of sketchy conditions for years. Though unable to work a smartphone, he was at home with the electronics on a boat. With one eye on the chart plotter and the other on the radar, he changed course slightly to the south. It wasn't the most direct line for Key West, but would put them offshore of Hawk's trawler when they passed. At their current speed, even with the course change, they would be in Key West at least an hour before Hawk. Fuel was a concern, though. Not knowing where this adventure was leading, he was worried at the rate of consumption. TJ might have a credit card, but he and Trufante did not have the means to fuel the boat. As soon as they cleared Hawk's boat, he backed off the throttles, dropping the fuel consumption into a more palatable range.

* * *

Alicia was so engrossed in her work that she didn't notice Hawk looking over her shoulder.

"I knew the tattoos were some kind of map," he said.

"Duh. But that's too wide a subject," she said. Then, realizing he was standing behind her, she hit the hot key combination and the screen went dark. Her fingers were poised to enter the last keystroke that would wipe the drive, but she waited.

"That kind of behavior is not going to help you," he said.

"And you are not going to get any more information. I think we are at a standstill," she said, not really sure she had any leverage.

"And there's no guarantee that what you find will be the answer, either. I've been around this game long enough to know things are not always the way they seem. People will go through such extreme lengths to hide treasure that they forget their own clues."

She nodded, acknowledging he was right. It was the same in data analysis. The high-end encryptions had dead ends and false trails laced throughout the code. She knew more than one programmer who had forgotten his key, making the data worthless. "What about a deal?"

"I'm listening," he said.

"You need me, or you would have found this already. What if we work together and split the find?"

He paused. "If you come up with the answer, we can work out a deal," he said.

She couldn't help but notice the smirk on his face. There was no way she could trust him, but she was obsessing about the riddle now. "Okay, but I need more power than this." She lifted her fingers from the keys.

"We'll be in Key West in a couple of hours. I'll see what we can do for you." He turned to walk away.

"What's in Key West?" she asked.

"Just work on the data. And I'll need some insurance." He called to Wallace, who set what looked like a shock collar for a large dog and several tools on the desk.

"That's not necessary," she pleaded.

"Like I said. Just insurance," Hawk said and nodded to Wallace, who placed the collar around her neck, adjusted it, and fastened the two bolts with a wrench.

She wiggled, trying to get as much space between the rough material and her skin, but as he tightened the bolts, she felt the two probes touch her skin. With a glare in Hawk's direction, she went back to work. He was right, the tattoos were a map, but that was the easy part. Assuming this was several hundred years old, she had her work cut out for her. Charts from that era were often more artistic than accurate. The cartographers took liberties where things were unknown and often hid ciphers in their drawings, creating a code within the chart. She entered another sequence and the screen lit up again. Studying the chart, she noticed the landforms resembled their present-day representations, but the accuracy was nowhere close to what they needed to even start a search pattern.

Splitting the window, she started to scroll through maps of the Keys. They were all similar, but none matched the patterns so carefully etched on Diego and Teqea's bodies. She got up and stood by the chart table next to the desk. She stared at a large-scale NOAA chart of the Lower Keys that was open on the table. Pattern recognition, whether in lines of code or in visual objects, was her specialty, but she knew it was her subconscious that solved the riddles, so she just stared at the chart, letting her inner processor work.

It was the grid lines drawn over the features and soundings that caught her attention. She studied the key with the help of a small magnifying glass she found in the drawer and was able to see that the lines indicated latitude and longitude. That all made sense. They were the means of locating a position, but in antiquity they were "undiscovered." Ancient mariners had a more instinctual method for navigation, using stars, swells, and experience to estimate their positions. Their GPS units were built into their heads.

She went back to the laptop and looked at the two tattoos side by side. Though the artwork was different, they too showed an underlying grid, but it didn't match the lines on the present-day chart. She closed the windows and opened the Internet browser, entering "ancient mariners charts" into the search window. The results were far-reaching, but slowly she narrowed down the results chronologically. Charts from the 1970s and 1980s were cluttered, not only with the latitude and longitude lines but also with Loran lines. This was closer to the patterns she was trying to match, but she knew they were too recent to be utilized in the tattoos, their lines based on signals from land-based radio towers.

The vibration of the engines changed and she went to the window, realizing it was almost dark. Land was ahead, and they passed a marker with a red triangle on top. The boat turned and slowed before heading into a harbor. The men were moving about the boat now, readying it for port. The collar bothered her, but it did have a benefit; she was deemed safe now and was given more freedom. Unwatched, she opened the cabin door and looked out at the harbor, trying to think of a way out.

* * *

"There he goes," Mac said as they watched the boat move past the former fuel depot, now a resort island, blocking their view for a minute before the boat reappeared and turned into the channel to the Key West Bight.

"What we gonna do now?" Trufante asked. "I'm getting hungry."

Pamela came by his side and slipped an arm around him. "Happy hour in Margaritaville!"

Mac expected he was thirstier than hungry, the lure of Duval Street so close whetting his appetite, and she was not exactly a good influence. "Let's make sure they get a slip here before we make any moves." The boat was out of sight now, but the radar showed it moving directly toward land. Soon it stopped, and Mac waited, assuming they had found a slip.

"Come on, Mac. It's almost dark. They're parked for the night," Trufante said.

"It'd be nice to have a closer look," TJ said.

Mac could tell Trufante was amped up and ready for a party,

but his mind was made up by TJ's plea.

"You're right. But I'm thinking we ought to go around to Garrison Bight. They won't know the boat, but they know us." Mac started the engines and hit the switch for the windlass to raise the anchor.

Trufante was clearly pleased and went forward to knock the mud from the hook before securing it in place. Mac zoomed in the chart plotter, checking the best route to the marina. He could have felt his way around the island, but he didn't get down here often enough to know it by heart. Actually, he avoided the place like the plague.

Twenty minutes later he called the harbormaster at Garrison Bight and arranged for a slip. They entered the harbor and docked. Trufante jumped out of the boat, gallantly extended a hand to Pamela, and helped her ashore. Hand in hand, they headed toward the restaurant at the end of the dock.

"What the…?"

Mac could tell TJ was getting anxious. "Let 'em go. He's a handful by himself. With the girl along, it only complicates things more."

"You're right. I'm just worried about Alicia," he said, checking his phone like there would be a miraculous message from her.

"I got a little cash. Let's grab a cab and do some surveillance." Mac fiddled with the electronics, shutting down the systems one at a time. He accidentally hit an unmarked switch and jumped when blue LED lights started flashing under the transom. Both men laughed at the display obviously intended to attract attention to the boat when it was tied up at the marina, spotlighting Celia's kids on her transom. He shut off the lights and the rest of the systems, then went below and turned off the battery switch just in case he had missed something.

Together they walked down the dock and passed the oyster bar. Mac was hungry, but it would wait. He wanted to make sure that Hawk was here for the night. A pink cab pulled to the curb, answering his signal, and they got in. Mac gave instructions to the driver, and ten minutes later they were standing at the end of Simonton Street, looking into the harbor. Mac paid the driver, noting his dwindling cash, and together he and TJ surveyed the harbor, looking for Hawk's boat. He breathed a sigh of relief when they saw it docked by the far corner of the marina.

"Come on. As long as we stay in the shadows, we should be okay," Mac said, leading the way around the first pile. Most of the boats had lights on, making it difficult to stay out of sight, but they reached the slip just before Hawk's, apparently unobserved. Mac pulled TJ into the shadows when he heard a loud conversation on the deck of the trawler.

"You are under orders," he heard Hawk say.

"You might be my boss, but this ain't the Navy." It sounded like Ironhead.

"If you care for your employment at all, you will stay aboard," Hawk said.

"I'll be back soon," Ironhead said.

They huddled together, out of sight, as the thug passed. He was clearly on a mission and walked right past them. Mac exhaled, watching the ship to see if Hawk would follow. He started to plan. Without his muscle, this might be as vulnerable as they were going to find him.

Chapter 15

A hand reached in and snatched the silver coin Trufante was bouncing off the bar. "True dat. Heard you got your ass run outta town."

Trufante winced when he heard the voice. He turned slowly and grabbed the man's arm, a large smile appearing on his face as he squeezed it until the coin dropped back on the bar.

"I was just playin', Holmes," the man said. "And whatcha got here?" From his stare it was obvious what he was talking about.

"Pamela, this here's Jimmy. A turd I know from a past life," he said.

"Shit. If I'm a lowlife, what does that make you?" Jimmy said and slapped him on the back.

She turned back to the bar and started humming "Ship of Fools." Trufante put an arm around her, but she ignored him and started tapping on her phone. He turned to face Jimmy, his larger-than-life smile gone.

"You're lookin' a little rough around the edges—even for you," Trufante said. The bare-chested man standing at the bar looked like a wannabe from *The Sopranos*. Even his half-fake New Jersey accent, carefully groomed to include all the right words, belied him. He stood a head shorter than Trufante, gaining a few inches with his trucker's hat complete with knock-off designer sunglasses set on the visor. A rip-off Tommy Bahama shirt was unbuttoned, revealing way more than anyone would want to look at. The outfit was completed by ratty board shorts in a different pattern than the shirt and rubber flip-flops. If his attire wasn't bad enough, it was capped with a continuous layer of sweat coating his entire body.

"Hey," he called to the bartender. "Send down a round, would ya?"

The only redeeming factor about Jimmy was his wallet. He was always flush with cash, buying him friends in a town where the natives barely got by. His means were unclear and his persona shady—also okay in a town that lived on the edge. The bartender set three glasses in front of them. Pamela finished her old one, pushed the glass forward, and started in on the new one, all without taking her eyes from the phone.

"So, whatcha been up to?" Trufante asked, feeling he owed him something now that he had bought a round.

"This and that. It's Key West. Always an opportunity," Jimmy said.

Trufante nodded his head. That was something he could relate to. Pamela swung around and, with a loud slurp and a giggle, finished her drink.

"Babe. You think we could get out of here? It's a little creepy-crawly," she said.

Jimmy appeared not to notice the comment was directed at him. He moved down the bar, slapped someone on the back, and reached around him, grabbing an oyster from the tray on the bar. He moved back to Trufante and Pamela, slurping the mollusk directly from the shell. Trufante felt a jab in his side, so he turned to the bartender and asked for the tab. Seconds later, as if the bartender couldn't wait to get Jimmy away from his customers either, he handed Trufante a slip of paper.

"Here, babe, ya got it?" he asked, his smile back.

She gave him a vacant look. "My purse is in the saddlebags

on your bike—back at TJ's place."

Trufante's smile faded.

"We've been on boats, like, nonstop. I didn't even think."

"Tru, Tru, Tru." Jimmy overheard the conversation and zeroed in for the kill. "Your old friend Jimmy knows you're good for it. You just give me that coin, and I'll hold it for collateral. From the looks of it, I could float you something extra on top."

The something extra got his attention. After all, it was Key West. If he could put some cash in his pocket and rid himself of Jimmy, why not? It was just another old coin. He reached into his pocket and pulled the dull silver out. Just as he was about to hand it to Jimmy, Pamela stopped him.

"Let me get a picture of it. I'll put it on Facebook, like we're real treasure hunters," she said, grabbing the coin and placing it on the bar. She stood hovering above it with her phone and took a picture of the front and back.

Jimmy reached in and grabbed it, biting it like a pirate before putting it in his pocket. He reached into his back pocket and pulled out his wallet. Close enough that Trufante could smell the horseradish from the oyster on his breath, he opened the wallet, wide enough for anyone nearby to see the stack of hundreds. With a flourish, he pulled out two and handed them to Trufante. "That'll be three bills when you want it back," he said, returning his wallet to his pocket.

"Three hundred? For two? That ain't hardly right," Trufante pleaded.

"Shit. A small price for saving your ass. I got no problem keeping the coin. Either way." He turned and walked down the bar, grabbed another oyster, and continued his search for more victims.

* * *

"Come on, babe." Trufante pocketed the money and led Pamela outside.

"Where we going now?" she asked. "You going to show me a good time in paradise? Sloppy Joe's, The Bull, Hog's Breath— let's do it up." She took his hand and started across the parking lot.

He pulled her back into a dark corner by the bar. "How 'bout a little Key West intrigue?"

"Intrigue? Like spy stuff?" She grinned. "That could be fun. Can we still get a drink?"

"As many as you want," he said, pulling one of the hundreds from his pocket. "Why don't you run on in there?" He pointed to another bar next door. "And get us a couple of drinks to go. I'll keep an eye on our friend here."

She took the money. "That guy creeps me out," she said.

"We gotta help Alicia, and I got a feeling he's gonna lead us right to her."

"This isn't going to get dangerous, is it? Like with those guys at the house?" she asked.

He leaned in close, flashing his vintage Cadillac grille smile. "Would I be asking you to get cocktails to bring to a knife fight?"

Reassured, she started bopping over to the bar. He turned to watch the door. Jimmy was seldom welcome anywhere for very long. He should be coming out any minute. As long as Pama-Bama-Jama got back with the drinks first, they were all good.

She came back from the bar carrying two large red cups and two miniatures. "Look, these are so cute, I had to get a couple."

He took the small cup, being careful not to spill it. "Jell-O shots?" he asked.

"Party on." She smiled and clinked the plastic cups together. They both placed their heads back and shook the Jell-O from the cup.

With the shot in his mouth, he reached in to kiss her, but Jimmy walked out of the bar, distracting him. Trufante took the larger cup and pulled her into the shadows.

"This spy stuff is fun," she said, kissing him.

He almost gave into the temptation to close his eyes and

enjoy it, but Jimmy was gone. Reluctantly, he broke off the kiss, giving her butt a hard squeeze. "007 here. Ready to roll?" If the spy stuff didn't work, at least they'd have a good time.

Slowly, he moved out of the shadows. He looked down the street and saw Jimmy bending over to unlock a scooter.

"Shoot."

"What's wrong?" Pamela asked.

"We'll never keep up with him," he said, pointing to the scooter.

"There's an app for that." She pulled her phone out and pressed an icon. "Two minutes," she said. Catching his confused look, she added, "Uber, dude."

He drew a blank and was about to ask what she was talking about when a rickshaw pulled up at the corner. She grabbed his hand and led him toward it. The driver, sitting on a bicycle with a small cart behind it, greeted them. "Your Uber is here."

Trufante was still confused when Pamela pulled him into the open seat behind the driver.

"I need your destination," the driver, a rail thin man probably in his mid-thirties, said.

"How about we go off the clock and do a cash deal?" Pamela asked. "And the first thing would be a drink."

"We got to keep him in sight." Trufante pointed Jimmy out to the driver.

"Jimmy Bones?" the man asked.

Trufante had never heard his last name, and he laughed, sure that he had fabricated that along with the rest of his persona. Jimmy was on the scooter now and pulling into traffic.

"Yeah, follow that scum," Trufante said, playing the odds that the driver probably didn't like Jimmy either. Keeping him in sight was not a problem. It didn't matter what you drove in Key West. A bicycle was as fast as a car on the narrow crowded streets, and the rickshaw had no problem keeping up with the scooter. Jimmy paused at the stop sign at Duval, and Pamela jumped out.

"I'm getting us a refill." She grabbed his cup and ran across the street to a counter that called itself The Smallest Bar in the World.

He would have stopped her, but with the traffic cruising Duval, she would easily have the drinks in hand before they were able to cross. Finally, the driver found an opening, pedaled hard across the street, and picked her up on the other side. Trufante took the cups, and she hopped in, a huge grin on her face.

Jimmy was a block ahead of them. He crossed Whitehead and started weaving his way to the water. Trufante and Pamela sat back, watching the Victorian houses cruise by like any other tourist couple, except their destination would be determined by Jimmy Bones.

* * *

Mac crouched down by the dock, watching the trawler. From his position, the windows on Hawk's boat were hidden behind equipment or bulkheads. The only way to see what was happening was to board one of the boats docked on either side. He looked at the boats adjacent to it, trying to see if they were empty and if they allowed for a better vantage point, but was distracted when he heard someone coming toward them. Turning for a better look, he caught the flash of a lighter and saw the red end of a cigarette. Before he got any closer, Mac slithered back to TJ, pointing to the approaching figure. He whispered for him to stay put and slowly moved toward the dock.

His eye followed the flare of the cigarette butt, as it caught its last breath of air, before being dowsed in the water. The man was still fifty feet away and looked to be approaching Hawk's boat. Creeping forward, Mac crouched down by the shore power box, fiddling with the cord like there was something wrong with it. Slowly he moved to the sailboat docked on the starboard side, rose to his full height, and approached it like he owned it. Just as he was about to step from the concrete section of the dock to the wooden finger pier, their eyes locked. The last thing he expected was to see someone he knew, or rather who knew him.

"Mac Travis? In Key West? I should have figured you'd be around if your boy Trufante was here. And a silver coin too." He reached into his pocket and pulled out the coin, flipping it carelessly in the air. Mac was about to snatch it from him, but was distracted by a tipsy couple turning the corner from Front Street, looking like they had enjoyed their evening in Key West. The couple turned at one of the finger piers, and he turned back to Jimmy.

"Where'd you get it, Jimmy?" Mac said quietly. He knew the man, having hired him years ago for a salvage job. Another half-bent Northerner making their way to Key West, needing some temporary work to make it the final sixty miles to what they thought would be their paradise. It was a pilgrimage of the misfits. They often stopped in Marathon, looking for work on the way down, quitting as soon as they had enough money to move on, their minds filled with dreams of the paradise just down the road. Then, disillusioned and often broker than when they had come through before, they'd come back, but with a different attitude. Mac could always tell the ones that would make it and those he would see on their return trip. Jimmy was one of those he'd never expected to see again.

He laughed, and with his face close enough that Mac was forced to step backwards, he whispered, "Payback's a bitch." He got in Mac's face. "Now I have something you want."

"Here to sell it to Hawk? He's here for a few hours and already the scavengers are coming in," Mac said.

"I ain't no scavenger. Nope, Jimmy's legit."

Mac was about to respond when he saw a movement in the shadows. Before the next words could leave his mouth, something smashed into his head and he fell to the deck.

Chapter 16

TJ sat motionless, blood pounding in his ears but unable to do anything as Ironhead picked up a boat hook, wound up, and swung. Mac dropped to the deck. The thug kicked him and then turned to look at the strange man who Mac had been talking to.

"What do you want?" Ironhead asked the man.

The guy who called himself Jimmy pulled something from his pocket and held it out. "Just want a minute with your boss."

"You on a fishing trip or you selling?" Ironhead asked.

"Maybe both. I think he'll want to see this," Jimmy said.

Ironhead grabbed Mac's legs and started pulling him to the boat.

"Wait, what about me?" Jimmy asked, clearly afraid to move closer.

"Just stay there. I'll be back with an answer," Ironhead said and crossed to the deck of the ship. He turned, pulled Mac across the void, and hauled him through a cabin door.

TJ was alone and far outside of his comfort zone.

* * *

Mac tried to lift his head, but it stuck to the deck. It took him several tries before the clotted blood broke free. He sat up slowly, waited for the room to stop spinning, and looked around. The cabin was windowless, leading him to believe it was under the waterline. It was empty—devoid of furnishings or supplies, just the steel floor and bulkheads. Placing his hand against the wound, he was thankful the bleeding had stopped. He sat still and listened for a few minutes, trying to get his bearings. The engines were off, and the gentle lapping of the waves against the steel hull told him they were still in the harbor.

Sitting against the wall, he tried to piece together what had happened. Jimmy Bones's face flashed in his memory, and he frowned. If there was anyone that attracted more flies than Trufante, it was Jimmy, but where the Cajun was just a magnet, Bones was actually shit. There was nothing accidental or unlucky about him; it was just bad juju.

Without warning the door opened, and Ironhead entered. Mac instinctively moved to the corner in case he needed to protect himself, but the larger man just smiled.

"Boss wants to see you," he said and moved out of the doorway.

There was no fight in him, and Mac slowly got to his feet. With a hand on the wall for support, he held up his other hand, signaling for Ironhead to hold on, and waited for his vision to clear. It was certainly a concussion, and he hoped nothing more, because he knew that a doctor's visit was not in the plan. Feeling stable enough to walk on his own, he moved to the hatch and stepped into the companionway. He looked around, forming a picture of the ship in his head. He already knew the main deck, and now he saw the two steel doors behind him and a flight of stairs in front. Ironhead pointed up, and he climbed.

"Well, Travis, we meet again." Hawk stood in the center of the room. "And it looks like I hold all the cards—or coins this time." He flipped something in the air.

Mac looked around the cabin. The large room held the living area and galley. The wheelhouse just forward of it stood higher and was accessible by a door to the cabin and one to both sides of the ship. The rear cabin door led to the aft deck. Alicia was sitting in the corner, carefully avoiding his eye, whether from fear of reprimand from him or Hawk, he could only guess. She looked tired, but at least she had not been mistreated. He noticed something around her neck, but Hawk distracted him.

"Catch." Something flashed from his hands, and Mac reached out for it but missed. Ironhead laughed, retrieved the object, and placed it in his hand. The silver had been cleaned and shined, but he knew the coin.

"You recognize that?" Hawk asked.

"Seen a lot of treasure and old coins in my day," Mac responded. The fresh air and daylight were helping clear his head and he felt better.

"Come, now. You are my guest for the time being. Let's not change that status," Hawk said, opening his other hand and showing Mac the remote control. He looked back at Alicia and realized he was holding the controller for the shock collar around her neck.

There was no point in subterfuge. "It's from your stash in the confiscated house," Mac said.

Hawk nodded and held out his hand for the coin. Mac rolled it between his fingers. Ironhead took a step toward him, and he handed it back. "There are plenty more where this came from."

Mac wondered what game he was playing. He had seen him place a load in the canal and had to assume there was more there than he had seen. "What do you want from me?"

"Quite simple, Travis. Legitimacy. You may have had some run-ins with the law, but I'm totally blackballed after that Marine and you ran my idiots aground. ICE bastards held a kangaroo court, confiscated the house and everything before I could even lawyer up." He paused and rubbed his bald spot. "They might have taken away your commercial fishing license, but I checked, and your salvage license is still in place. Mine, on the other hand, is suspended pending an investigation."

"You were dirty long before Jesse and I grounded your goons," Mac said, biting his tongue. He knew he shouldn't have gone that far. The only way out of this was to wait and find an opening, for both his sake and Alicia's. He had dealt with Hawk before and seen firsthand how devious he was.

Ironhead stepped closer again, but Hawk ignored him, holding up a hand to stop him. "With the help of your friend here, we are close to the location of a major haul, but I'll need you to pull the permits."

"Why should I do that?" Mac asked.

Hawk pressed a button on the controller. Alicia jerked suddenly and slumped over. Mac took a step toward her when Ironhead stepped in front of him.

"She'll be all right. And just so you know, that was the lowest setting," Hawk said, pocketing the device.

"So, if I do the paperwork, you let her walk?" Mac asked.

"Something like that, but she's running a little behind on her research."

This was not going the way Mac had planned it. After running into Jimmy and seeing the coin, he could only guess where Trufante was. His only backup was TJ, and for all he knew, he could be locked up below. He had to solve this with what he had in front of him.

"Okay. Alicia figures out the riddle, and I run the paper. Then what?" Mac asked.

"That would all depend on you, Travis. Cooperate and I could even cut you in for a share. As far as divers go, you're one of the most respected down here. Put away your pride, and you can have the hermit's island, get your boat back, and maybe a pile of cash to do what you want. If the score is anywhere near what I suspect, you could be set for life."

Mac knew that plans seldom worked out as they were conceived, but he had no other choice than to play along—for the moment.

* * *

"This is fun," Pamela said, slurping the remainder of her drink through the straw.

They had followed Jimmy to the marina and were sitting on a dock box by one of the finger piers several slips down from where Hawk's boat was tied up. Jimmy had been aboard for ten minutes, and Trufante was getting anxious. It was not often that anyone, especially Hawk, would put up with him for that long. It had to be the coin, he thought.

"Gonna need another round of brews, and then why don't we—" Pamela started.

Trufante put a hand on her knee, stopping her. Jimmy appeared in the doorway of the cabin, and he needed to decide what to do—follow him or stay with Hawk. Deciding that whatever worth Jimmy had, he had just traded or sold, he decided to stay with the boat.

"Right on, babe. I'm in for that," he said, gathering their empties and leading her away from the dock. He paused to see which direction Jimmy was going and took her hand, leading her in the opposite direction. They found a bar a few blocks away, refilled the drinks, and started back to the dock when she pulled her hand out of his.

"This is getting boring," she said, raising her hands over her head and shaking her hips. "Let's go dancing." She put her arms around his neck.

His train of thought jumped the rails and headed for a deep ravine. It didn't take him long to rationalize the change of plans. The boat was obviously in Key West for the night. Why watch it? Maybe after a few dances, and a couple more shots, they could head back to Garrison Bight and check out the cabin on the boat. If the sucker had four engines, he could only imagine what the berths looked like.

"Right on," he said.

"Then show me the way to the next whiskey bar," she said, following him towards Duval Street.

* * *

TJ sat in the bushes feeling helpless. He knew Mac and probably Alicia were aboard the steel trawler, but he was at a loss as to what to do about it. To make matters worse, Trufante was missing, and now he was here alone.

Closing his eyes, he tried to envision the scene in front of him as if it were a challenge in a video game. Something he was good at—very good. In a hostage situation, the best plan of attack would be a diversion. His brain was clicking now, and he thought through his options and available resources, trying to decide if it should come from land or sea. Running both scenarios through his head, he thought about the pros and cons of each, deciding on a water-based attack. Anything emanating from land would have the chance of a random person interfering with his plan, and the increased chance of police intervention. An attack from the water, although harder to execute, would have a better likelihood of success.

Taking one last look at the trawler, he moved away from the cover of the bushes and headed back toward town. With his phone held in front of him, he followed the map. Staying on Front, he skirted Whitehead and Duval and then followed side streets. A half hour later, he reached the marina and paused for a minute before heading onto the dock. The boat looked like it was rocking. Studying it, he disregarded the action, possibly the result of an unseen wake, bouncing back off the seawall.

He approached the boat and heard an unmistakable sound coming from the partially open hatch in the forward berth. Hoping they wouldn't last long, he walked back to the main pier and started to work on his plan of attack. Taking a docked boat in the middle of a busy harbor was not the easiest of problems, but after a few minutes several options came to mind. He looked back over at the boat, now settled and swaying in rhythm with the other craft, and approached, making enough noise to rouse the occupants.

Trufante popped his head out of the cabin. "Yo, TJ, what's shakin'?"

"Just you, my friend," he said, hopping over the gunwale and going to the helm. "Get your act together. We're going on a sortie."

"What's that, Tru?" Pamela asked from below. "Another adventure?" She appeared behind the Cajun, buttoning her blouse. "Can we get another drink first?"

"Excellent idea." Trufante dug in his pocket and pulled out a handful of bills. "Why don't you procure us some cocktails?" He looked at TJ. "You in?"

"I'd go for a bottle or two," TJ said. Alcohol was part of his plan.

Chapter 17

Mac was already awake when the door opened. He had been for hours, trying to figure some way out of this mess. There was always a chance to make a break for it when they went ashore to file the paperwork, but Alicia would pay for any actions he took—Hawk had made that clear. One thing he had decided, after thinking about it, was that having his license on the paperwork was not a bad idea.

Ironhead led him back up the short flight of stairs leading to the main cabin. Hawk was already sitting at the table eating breakfast. Another place was set, and he motioned for Mac to sit.

"Go ahead and eat," he said.

Mac sat, but pushed away the food. He wanted no part of this attempt to ally with him. "There's no Department of Historical Resources office here," Mac said. He had always had to deal with the bureaucracy in Tallahassee whenever he had obtained exploration or salvage permits before.

"Been a while, I'm guessing," Hawk said. "The code is so comprehensive and ridiculous now, you need a lawyer to file. You'll be visiting an associate of mine. He's got connections there. Once you sign, we should be up and running in a few days—provided your friend here closes in on the location."

"How can you file for the permit without the coordinates?" Mac asked.

"It's an exploration permit. The exploration area is quite a bit broader than an actual salvage permit."

"And you won't be getting one of those, I expect," Mac said. The exploration permit would allow them to search, unrestricted and unregulated, as long as they didn't disturb anything; a salvage permit would require inspectors and archaeologists.

For now, he would cooperate. After breakfast, Wallace escorted him off the boat, leaving Ironhead to watch Alicia. She was already working; two computers now sat in front of her, doubling her resources overnight. They had exchanged a look of mutual reassurance before he had left. He knew her well enough that she would hide whatever she discovered until he returned.

Everything in Key West was more colorful than you would expect in the rest of the world, and Hawk's lawyer was no different. Located on the first floor of a brightly painted, meticulously restored Victorian home were the law offices of Wallace and Wagner, LLC. Mac looked at the sign and back at his escort, wondering what the relationship was. He soon found out when they entered the foyer of the house and were greeted by a flamboyant man who bore a strong resemblance to the man standing next to him, the one he called the weasel. They were so close, in fact, that he suspected the only difference might be their sexual preference.

Their reunion was curt, merely a nod to each other.

"I have the papers drawn up in the office," Wagner said.

Mac followed the men across the freshly oiled Southern yellow pine floor into a tastefully decorated, paneled study.

"Please," Wagner said, indicating the two chairs in front of his desk.

The men sat, and the attorney pushed a sheaf of bound papers across the large desk to Mac. He started reading.

"Standard filing," the lawyer said. "The yellow tabs are where to sign, and I'll need a current address."

Mac took the papers and started signing. He paused when he

came to the address, then entered Trufante's. Finished, he slid them across the desk to the lawyer, who scanned them to make sure the fifteen signatures required were completed, and smiled.

"Very good, then," he said, rising from his chair to dismiss them.

Before they left, he handed a copy to Wallace.

* * *

Alicia didn't turn when they entered the cabin, but Mac saw one of the screens change.

"Here's your copy." Wallace handed the manila envelope to Hawk.

Without looking at it, he opened a drawer in the cabinet behind him and dropped it in. "Let's go. Nothing else to be gained hanging around here."

The two men nodded and went to work, both knowing their duties. Wallace went into the wheelhouse and Mac felt the deck vibrate when the engines started. Ironhead had already released the stern lines and was standing on the bow, waiting for Wallace to pull up next to the piling that the fore and spring lines were hooked over. Alicia shot Mac a panicked look, but there was nothing he could do.

"Where are we headed?"

"Not your concern, Travis. It's up to your friend there, and I'm giving her four hours to figure it out."

Mac got the threat. He looked at Alicia, but she was staring at the data scrolling down the screen.

"At least let me help her, then. No harm in that, is there? I've been staring at those pictures for years," Mac said.

"Suit yourself," Hawk said and went to the wheelhouse.

Mac moved a captain's chair next to Alicia and looked at the display. He was about to say something when she tapped his hand and pointed at the screen closest to her.

"Type it, if you don't want them to hear," she whispered.

She had opened a small window in the corner of the display. "Any luck?" he said, wanting at least some conversation to appear normal.

"I've got some of the patterns translated into a chart of sorts," she said, then typed, *But there's something missing.*

"Show me what you have," Mac said.

She changed the display of the screen to show a chart of the Middle Keys with lines crisscrossing from all angles. Next to it, she opened another window showing the tattoos. The lines matched.

"What am I looking at?" he asked.

"It's a portolan chart. The lines emanate from several compass roses set at specific locations. Each one has thirty-two lines showing what they called the wind points, but they're really just degrees or bearings on the circle." She started to eliminate lines. "Just offshore of Marathon is where I expect the location is, based on the center of the pattern on the tattoos."

He slid closer and typed, *Too much information.*

She continued, "It would appear you could locate whatever we are looking for by just transposing the lines onto a current chart, but it's not quite so easy. There is no projection—you know, the true shape of the Earth's surface—represented here. These lines assume that the planet is flat. We also don't know what year this was drawn in. The lines are all based on magnetic north, which is the point a compass shows."

"Right. We need to account for declination," Mac said, starting to understand that the information she had uncovered was useful, but the search area was still close to ten square miles. Too large for an effective operation. It was discovered early on in China, and then later in Europe, that the magnetic pole moved over time, but calculating it was more of an art than a science. These charts had no reference to declination or even the date they were drawn. He leaned over and typed, *Any ideas?*

She shook her head. "There has to be a key to tell us the year this was drawn. Without that, we're lost."

"What's the range?" he asked.

"Somewhere between two and two and a half degrees every hundred years," she said.

Mac did some quick math in his head. Averaging the distance of a degree at sixty miles, that could mean over a hundred miles a century, and they had no idea how old the map was. "So what is the missing link?" Mac wondered aloud.

Hawk came up behind them. "Missing link? It looks like you're making progress."

Mac looked at the screen, but Alicia had already entered the sequence of keys and it was dark. "Yeah. We're getting there," he said.

"Two hours," Hawk grunted and walked away. Mac got up and looked out the port window. There was nothing but water. He figured they had cleared the Northwest Passage and were now cruising east toward Marathon. He had only a few hours to figure a way out.

* * *

TJ had been waiting long enough. His work was complete, and he banged on the cabin door. Several minutes later he heard movement, and a shirtless Trufante emerged, squinting in the morning sun.

"Top of the morning to ya." He smiled, showing off his thousand-dollar grin.

"Come on, man. We gotta go," TJ said.

"You been busy," Trufante said.

On the deck were a dozen beer bottles of different varieties that TJ had scrounged this morning from the trash cans around the parking lot. "Had to fight some bums for the bottles," he said.

"Molotov freakin' cocktails," Trufante said. "What's your

recipe?"

"Fuel and oil for the contents. Some torn clothes soaked in alcohol for the wick. Sealed it up with some candle wax I found in the emergency kit."

"Right on," Trufante said. "What's our plan?"

Pamela appeared, shaking her hair out but ignoring them.

"We gotta get Mac and Alicia."

"Right!" Trufante said. "Fire 'em up and let's go."

"How about some breakfast first?" Pamela asked.

TJ was prepared. "Danish in the bag there."

She brushed past him, took one, and sat on the transom, picking pieces off and eating it, oblivious to what was going on around her. Trufante went to the helm and fired the engines while TJ packed the bottles in an empty beer case he had found. He stashed it in the cabin and released the dock lines. Seconds later they were in the channel, heading toward open water. Once clear of the last marker, Trufante turned to port, and they followed the coastline around Mallory Pier, staying between the markers of the deep channel leading to the entrance of the bight.

"Shit. She's gone," he said after they reached the inside marker and had a clear view of the harbor.

TJ looked around, his head falling to his chest. They were too late.

"Not to worry, dude. Mac found them on the radar before. We can do it again."

"Head offshore toward Sand Key, and we can lose some of this traffic," TJ said, sliding next to Trufante and pressing the power switch for the electronics. Seconds later, the screen populated, and he studied the boats. He had an idea what he was looking for, but he had to be patient. Soon, several miles from land, the clutter started to clear. The screen showed mostly boats now, and they saw a small blip, moving slowly east on the Gulf side.

"That's them," TJ said.

Trufante pushed the throttles down, letting out a whoop as he cut the wheel. The boat pivoted and sped toward the Gulf. They were on plane in seconds, cruising at fifty knots into a light chop. TJ studied the blip. It was at the edge of the third ring, fifteen miles ahead. At their current speed, they would be on them in an hour.

"What we gonna do when we catch 'em?" Trufante yelled over the engines.

"Pirates of the Caribbean," Pamela said, smiling.

* * *

The closer they got to Marathon, the more distracted Mac became. Somehow he needed to give Hawk enough of the puzzle to buy some time. He briefly wondered what had happened to Trufante and TJ, but from his experience with the Cajun, he'd show up when you least expected or needed him. TJ might have a plan, but Mac couldn't wait. He would have to act on his own.

Mac typed, *Transpose the lines onto a chart and give him something.*

Alicia looked at him and nodded, then closed the window. She was working in one window with all the data in what appeared to be layers. Hiding the tattoos and land features from the screen, she left the grid. Next, she opened the NOAA chart labeled 11453 and placed it in the background. Manipulating the size of the grid she estimated the scale.

"There are no landmarks on the tattoos. Where do we put the compass roses?" she asked.

Mac rubbed the stubble on his face. That was one of the parts he could never figure out, but now with her computer wizardry, it became clear. "There are three, right?"

She nodded and looked at him, her fingers poised on the keyboard.

"Indian Key, Marathon and Key West. See if they'll line up with Boot Key Harbor and the bight in Key West," he said, tapping the locations on the screen with his finger, hoping at least the two roses would fall on the two natural harbors. He watched, nervously tapping his foot. Almost forgetting about Hawk and their circumstances, he was excited—after all these years, he sensed they were on the verge of solving the mystery. Anxiously he watched while she moved the grid to the two points he indicated. They fell into place, and he studied the chart.

The two roses fell directly in the center of the harbors, the third near Indian Key, an old wreckers' port near Islamorada. Those would have been the three best landmarks in the early 1700s, and he sat back, wondering if he had been wrong all along.

"Give me the coordinates of these points." He tapped the screen with a pen to show her three spots offshore of Marathon where all three sets of lines intersected. Hopefully this would buy some time.

Chapter 18

Mac handed the coordinates to Hawk, who took them to the chart table. "You're sure about this?"

"You know as well as I do that this is not an exact science," Mac said.

"You lead me on some kind of wild goose chase, and this partnership is not going to end well," Hawk said.

Frustrated, Mac got up, but Ironhead moved toward him, a pained look on his face. "We've been at this a long time. Mind if we go out on the deck and get some air?"

Hawk looked up from the chart where he was plotting the coordinates and nodded. "Looks like deep water," he said.

"If it wasn't, whatever it is would have been found already," Mac said, pushing the door open.

He stood on the deck with Alicia. Looking out at the small puffy clouds and the light chop on the water, he shook his head. "What's missing?"

Alicia was sitting on a small built-in bench backed up to the cabin. Mac motioned her toward the transom where they were less likely to be heard. "A key—there's got to be one thing that will align everything."

Mac stared at the wake of the boat, thinking of how, if it was him, he would have hidden a reference for the chart. Before electronics, mariners relied on sun and star sightings using sextants and backstaffs to estimate their position. The chronometer and then the GPS came along later, adding accuracy, but ancient mariners, no matter their origin or technology, all had one thing in common. "Stars," he said.

"Maybe. That would date it, clarifying the declination," she said. "Let me go have another look."

"No," Mac said. "He's happy for now. Let him be." Mac could see Hawk through the tinted windows, bent over the table studying the chart. The northern tip of Big Pine Key had just come into view, and they sat in the sun, watching the small islands pass by on the starboard side. "That's it," Mac said, studying the island. "Cheqea is the only one I don't have pictures of."

"Cheqea?" Alicia asked.

"Teqea's twin sister. She's a bit of a recluse. Lives out there somewhere on state land."

She followed his gaze to Big Pine. The key was considerably larger than most, famous as the last refuge of the protected Key deer. The undersized deer were given thousands of acres of government land to roam. Somewhere in the scrub that comprised the landscape of the key, Cheqea could be found. The twins had a unique relationship, never understanding that their parents had put them, and their cousin Diego, in a position to find the treasure— whatever it was. If they could have worked together, they had the clues, but they hated each other. It must not have been the first time. The tribal elders had accounted for this, passing the tattoos down for generations without the treasure being found. But now two of the three were gone and the tattoos with them. Teqea and Diego's tattoos were on the disk—Cheqea's were missing. It had to be the answer.

* * *

"Dead ahead," TJ said, looking up from the radar.

The boat was a thin line on the horizon, growing quickly as

they closed the gap. They had just passed the Content Keys. The music blared through the sound system, rivaling the roar of the four engines on the transom. Trufante was still at the helm, and Pamela, who had figured out how to run the sound system, swayed to some Jimmy Buffett.

Trufante looked up from the gauges and saw it too, slowly growing, the tower of the trawler barely visible on the horizon. "Content Keys are coming up. We better make our move soon," he said. Civilization would soon encroach on their efforts. This far out, the backcountry was the domain of smugglers, drug runners, and a few fishermen; another five miles would bring boat traffic and witnesses. He pushed the throttles forward, redlining the engines. They wailed in protest, but he ignored it and sped after Hawk's boat. They were close enough to make out the details of the trawler, and he backed down the rpms before they were spotted.

"What's the plan, man?" he asked TJ.

"Run 'em aground and then firebomb them."

Trufante looked at him. "Dude, they're going to have weapons. We need to figure this shit out."

"Look." TJ pointed to the trawler, its distinctive shape now clearly visible. "They're turning."

Trufante put his hand to his brow, shielding his eyes from the sun. "Wood's old place."

"Out here?" TJ asked.

Trufante ignored him, trying to think how they could parlay this development into a plan. "Not sure what the buggers are up to, but we can anchor off the back side, and they'll never see us. Take 'em on land."

"You sure that's a good idea? That water looks pretty skinny."

Trufante stared at the turquoise water, the color lightening the closer it got to shore until it was almost clear. Ignoring TJ's concerns, he steered toward it. Hawk's ship was around the corner now, needing the deeper water of the channel, but with their own outboards tilted up, he figured they only needed a few feet of water.

With a loud thud, all three passengers were thrown forward. They had bumped bottom before he expected. The engines screamed in agony as their water intakes, covered in the sand, were unable to suck the water needed to cool them. Alarms sounded, but Trufante reacted quickly and hit the tilt. All four engines lifted, and the change in weight distribution allowed the hull to float. He looked back at the array, letting the outside two down just enough for water to cover the propellers and submerge the intakes. Leaving the two longer-shaft inside engines in the air, he started the short-shaft pair mounted on the outside and backed off the shallow flat.

"That was freakin' close," he said, exhaling and smiling. "Maybe we need to reconsider our attack plan. It'd be a bad thing wrecking Celia's babies."

* * *

Hawk came on deck just as they turned toward Wood's place. He looked at Mac. "We're going to stop so you can get your gear. That's it. No screwing around." He took Alicia's arm and dragged her toward the cabin door. "Don't forget about this," he said, holding the controller in his free hand.

Mac saw the fear in her eyes before Hawk pushed her inside. He tried to put it out of his mind, focusing his attention on Ironhead, watching him as he picked his way through the shallows, easily finding the cut channel. They coasted up to the piling, and Mac jumped off. He splashed through the waist-deep water and started toward the shore, but his foot caught something, causing him to fall. It was the old cable from the boom. Pushing forward, now totally wet, he gained the small beach and followed the trail to the clearing. Ignoring Ironhead, who was about ten feet behind him, he entered the shed and started tossing gear on the floor.

"Come on. Just grab it all," Ironhead said, standing in the doorway.

Mac found a mesh bag and started stuffing the dive gear into it. He looked around as he packed, trying to find anything he could include that could later be used as a weapon, but there was nothing that wouldn't be obvious. He knew Ironhead was a skilled diver and would catch anything at all out of place.

"What are we diving?" he asked, picking up an old dive computer.

"You won't be needing that. We'll be using rebreathers with side-mount tanks for decompression and backup," he said.

Mac set down the computer but picked up a compass attached to a retractable lanyard that sat next to it. Ironhead watched but didn't say anything as he tossed it into the bag.

With no reason to delay and an idea forming in his head, he closed the zipper and rose, slinging the heavy bag over his shoulder. He left the shed and started down the trail.

"Here, take this," he said, handing the bag to Ironhead. "I've got something over here." Without giving him a chance to react, he took a small path to the right and found himself in a clearing. He went right for the winch, hoping the years of neglect had not frozen the mechanism. The last time he knew it had been used was a dozen years ago, during a chase, when Wood had used it to disable the boat of a crazy German couple colluding with a high-ranking government official to find oil out in the backcountry. Mac almost laughed remembering when some had thought the Keys were the next great American oil field. Now, with the production in the Dakotas, that was a distant memory. A quick look back confirmed he was alone, and he released the latch, allowing the cable to free-spool. The clicking sound would alert Ironhead if he used the ratchet to maintain the tension.

Initially he was discouraged when the cable didn't move, but the handle broke free, and the slack started coming in. Increasing the speed, he cranked for all he was worth, trying to keep the line taut, but it was coming in too easily now and a frayed end appeared. Discouraged, he rose and went back to the main trail.

"What the hell are you up to?" Ironhead asked.

Mac looked at him and shrugged his shoulders. "Call of nature," he said, taking the bag back. Together they walked to the beach and waded to the trawler.

With both men and the gear back on board, Ironhead went to the wheelhouse and started the engine. Mac peered into the clear water, cursing under his breath. Slowly the boat backed out of the canal, and he let out a sigh of anguish as he stared at the open water. If the cable had been intact, the propeller and shaft would be disabled now. Ironhead expertly negotiated the channel, turned into the deep pass, and accelerated.

Mac was out of ideas, but he hadn't raised any red flags either. There would be another chance. He would just have to be ready. He looked back at Wood's island, hoping he would see it again under better circumstances, when he noticed a large boat cut the edge of the channel, heading toward them. Not many would be brave or dumb enough to cut the channel like that unless they knew it well. The boat was closing on them, and he recognized the four rooster tails coming from behind it. He tried to see who was aboard, but the only thing recognizable was Trufante's smile.

There was no reaction from Hawk or his men. The boat meant nothing to them, just another charter coming back from a day out in the Gulf. Mac slid over to the port side. From their current course, Mac guessed that they would pass on the starboard side, and he wanted to be downrange of whatever they had planned. The boat was within a hundred feet, and he could clearly see Trufante, TJ, and Pamela. As he suspected, Trufante was at the wheel and TJ was huddled by the transom. Slowly he rose, and Mac could see the lit rag sticking out of the bottle.

With a roar, the boat was past them. Mac ducked behind the crane, knowing what was coming. Just as the bottle smashed against the deck, Ironhead and Hawk emerged from the cabin, their pistols already extended. They aimed and fired at the speeding boat, stopping when the glass bottle shattered. Fire spread across the deck.

"Get a fire extinguisher," Hawk yelled at Ironhead, then laughed when he saw the small pool of flames on the steel deck. There was nothing flammable, and the fire was too small and not nearly hot enough to do any damage. "And bring the big gun," he called after him.

Ironhead appeared a minute later with a white fire extinguisher in one hand and what looked like a bazooka in the other. The fire was gone with one quick squirt. He handed the extinguisher to Hawk and raised the gun to his shoulder. The boat had turned and was coming back at them now, preparing to pass on the port side. Ironhead lined up the shot, but at the last minute, Trufante cut the wheel, changing their trajectory to pass on their starboard. Mac grinned at the subterfuge and moved across to the port side, when another flaming bottle came toward them. Again, it landed but did no damage.

Mac knew it was only a matter of time before either Trufante made a mistake or Ironhead got a lucky shot off. He had to do something to increase the odds. They were coming back for another pass. This time, both boats would be facing in the same direction. The ruse Trufante had employed last time would not work. Ironhead would have a clear shot toward the boat's stern as they passed.

Inching over to the crane, Mac grabbed the control box. He was already familiar with the controls from the other night, and he slowly reached over, releasing the hook from its keeper. Ironhead was in front of him, bracing himself, using the transom and gunwale for support, preparing his shot. Hawk was firing at the approaching boat, but his shots went wild. With both men occupied, Mac hit the power switch, relieved that the noise of the engines covered the mechanism's whine. The boom swung toward

Ironhead. Mac hit the toggle to slow it and waited.

The boats were neck and neck. Hawk was firing at close range, but the motion of the boat was throwing his aim off. Ironhead was patiently waiting for his shot when the next bottle came over the gunwale. Both men ignored it, knowing it would be ineffective. The backs of the four outboards had just passed the transom of the trawler when Mac saw Ironhead tense and squeeze the trigger. Anticipating the shot, he moved the toggle. There was a long pause before the boom built up momentum and slammed into him, taking him over the side, but the projectile had left the muzzle a fraction of a second earlier. Mac watched in slow motion as the heat-seeking missile found the four blazing engines and the boat erupted in a ball of fire.

Chapter 19

They stood by the transom, surveying the water, each looking for something different—Hawk and Wallace for Ironhead; Mac and Alicia for any survivors from the explosion. Alicia stood next to Mac, trying to look stoic, but he could see tears running down her face. A low cloud of smoke still hung over the water, concealing the crash site. Slowly it lifted, and they saw the wreckage.

"Wallace," Hawk yelled. "Get in there and steer toward the debris."

He started toward it, but they stood, jaws dropped, as they watched what was left of the boat slip below the surface before they could reach it. There was still hope, with patches of debris everywhere, and Mac scanned the surface, desperate for survivors.

"Careful that trash doesn't wreck the prop," Hawk yelled to Wallace.

Mac continued to scan the water as the boat moved through the flotsam. Several bright orange life vests could be seen floating near the spot where the boat had sunk, but they were vacant. They continued to work the perimeter of the site, and finally Mac saw something move.

"There!" He pointed to a section of wreckage that looked like the console of the boat with three heads clinging to it. Somehow they must have been hanging on when the boat blew and the force of the explosion separated the prefabricated unit from the hull. From this distance there was no way to tell if they were dead or alive. Wallace ignored him.

Mac moved next to Hawk and pointed out the bodies. "You have to save them."

Hawk looked at him, unconcerned. "Right, let's see if they're still alive." He pulled his pistol above the transom, ready to fire, and called to Wallace to move toward them.

Slowly the boat picked its way through the wreckage, and they reached the console. What had been the small cabin was now bottom-up, giving the unit enough buoyancy to stay afloat. But instead of rescuing them, Hawk called for Wallace to stop, raised the gun, and aimed at the three heads, now looking to them for help.

"Get under!" Mac yelled at them and went for Hawk, pushing him off balance.

The gun fired and Mac was on him. Both men were on the ground now, Mac clawing at him, trying to get at the weapon.

"Back off, Travis," Wallace called.

Mac chanced a look up and saw Wallace with his gun pointed at Alicia's head. Reluctantly, he backed away from Hawk and crawled to the transom, where he looked over the edge to see if the shot had hit anything. With one hand, Wallace helped Hawk to his feet, but the other still had the gun trained on Alicia.

The calls for help were louder now, and Mac moved to the gunwale, where he looked at the console. The current had moved them close enough he could almost reach them.

Hawk was on his feet now, taking aim again. The range was almost point-blank, and he knew he had to do something quickly. "There—" He pointed to another piece of flotsam. "It's another body."

Hawk turned, following Mac's outstretched arm. From this distance it did look like a head on the surface. "Go," he called to Wallace and put the gun in his waistband. Sticking his hand in his pocket, he withdrew the controller for the shock collar. Waving it so they could both see it, he said, "Don't do anything stupid."

Mac looked back at the wreckage, trying to find Trufante. They were even closer than before, but quiet now after seeing Hawk with the gun. Hoping Hawk was too distracted to hear, Mac leaned over the gunwale and yelled, "Cheqea. Find her." Hawk's gaze moved to him, and he turned away from the wreckage, but before he did, he caught a look of understanding on Trufante's face.

* * *

The last thing Mike remembered when he woke up, tangled in a mess of mangroves, was the blast when the boat blew. He recalled being thrown from the deck into the water, but besides the pain in his side, he had no idea what had happened. Slowly, he fought the mud sucking at his feet and used the branches from the mangroves to pull himself onto the small key. His side felt warm, and he looked down at the gash. A pool of blood was accumulating at his feet. He looked back to see a trail floating on the water like an oil slick. Feeling fortunate he hadn't attracted a shark, he lifted his T-shirt and looked at his side.

It was hard to get a good angle, but he knew he needed medical attention—and now. Pulling off his T-shirt, he wrapped it around the wound, tying it as tightly as he could. With the blood flow stemmed, he looked around, surprised to see the mainland only a few hundred yards away. Fortunately the current had pushed him toward shore. An outgoing tide would have pulled him into the deep waters of the Gulf, where he would have been easy prey for a cruising shark or just lost at sea. He looked across at the mainland, not recognizing where he was, but it didn't really matter—it was close enough to swim. Feeling light-headed, he got up and waded toward shore. The sun was behind him, starting to set, but daylight was not a concern.

The mud sucked at his feet, but he fought through it until he was deep enough to fall forward on his hands and knees. With his weight distributed on all four appendages, he was able to make it past the flat into a channel, where, with the help of the tide, he sidestroked for the shore.

Exhausted from the effort, he climbed out of the water, sat on a small beach, and caught his breath. His side pounded in pain. Remembering the pills he had gotten from the VA clinic, he reached into his pocket, pulled out the bottle, and turned the lid. Though he had been hitting it pretty hard, he thought there should be a half dozen left, but the inside was half-full with cloudy water that had leaked in, dissolving the pills. He drank it like a shot, hoping that some of the contents remained, but the minute it hit his mouth, he gagged on the bitter mixture of the pills and seawater and threw it back up. Whatever medicinal value it had was gone now. To make matters worse, the mosquitoes had found him and were swarming around the wound and his head. He brushed them away and tried to rise. It took everything he had to make it to his feet, but one step at a time, he started walking to a light in the distance.

* * *

Trufante, TJ, and Pamela clung to the console, not sure if they were better or worse off. They watched Hawk's boat as it turned to the west and made for Moser Channel. They followed its path into the channel but lost sight of the boat when it passed under the tallest section of the Seven Mile Bridge.

"What did he say?" TJ asked.

"Cheqea. A name from the past," Trufante said. "Bet it has something to do with the tattoos. Her brother and cousin had them too." He turned to Pamela and saw her shivering. "Hang on there, Pajama Bama, we'll get you out of here." She didn't respond, and he started to worry that she was injured or becoming hypothermic.

The water was in the low eighties, but with enough time, coupled with the shock from the explosion, it would take its toll—she looked to be in bad shape.

The first responders had arrived just after Hawk left the scene, but had not spotted them yet. A helicopter had been overhead circling for the last twenty minutes or so, and they could hear several boats nearby. TJ climbed higher on top of the console, pulled off his shirt and started waving it in the air. The helicopter must have spotted him. It changed course, heading in their direction. Seconds later, Trufante heard an outboard closing on their position.

The sheriff's boat idled toward them, and Trufante could see the deputy at the helm. He spun the wheel, and for a moment he thought they were moving away, but the transmissions clicked and the boat backed down on them. Minutes later they were pulled out of the water and onto the deck of the sheriff's boat, where they sat wrapped in blankets.

"What happened out there?" the deputy asked.

TJ was about to respond, but Trufante cut him off. "Damn engine blew. Never seen anything like it."

The deputy looked at him warily, knowing him, at least by reputation. "Is that what happened, sir?" he asked TJ.

TJ looked dead ahead and followed his lead. "Yeah. Don't know what happened." He turned to Pamela. "Is she okay?"

"Just shock, I think. Soon as the chill wears off, I think she'll be fine." He turned back to TJ, obviously wanting no part of Trufante. "Whose boat was it?"

"Celia over at the marina by the Keys Fisheries loaned it out," Trufante replied.

"I wasn't talking to you," the deputy said, looking at TJ, who just nodded.

Trufante could see the look of distress on the deputy's face. He knew firsthand that Celia could have that effect on people. He looked around for the first time, noticing that the boat was just entering Boot Key Harbor. "Where are you taking us?" he asked.

"Not really sure. I've got nothing to hold you on. Do you think she needs to go to Fishermen's?" the deputy asked.

Trufante looked at Pamela. Her color had returned and she shook her head. "No hospital. We're good. How 'bout you drop us over at Pancho's?"

"That's fine, but I'll have to get a statement from you when we tie up." The deputy went to the helm and spoke to the officer at the wheel.

Five minutes later they were tied up off the side of the fuel dock answering questions. Trufante did most of the talking, although the deputy was clearly looking to TJ for a more substantial or truthful version. He finally gave up and looked squarely at Trufante.

"You know the deal. Don't leave town," he said.

Trufante climbed onto the dock and helped Pamela off the boat. TJ followed, and together they watched the deputy pull away. "We gotta get your boat and go to Big Pine," Trufante said as soon as the sheriff's boat was out of earshot.

"I'm for getting my boat, but what about Alicia?" TJ said.

"Mac said to find Cheqea. That'll lead us to her. Probably thinking a trade or something," Trufante said, knowing it was not going to be as simple as that—anyone crazy enough to want to deal with the old chief was in for a load of trouble.

"Can we get some food and maybe a drink or something while you guys figure this out?" Pamela said.

Trufante went to her and put an arm around her. She was still wrapped in the blanket, but had stopped shivering. "We'll take care of you, babe."

"How far is Mac's?" TJ asked as they started walking away from the water.

"Couple of miles, but I got a plan. Look." He pointed to the end of the parking area. "There's a gang of bikes over there." Trufante pointed to several racks crowded with rusty bicycles. "It's the liveaboards. They leave 'em here. Bettin' a bunch are abandoned and don't have locks." He went to the rack and pressed the tires of a dozen or so bikes to make sure they still had air before pulling three from the rack. "This'll do."

They left the marina, wound past the ballfields of the community center, and turned right onto US-1. Several blocks later, they turned again and rode to the end of the street. Portable sections of chain-link fence surrounded the property that had once been Mac's house, but at least the police tape was down.

They left the bikes and looked for a way in. There was a gate with a chain and padlock out front, but after a few minutes, they found a section of fence by the corner that wasn't secured to the next panel. Trufante pushed against it and slid through the opening, signaling TJ and Pamela to do the same. Once inside the perimeter, they took a circuitous route around the demolished building and were about to approach the dock when the security lights on the house next door turned on. A door opened and a man appeared.

"Can I help you with something?"

Trufante saw something long in the man's hand. "Just gettin' the boat. We ain't lookin' for no trouble."

"The whole lot of you's trouble—Travis, you, that lawyer woman. I'm still fighting with the insurance company for my sailboat that Travis took and wrecked."

Trufante ignored him and kept walking toward the dock.

"Why don't y'all wait right here?" The man pointed the gun at them. "Sheriff'll be here shortly."

* * *

Mac looked back at the Seven Mile Bridge, wondering what had happened to Trufante, TJ, and Pamela. The sun was setting off to the side, and from this distance, only the arch at the center was visible. Hawk had ordered them off the scene quickly, before the first response boat had arrived. The trawler had escaped unnoticed and was now cruising toward the lighthouse on Sombrero Reef. He had to assume they had been rescued. The explosion had happened only a mile or so from land, which would reduce the search area significantly.

Hawk moved behind him. "Better get some rest. We're diving in the morning," he said.

"Don't think rest'll be happening," Mac said.

Hawk thought for a second and then, apparently realizing there was no harm in telling him, said, "Sombrero Light. We'll tie up on one of the balls out there."

Mac couldn't knock his logic. The mooring balls were safer than anchoring, and they were also in federal waters, which would keep the local sheriff away. They were moving towards one of the deeper balls, frequented by dive boats during the day, and away from the swells created by the shallow water around the light. "Where's Alicia?"

"She's resting inside. I had to sedate her."

Mac thought that was probably for the best. There was nothing to be gained until Trufante found Cheqea. If he was able to enlist her help, they might have the final clue to the puzzle and a bargaining chip.

Once they tied up to one of the buoys, he went back into the cabin and grabbed a plate of food that Hawk offered. Sitting down to eat, he thought about what would happen next, knowing that having to rely on Cheqea was not going to make this any easier.

Chapter 20

They froze at the sight of the shotgun pointed down from the balcony of the house next door, but Trufante was not going to wait for the sheriff.

"Nice and slow," he encouraged them. "Damn fool's always been cranky. Don't mind him," Trufante whispered to TJ and Pamela. They started walking.

"I'm serious," the man yelled.

They heard the sound of the shotgun chamber a round, and Trufante turned back to him. The man stood above them on the second-floor porch. He had a clear shot if he wanted it. "Go on," he whispered to TJ. "I'll deal with him." TJ went for the boat, pushing Pamela ahead of him. "Easy, now. We don't want no trouble," he called to the man. Headlights hit Trufante in the face, and he looked toward the street, his view unobstructed now that the house was gone. The sheriff's car came to a stop. "See that?" he yelled up to the man. "Sheriff's here. He'll take care of everything. For once he was thankful for the law's prompt response."

The sound of the boat engine starting broke the silence, and Trufante used the distraction. He took off just as the beam from a spotlight coming from the sheriff's car caught him, but he kept going.

"Son of a bitch," he heard the man yell.

A shot was fired, and he ducked. The spotlight shifted to the house next door where the shot had come from, and he ran for the boat. "Go," he yelled to TJ, who was already at the wheel. Trufante untied the dock lines and kicked the bow away from the pilings. The boat was already moving when he jumped. Barely clearing the gunwale, he landed on the deck.

A bullhorn blasted. "You there. Return to the dock."

TJ was halfway through his turn when the order was repeated.

Trufante climbed up to the bridge. "Can't hear what he's saying. Can you?" he grinned at TJ.

"What? I really need to do something about these engines," TJ said, laughing with him as the boat made the turn and headed toward the harbor.

Pamela climbed up just as they turned out of Mac's canal. She started singing "On the Road Again" and sat beside them. "You guys ever do anything boring?" she asked.

"Just wanting to keep you entertained," Trufante said.

"Where are we headed?" TJ asked.

They were in the main channel of the harbor now, passing several rows of sailboats tied up to white mooring buoys. "Cheqea's bad business when the sun goes down. Don't think we want to mess with her tonight."

"Where to, then?"

"I could use a bite to eat. Let's head over to the Rusty Anchor. Rusty'll let us tie up overnight. We can head to Big Pine at first light. Damn, I can smell Rufus's hogfish sandwich from here."

* * *

The pain was intense, but Mike continued toward the light, which had turned into the back of a house. It was an older-style home built in the '70s, before all the houses were required to be elevated above the flood plain. The main floor was just above the ground—a good thing, because he didn't think he could climb stairs right now. There was music coming from an open window, and he thought he smelled the bittersweet aroma of pot. He banged on the door then backed up several feet to be less intimidating. A few minutes later, after another attempt, a woman came into the room. She walked to the door and peered out.

"Help me, please. I've been in an accident," he said meekly.

The door opened and she stepped outside. "Wow, you look bad."

"I could really use a ride to the hospital," he said.

She rubbed her head. "I've been smokin' a little. Maybe I should call an ambulance, or the sheriff."

"Oh, no. That won't be necessary. A little bit of smoke would be cool, though," he said, cursing that the painkillers had been ruined by the water.

She walked back into the house, closing the door behind her, and he considered his options. The hospital was out of the question. The police would have alerted them to be on the lookout for survivors of the explosion, and there would surely be questions. There had to be a better way—maybe a vet, or a private doctor.

The door opened and the woman came out holding a pipe. Flicking the lighter, she pulled the flame into the bowl, held her breath for a second, and handed it to him. He took it and inhaled deeply, immediately feeling the smoke enter his lungs. While he waited for the magic to happen, he took another hit and handed the pipe back to her. He followed her gaze to his feet. Blood was pooling on the tile floor.

"I don't care what you say. I'm going to call for help," she said, going for the door.

He had to act. As fast as his injury would allow, he sidestepped around her and put his hand on the door. "That won't be necessary. Maybe we should go inside and see about patching this up—see if you've got anything stronger than the smoke too."

She was scared and looked like she might scream. He was

about to reach out to stop her when he saw her tank top. "What's this Turtle Hospital?"

"Just a place down the road. Takes in injured turtles and stuff," she said, calming slightly.

"Call them. Tell them an injured turtle washed up on the beach."

She looked at him strangely.

"Look, you want me out of here. Make the call and I'm gone. Nobody gets hurt," he said, moving away from the door. Either she was going to do what he asked, or he would take matters into his own hands.

"Okay. I'll get my phone," she said and went inside. A minute later she was back. "They're on their way, but you've got to promise this is going to be cool."

"Yeah, sure, I promise," he said. "Now this is how it's going to go. All you have to do is direct them to the beach down there." He pointed to a spit of sand just outside of the reach of the lights.

He waited with her in an uneasy silence, passing the pipe back and forth several times before they heard the sound of a car pulling in the driveway. "Remember," he said as he walked away from the patio. Looking back, he saw her meet a man and a woman who exited what looked like an ambulance. Suspecting a trick, he crept around the side of the house, surprised to see the markings on its side said *Turtle Ambulance.*

Hobbling down the beach, he moved behind a cluster of scrub palms and hid. Without a weapon, he was counting on surprise to take one of the pair coming toward him. The woman was leading them to the spot he had pointed out. Just as she passed him, he lunged forward from his knees and grabbed the ankles of the man. The surprise was total, and he met little resistance.

He had the man by the legs and quickly reached up for his arm before he could react. With a twist, he grabbed his hand, pulling it behind the man's back. "Okay. Everyone is going to listen carefully and we'll be fine." They stood in a semicircle, the girl and woman on each side of the man. "Let's take a nice walk back to your little ambulance and go see this hospital of yours." They didn't move. "All I need is one of your doctors to stitch me up, and you'll never see me again." Their eyes were bugged out, but they nodded.

Leaning heavily on the man for support, they walked back to the ambulance. "You two in back," Mike said to the women. They climbed in, and he shut the door. "And let me have your phones." He collected their phones, closing the door behind them. Having to contort himself to ease the pain, he made it into the front seat. "Drive," he ordered the man.

They turned onto the highway and followed US-1 north for about a mile before making a left into the hospital's parking area. The driver clicked a remote. Before Mike could say anything, an automatic gate slid open, he drove in, and they parked by the office of what looked like an old motel.

"Get out," he ordered the driver. He opened his door and slid out. With an eye on the man, he hobbled around the orange-and-white ambulance and let the women out of the back. "Okay. All together now, let's find a doctor."

"I am the doctor," the girl said. "If you'd given me the chance, we could have fixed you up back there."

He shot her an angry look. "What's your name, honey?"

"Jen. Now let's get you inside and patch that up," she said, leading him around the front of the office to a glass door. She reached into a pocket of her lab coat, and he grabbed her hand. "Easy there. You're going to have to trust me a little," she said, pulling out a key. The door opened, and she led them to a small exam room.

"Looks like a regular doctor's office," Mike said.

She ignored him and went to the side table, where she started putting supplies and instruments on a metal tray. "You want to take that off, or do you want me to do it?" she asked, looking at his shirt.

He peeled it off, wincing when the dried blood pulled away. "Those are sterilized, right?"

"Yes, we care about our patients here." She moved around to look at him. "Lie down on your good side."

Moving to the table, he lay as she requested. "You got something for the pain?" He glared at the man and woman, also in the room. "Nothing that'll knock me out."

"I can give you a local," Jen said, loading a syringe with a clear fluid. Without warning, she reached over, stuck him, and pushed the plunger, releasing the anesthetic. "That should do it. Lidocaine."

His side immediately went numb, and she went to work stitching the wound. He watched as she opened the seal on an envelope and extracted something. With her back shielding her, he couldn't see what she was doing.

"Hey. What's that?"

She hesitated. "It's a delayed release antibiotic. State of the art."

"Damn turtles got it good," he said.

Just minutes later, she wrapped a fresh bandage around it. He got up and turned to her. "And something for the pain."

"The lidocaine should hold you for a while. I guess you're not the type to listen if I warn you about getting it wet." She started cleaning up, returning the unused supplies to the shelves.

He looked around but didn't see any pills. But it was a hospital—there had to be painkillers here someplace. Didn't turtles feel pain? "When I ask for something, I usually get it," he said, moving to the table and taking a scalpel. Rubbing the blade sideways with his finger, he glared at her.

"Just a minute," she said and left the room.

"You two stay here," he told the man and woman, then went to follow Jen. She unlocked a door and went into a small storeroom, took a bottle off the shelf and dumped half a dozen pills into her hand, almost dropping them when he reached for her arm.

"Put them back, I'll take the bottle." He grabbed the bottle and pills from her, popping three in his mouth and dry-swallowing them before closing the cap. "Thanks for your help." He walked back the way he had come and turned into the hallway, where he found the door leading to the parking lot. Outside, he looked at the street, then back at the water. His mind started to clear as the painkillers took effect. He went back inside.

"All of you. Into the office," he ordered.

He walked around to the wrapping station in the gift shop and grabbed a packing tape dispenser. One at a time, he bound and gagged them. On his way out, seeing the T-shirt display and realizing he was topless, he grabbed an XL from the shelf before leaving.

He needed a way out. It wouldn't take long for them to free themselves and call the police. Walking away from the street, he looked for a place to hide. They'd never suspect him of staying on the property.

Near the water, dark netting surrounded a fenced-in area holding huge black water tanks. He opened the gate and entered. The tanks were lit from above, and he could see turtles in most. Too exposed to hide, he left the pen and walked to a small cove on the right. To the end, just hidden behind the tanks, was a twin-engine center-console, hanging above the water from two steel arms. Staying to the shadows, he approached it, found the control box, and lowered the boat into the water. Careful of his side, he slid down into the hull, unhooked the cables, and looked at the helm. The keys were in the ignition, and he took one last look toward the hospital and street to see if anyone had seen him. One at a time, he started the engines. The transmissions clicked when he pushed down the throttles, and the boat started forward. Slowly, to keep the engine noise down, he idled out of the cove and into open water. Once clear of the breakwater, he turned to the west and pushed the throttles down to their limits, steering a course that would take him under the bridge.

Chapter 21

Around midnight, the wind strengthened, kicking up the seas and making sleep difficult—not that he would have had much luck anyhow. It had still been dark when they had released him from the hold, and now the first rays of light were just breaking the horizon. Usually it was his favorite time of day, but sitting on deck under the watchful eyes of Ironhead, the sunrise was ruined. Alicia was back in the cabin, refining the chart, but they still needed the missing information. Without it, this might be a very long day.

Sometime last night, he had heard the sound of an outboard motor approach and what he thought was a hull scraping against the boat. Now the boat was gone, but Ironhead was back, looking uncomfortable, wearing a Turtle Hospital T-shirt. He wasn't sure how he had found them, but the reef was less than a mile wide, running parallel to land. There were few boats out at night, and finding a ship the size of Hawk's trawler would have been easy.

He looked toward land. Marathon was just visible—a thin line on the horizon, the high-rise at Key Colony Beach to the right the lone identifiable landmark. With the right tide, he could swim it, but the ebb tide removed the possibility for now. With the near full moon, he estimated current would be running at almost two knots, moving away from land faster than he could swim. But even with the right tide, he couldn't leave Alicia. Ironhead sat there glaring at him, a strange look on his face. Hawk called for him to take the wheel, and Mac noticed that he was favoring one side when he moved. There was no apparent injury, but he filed away the observation, a plan for the thick-necked thug forming in his mind.

The engines started and Hawk called for Wallace, who was standing on the bow, to release the line attached to the buoy. He slid the dock line through the eye of the mooring line and signaled that they were clear. Ironhead steered a large circle to escape the other buoys, then headed just south of east. Mac stared down at the water, changing from almost clear to green to blue as the depth increased.

"Get your gear sorted," Hawk ordered him. "We'll be on the first numbers in twenty minutes."

Mac was surprised they would be diving this quickly. "Don't you tow an array first and make sure something's down there?"

"If you want a neon billboard that says you're searching for treasure, that'll work great, but we're going to do this the old-fashioned way," he said.

Mac understood his point, though it would mean a lot of bottom time for him. Pulling a side-scan sonar array was the simplest and most effective method for locating anomalies like shipwrecks underwater, but anyone fishing or diving nearby would quickly notice them. Commercial fishermen would easily pick up the search grid and know they were looking for something. They had a permit for exploration, but it wouldn't stop everyone else from just "diving" the area.

He went into the cabin. "You having any luck?" he asked Alicia.

"Kind of tweaked the coordinates a bit by adding the projection of the Earth's surface to the chart," she said, moving to the side to give him a view of the screen.

The straight lines he had seen yesterday now had slight curves to them, adjusting to the round orb. "That should help a little, but this is still a wild-ass guess."

Hawk came over. "I'll need the first pair of coordinates now."

"You know this is a shot in the dark," Mac said, trying to take some of the pressure off of her. "You can't think that we are just going to stumble on a ship that's been lost for hundreds of years on a handful of dives."

He looked over to Alicia. "If she's as good as her reputation, we ought to. If not, I have no use for her." He turned to him and smiled. "Or you."

Alicia wrote down the numbers on a piece of paper, and Mac watched as Hawk plotted them on the chart.

"Two hundred and ten feet, Travis. Better put your big boy pants on," he said. "That's why no one has found it—too deep."

Mac knew he was right. One hundred thirty feet was the maximum depth for recreational divers, and until recently, unless you had a submersible vessel, the depth would have discouraged anyone who'd thought to look.

The dangerous shoals and proximity to the Gulf Stream virtually guaranteed that early Keys inhabitants were all in the wrecking business in one way or another: either recovering or brokering the goods that washed up on shore. As technology improved, they were able to dive the shallow wrecks.

But what if the wreck was deep, and valuable? The European settlers and sailors were notorious for being shortsighted and closed-minded. Hundreds had died by their refusal to adopt local diets. Their views toward navigation had leaned toward the scientific, and where the rudimentary instruments and technology had fallen short, they'd filled the gaps with fiction. They would have had no way of recording a deep wreck.

Indigenous tribes had accurately navigated the oceans for a thousand years, relying on more natural methods. They used the stars, of course, but learned the subtle feel only acquired through generations on the water to learn the swells and currents that would push a boat off course. With their instinctive feel for the ocean, they could easily have marked a treasure, hoping a future generation might profit by it.

He'd been thinking last night about the Indians that had inhabited the islands in the seventeenth and eighteenth centuries. The indigenous people had been the original wreckers, salvaging long before Europeans had settled in any numbers. They were so skilled at recovering the bounty of the sea that when the Europeans finally realized the financial rewards, they had hired them to do the work. As news spread of the treasures being dumped on the ocean floor, clusters of settlers built Key West, Vaca Key, which was now Marathon, and Indian Key. Was it possible that this was a treasure map leading not to some ancient Mayan ruin, but to a more recent wreck? The relics that he and Wood had found years ago dating from an old Mayan canoe had been inshore. There was no reason for the elaborate tattoos to conceal the location.

"You going to get on with it?" Hawk asked.

Mac snapped back to the present and went out on deck. His gear was still in the mesh bag. Ironhead was gearing up and Mac studied his setup.

"Side-mount?" he asked.

"Bloody back is a problem. You ever try it?" he answered.

When it came to talking diving and equipment, the barrier between the men broke down. Mac had used the harness system, allowing multiple tanks to be carried alongside your body instead of on your back while cave diving. "Yeah. It would be good to have two tanks, especially if we're going over two hundred feet."

"Here." He tossed Mac a harness. "There's a rebreather setup under that bench."

Mac had wondered how they were going to get any bottom time at that depth. The maximum depth for nitrox, a standard gas mixture with an increased oxygen content, was much shallower, and he didn't see any equipment for a helium mix, which negated the risk of oxygen toxicity. He opened the lid and pulled out the backpack-mounted gear. His confusion must have been evident, his experience with the equipment limited.

"Let me give you a rundown," Ironhead said.

Mac was cautious as the man ran through the system setup and operation. Above the water they were enemies, but forced to work in the conditions below, they would need to count on each other for support. The mixed-gas closed-circuit rebreather would allow them time at depth without the risk of oxygen toxicity. The side-mount tanks would be used for the lengthy decompression stops, and as an alternate air source if the more complicated equipment failed. With just a single regulator attached to each tank, the redundant and simple systems provided a degree of comfort.

The boat slowed, and he grabbed the gunwale as they turned abeam into the waves. This was a day better spent under the water.

"Get ready," Ironhead said. He turned away and inspected the bandage on his side. Using his teeth to hold the end of the roll, he pulled off several feet of duct tape, wrapping it tightly around the bandage to protect it. Satisfied with his work, he reached into his gear bag, removed a container, and dumped several pills into his hand. Placing them in his mouth, he grabbed a bottle of water and swallowed.

Mac heard the anchor drop and the chain roll through the guides. "You sure you're okay with that? It looks pretty bad," Mac said. If they were going to be buddies underwater, he needed to know Ironhead's mental and physical state—and both looked bad.

"Boss ain't going to listen to any excuses," he said, struggling into a heavy wetsuit.

Mac followed his lead and put on the thick suit. The seven-millimeter cold-water suit was bulky, but at the depths they were diving, the water would be considerably colder than the surface. He calculated the extra weight he would need and then subtracted four pounds for the second tank. On his right arm, he strapped the computer matched to the rebreather equipment and scrolled through the screens, familiarizing himself with its operation.

The bow turned into the waves when the anchor grabbed, and a horn chirped.

"That's it. We go." Ironhead sat on the gunwale, wincing as he tried to attach the tank to the harness on his wounded side.

"Here," Mac said, helping him.

Ironhead nodded, pulled the mask he had placed backwards on his head around to the front, and made a few final adjustments before rolling over the side. Mac attached the two tanks to his harness and duplicated the process before dropping into the water.

It took a few minutes to adjust the equipment, but considering the two tanks plus the rebreather, he was balanced and comfortable. Ironhead gave him the okay sign and, without waiting for an answer, started a fast descent. By the time Mac had cleared his ears and made a few tweaks to the harness, they had dropped past one hundred feet. The water was getting darker, and the visibility degraded as they descended, the angle of the early-morning sun not allowing the full spectrum of light into the depths. At a hundred eighty feet, he followed Ironhead's lead, switched on the LED light attached to a headband, and for the first time saw the bottom.

* * *

TJ paced the deck. "Why wait?"

"Goddamn, son," Trufante said. "Ain't gonna do us no good, back there during the low tide. This thing draws some serious water."

TJ nodded. "We can at least head over there."

"Pama Bama's still asleep down there. Not a real morning person—if you know what I mean."

Frustrated, TJ went below and came back with another cup of coffee. "An hour."

"That's all I ask," Trufante said, sipping on his Coke.

"You think we can find her?" TJ asked.

"It's not the *finding* part—it's the *her* part that worries me."

They sat in silence, each contemplating their own problems. TJ obviously worried about Alicia, and Trufante about how to handle Cheqea. There were not many people that scared him, but she was one.

They were on the flybridge of TJ's boat, looking at the area on the chart plotter. "We draw a lot of water to be on the back side," TJ said, pointing at the shallow water surrounding the area where Trufante expected to find Cheqea.

"I want to get close as I can," Trufante said. "There's snakes and shit in that scrub. Big Pine, my ass. There ain't nothin' taller than me on that pile of sand."

"Well, you tell me how we're going to get in there drawing six feet of water," TJ said, staring at the chart plotter.

Trufante reached across and panned the chart to the northern side of the island, where he traced a line with the tip of his finger up the Bogie Channel to a point of land across from Porpoise Key. "Can you get 'er in there?" he asked, knowing there was no other option than a hike.

"Yeah, and then what?" TJ asked. "You gonna swim?"

Trufante looked over the windshield and pointed to the white container strapped to the bow. "That'll work."

TJ thought for a moment. "Okay. Your hour's up." He started the engines.

Several minutes later, with Pamela sunning herself on the back deck, they were underway. Running parallel to the Seven Mile Bridge, they followed the curving shoreline. When they passed the beach at Bahia Honda Key, TJ cut the wheel to starboard. They passed under the new bridge and then, a hundred feet later, through the open section of the old railway bridge, where they entered Bahia Honda Channel. About a mile in, with No Name Key on the port side, he kept the red 22 and 22X markers to starboard and entered Spanish Channel. A quarter mile later, with the mangrove-covered Little Pine Key off to the side, they moved to the west side of the channel and anchored.

Trufante climbed around the cabin and unhooked the straps holding the container to the deck. He dropped the container into the water. On impact, the unit separated and a large raft self-inflated. It was soon bobbing by the transom. TJ opened the transom door, and from the swim platform, he grabbed the floating line. He tied it to a cleat, then took a knife and cut away the tent-like structure. It was designed to protect the occupants from the elements, but the bright orange material would only attract the wrong kind of attention here.

Trufante stood by him, staring at the shore, still a hundred yards away. "How'm I gonna get there?"

TJ pulled two dive tanks out of a rack by the cabin. "Here you go. One for the way there and one for the way back."

Trufante grinned at him and loaded the tanks. He waved to Pamela and released the line. With one of his long arms, he reached into the water for the valve and cracked it slightly. Nothing happened, and he opened it more. The raft started to slide across the water, emitting a trail of bubbles behind it. It was awkward holding the tank in the water, but if he stayed on his belly, he was able to hold the cylinder over the edge and manipulate it enough to steer.

Chapter 22

Mac glanced at the dive computer. They were at two hundred twenty feet. Huge schools of ten-pound yellowtails, or flags, as the locals called them, huddled together around the small coral heads rising from the sandy bottom. Otherwise they were finning over a desert, but that was what Mac had expected. The shallower, more famous reefs just inside of their position had probably taken the ship down, and either the tide or a storm had dragged it back to deeper water before it sank. Ironhead swam ahead, with Mac staying about ten feet behind. On his left arm was a dive computer, constantly updating their depth, bottom time, and anticipated decompression schedule. He glanced at it often—vigilance was needed at this depth. They had long ago passed the no-decompression limit that recreational divers were familiar with.

With his right hand, he pulled off the retractable compass clipped to his vest and held it straight out in front. The needle showed them moving in a straight line directly south. Suddenly Ironhead turned to the right, and Mac checked his computer and then his compass. They had been moving south for ten minutes and now were heading due east, which Mac expected they would continue for the same amount of time before turning north and then west—a square search pattern. Every so often, Ironhead kicked out several times with his right fin to counteract the current, but otherwise he held his course. With the LED light synchronized with his head movements, he was able to watch his gauges and search at the same time. The big question was, if Mac did see something that Ironhead missed, should he call attention to it or file it away to check later?

For now, there was no conflict. They were back at the start of the search grid, and Ironhead gave a thumbs-up sign to start the long ascent. They stayed together on the decompression stops, but rarely faced each other, the brotherhood and goodwill Mac had felt with a fellow diver already fading. He expected trouble soon.

* * *

Trufante hit a small section of beach, jumped out, and pulled the life raft ashore. He closed the valve on the tank and tested its weight against the other. It was considerably lighter, and he suspected TJ was right; he would need both to return to the boat. He pulled the raft above the high tide line and set the tanks in the bow to secure it, then started walking inland.

Mangroves lined the adjacent shores, but there was a narrow path leading through the massive bushes in front of him. The trail ended after a few hundred feet, with a few boulders marking the end of a road. Like most through Big Pine, the pavement ran straight as an arrow, its end invisible over the immediate horizon. Fighting the morning humidity, he started out along the shoulder, tucking his shirt in and slicking back his hair in the hopes he could hitch a ride from one of the rental cars that cruised these roads looking for Key deer.

Several couples riding bicycles passed by, obviously residents, smart enough to get in their exercise before the real heat hit. The tourists were not as savvy and would come later. He walked for what felt like an hour, passing several small neighborhoods, but for the most part, the landscape consisted only of the low scrub and stubby weatherworn pines prevalent on the key. Soon he came to a paved street, which he crossed, and saw a sign for one of the few attractions on the island besides the deer. The Blue Hole was nothing but an old quarry, but it had an interesting name and a deck overlooking it. The only thing it really had going for it was the birds it attracted.

He left the road at the parking lot by the trailhead and started walking the well-trodden path. The Blue Hole was on his right, but he continued until the maintained trail became nothing more than an overgrown game path plowed by the small deer. It was somewhere in this uncharted protected area that he expected to find the old chief. Searching through this jungle of scrub and rattlesnakes was not a task he relished. Needing some kind of a vantage point, he looked around for the largest tree he could find and, ignoring the brush cutting his legs, headed straight toward the tallest one in sight.

Standing ten feet above the ground, the dead-looking trunk may have once been more substantial, its life probably taken by a hurricane, but for his purpose it would work. The slick trunk had no footholds, forcing him to jump for the lowest branch, which he reached after several misses. Hanging from the thick limb, he swung back and forth until he had enough momentum to swing a leg around it. He crawled on top and went for the next level. The branches were closer together now, but as he climbed higher, they became thinner, and he heard something crack beneath one of his feet. Until now, he had been so focused on climbing that he had ignored the landscape, but after deciding this was as high as he was going to climb, he looked around.

The few extra feet gained him what he needed. Now able to see the shore of the western end of the key, where he suspected he'd find her, he searched for signs. Just before giving up, he saw what he thought was a thin wisp of smoke being carried on the wind to the southwest. Taking a bearing on the sun, he climbed down, having to jump the last few feet. Once on the ground, he turned to the sun to reorient himself. He started moving cross-country, further cutting his legs on the sharp palmettos and hoping he would avoid the rattlesnakes he knew were hiding in the shade at their bases.

He made it to the shore, but there was no sign of life, and he sat down on a piece of driftwood to catch his breath and rest. There were no trees to climb this close to the water, and he was about out of energy, not even sure if he wanted to walk back across to the raft, when he smelled the unmistakable aroma.

"Trufaaante?"

He jumped in surprise, turning to see the woman he sought standing in front of him, smoking a long pipe. "Cheqea. What's shaking?"

She laughed deeply and started hacking. Regaining her composure, she looked at him. "You always make me laugh, but now it hurts." She took another pull on the pipe and handed it to him.

He took it and sucked deeply, wondering where she found weed of this quality out here in the boonies. Releasing the smoke slowly, he studied her. Although it had been at least ten years, she still looked the same, her grey hair roughly plaited, the split ends shining in the sunlight. Her face had the rutted look of someone who spent all their time outside, and she was dressed in clothes a thrift store would have passed on.

"Mac sent me to find you," he said.

"Mac Travis?" she asked, reaching into her pouch to refill the pipe.

Under other circumstances, he would have been happy to spend the afternoon smoking and laughing with her, but he needed his head clear and declined when she passed the pipe to him. "There's some trouble and he needs you."

"Cheqea is not in trouble. This is federal land and I have a paper saying it is a reservation."

"No, not you, old mother," he said. "Mac and another woman are being held by Hawk."

She spat at the name. "Hawk is no good man," she said and

coughed.

Trufante waited until the fit passed. "Will you come help?"

"I will help Mac Travis, but I need a favor in return."

Here it comes, he thought. Cheqea was well known for her favors. Many had courted her to benefit from the privileges, as she called them, or entitlements, as others saw them, granted her by the government. As the last remaining member of her tribe, she held power, especially in the current political climate of appeasement.

"How 'bout you and him talk about that?" he offered, starting back along the path, hoping she would follow.

"You must make treaty now."

He turned and smiled hoping to defuse her. "You know ol' Tru will take care of you."

"Trufaaante. Yes, you are my friend."

He started back along the path, but she called to him. "I'm not walking across this island. Follow me." She started walking along the thin strip of beach. In a hundred feet, the path cut just inshore, and they entered a well-concealed clearing screened by thick mangroves. To the side was a small structure pieced together from pallets and tarps that had floated up on the beach or were entrapped by the mangroves along the shore. She entered and came back a few minutes later with a small knapsack.

"What are you looking at?" she scolded him.

Trufante was standing by the other side of the clearing by a small still. "Got any samples?"

She spat again, "Trufaaante. Never the smoke with you, but the alcohol is your ghost," she said and led the way to a trail he had not seen. Twenty feet later, they stood by a small wooden boat with an ancient outboard motor.

"This works?" Trufante asked, thinking his life raft with the scuba tank propulsion would be better.

"Push it in. Cheqea is losing patience with you."

He pulled the boat to the edge of the mangroves, where he saw a gap in the brush. Moving behind the boat, he pushed it through the opening and then crawled after it, immediately sinking in the muck.

"What the—"

"Do not speak that vile language in front of me. If you would have come at high tide, we would have floated right out."

Like it was his fault they had come at low tide. He fought through the muck, finally finding enough water for the boat to float freely. They climbed in and he primed the engine, worried about whether the sunbaked, cracked bulb would still provide enough suction to pull gas from the tank, and opened the choke. Surprised when the engine started after two pulls, he pushed the choke in and spun the motor to steer to deeper water.

* * *

Mac climbed aboard after Ironhead. Alicia was on the platform to help, taking first the near-empty tanks clipped to his side-mount harness, then his fins. With only the rebreather on his back, he climbed aboard and sat on the platform. Though the wetsuit was thicker than any he had used in the Keys before, he was still cold after almost two hours in the water. The search had lasted an hour, and the decompression stops had taken the balance.

Hawk came to the transom and glared at him. "I was expecting results," he said, moving closer to Alicia than Mac liked.

"You know the odds of finding something on the first drop— zero," Mac said.

"This leaves me to question how valuable our computer whiz is." He grabbed the collar around Alicia's neck and pulled her toward the gunwale. "This deep, on an outgoing tide, if the sharks don't get her first, she'll be dead by the time she reaches the Bahamas." He released his hold on her and took the controller from his pocket.

"Stop the threats. If you want it, we need more information," Mac said.

Hawk's face turned red. "We will do another dive this afternoon and then two more tomorrow. After that I will determine if either of you has any value."

He walked into the cabin, leaving Mac under the watchful eye of Ironhead, who was stripping out of his wetsuit. The man was larger and had already bested him once, but he was injured and Mac expected the pills would be wearing off. He would only have a few seconds while his arms were still entangled in the neoprene. Mac took the opportunity. Turning his back to the man, he grabbed a gaff from its holder under the gunwale, spun, and swung toward him, but Ironhead ducked under the hook, still struggling to free himself from the suit. Under normal circumstances, taking off a wetsuit was a strenuous process, but struggling seemed to make it worse.

Mac took a step forward and jabbed the stainless steel hook at him, feinting to the left before swinging from the right. This time Ironhead was too slow, and the hook hit him in the ear. Blood streamed from the wound, but before Mac could strike again, Ironhead reacted. Like a raging bull, he managed to extract one arm from the suit and grabbed the shaft of the gaff on the next swing. Using his one free hand, he pulled the shaft, and before Mac could release the handle, Ironhead cocked his head and butted him between his eyes. Mac crumpled to the deck.

Chapter 23

Standing in the door of the plane, Mel hesitated. It was the first time she would set foot in the Keys in almost a year—not her longest absence, but her most emotional. An anxious couple pushed behind her, ready to start their party, and she reluctantly walked down the steel stairs pulled up to the small plane at the Key West airport. The breeze whipped her short hair into her face, forcing her to shield her green eyes from it, and she smelled the humid breeze. Stepping down onto the tarmac, she knew that whenever she touched the soil of the islands, things changed for her.

She was sure that Mac had saved her life that night on the sailboat, sacrificing his safety for hers when he released the life raft just before the boat sank. Finding out he was all right had taken a weight off her, but she felt deep down that, regardless of her feelings for him, their relationship was over. Trouble followed him everywhere he went, and although he was not responsible for it, the outcome was always the same—disaster. First her father, losing his life while saving the future president's, then a crazed drug dealer, and finally, the incident with the rogue CIA agent that had led to the wreck that had almost killed her.

Fully recovered, at least physically, she grabbed her briefcase from the cart and followed the line of passengers moving toward the small terminal. There was no need for a carry-on—she had no intention of staying overnight. The group entered the glass doors, heading for the baggage carousel, but she walked right through the terminal, crossing the street in front of the obligatory pink cabs, and entered the covered garage. Scanning the line of cars, she checked the text message on her phone for the space number of her rental.

Finding the car, she stashed her briefcase in the backseat and got comfortable with the controls, especially the AC. Satisfied, she pulled out of the space and exited the lot. Turning left onto US-1, she saw the emerald water from eye level for the first time in a year and felt a pang of remorse for all that had happened. She turned right off the island and drove the sixty miles to Marathon. Now that she was here, she was unable to get Mac out of her mind. Surprisingly, she had become more like him in the last year than she wanted to admit. After taking nearly six months to recover, she had done nothing to move her life forward, either professionally or emotionally. In fact, she suspected she was depressed, and felt almost invigorated by the challenge of dealing with the building department.

She walked through the doors of City Hall, not sure if she should go into lawyer mode or just be another landowner. Before she could decide, a familiar face met her at the counter. They exchanged gossip about their high school acquaintances while she waited impatiently for the head of the building department to see her.

A balding, slightly overweight man came toward her, and she breathed in deeply, readying herself to present her rehearsed argument. She had fought with herself after receiving the copy of the notice by priority mail. In many ways she wanted her past to disappear, and that meant leaving everything Keys-related behind. But she knew how precious that island had been to her father, and now Mac. A piece of her felt she owed it to both of them to help preserve it, and letting Mac have the property might ease her guilt over their breakup. All those feelings aside, the notice just plain angered her.

She had escaped the Keys after high school to attend college and then law school in Virginia. During her time there, she had fallen in with a group of activists and interned for the ACLU, who had offered her a job after graduation. For a decade after passing the bar, she had fought the government, arguing for the activist causes the group represented. Her view of the world had changed over the years and now she considered the time wasted, but politics aside, this was just wrong. She had clear title to the island, and if Mac wanted to rebuild her dad's house, he should be allowed.

The man stopped short of the counter, his bureaucratic radar alerting him to the danger ahead. Mel had already spoken to him on the phone, and he had expected the meeting, but from the look on his face, he was regretting scheduling it.

"Mr. Baldwin," she said, extending her hand. "Melanie Woodson. But just call me Mel."

He inched forward and shook, his grasp feeling like that of a ten-year-old girl. "Why don't you come back to my office?" he said, lifting the counter.

She shook her head, wanting witnesses. "Out here is fine," she said, opening her briefcase and pulling out the certified letter. "In my opinion, this notice is in error."

"And how's that?" he asked.

She pulled out a sheaf of papers copied from the building code. It was neatly bound in a folder with yellow highlights throughout. "How many examples should I cite?" She sensed he was close to folding and backed off. "Surely we can find a section somewhere in here." She lifted the folder, flipped through the pages, and dramatically set it back on the counter. "That allows a property owner to rebuild damaged property."

Every eye in the room was on them, and he turned red. "But you see," he stuttered, "it was never permitted."

She cleared her throat, making him jump. "Well, what if we paid the original permit fees from the nineties, when it was built?"

She sensed this was about the money.

He thought for a second. "That might be acceptable," he said and gave instructions to one of the clerks. "If that is all.... "

"Thank you so much for your time," she said, about to shake his hand, but his back was already turned to her. Walking over to the woman he had assigned the task, she removed her checkbook and waited for the bad news.

A half hour later, she stood outside the building wondering what to do. The permit was settled, for a fraction of the cost they had wanted, and she felt drained, the emotional buildup of coming here and then the petty negotiation with the building department leaving her hungry. She looked around for a familiar place to eat, or maybe avoid. A sandwich shop across the street caught her eye—one that she didn't remember, which was a good thing. She walked over, ordered, and took a table by the window. While she waited, she grabbed a copy of the *Keynoter* from the next table and stared at the headlines.

* * *

"That your boat, Trufaaante?" Cheqea said when they pulled up to TJ's boat.

"You know better," he said, cutting the engine and coasting up to the swim platform. Pamela came through the transom door to help with the line.

"That's a nice-looking chiquita. She yours?"

Pamela smiled. "I'm Pamela, but you can call me Pajama Bama, like Tru does."

"I like her," Cheqea said, taking Pamela's hand and climbing out of the boat. "Where's Mac Travis?"

"It's like I told you, he's in trouble," Trufante said.

Cheqea started to shake. "Don't you talk to me like I'm some old fool. I ask you a question, I want an answer."

Trufante was starting to wonder if dealing with her was such a good idea when he saw Pamela go to her and whisper something. They both giggled, and he suspected whatever she said was at his expense. Leaving them to each other, he climbed the ladder to the bridge to talk to TJ.

"Well, now that you have her, what are we going to do to get Alicia back?" TJ asked.

Trufante rubbed his face, thinking a beer would be good around now. He was tired from the cross-country hike across the island, and now that she was here, he had no idea what to do with her. He avoided TJ's stare and looked down at the two women sitting next to each other on the transom.

"She says she can find him," Pamela called up.

Trufante wondered where this was coming from, but with Cheqea involved, anything was possible. The woman was a reputed mystic, according to some New Agers who thought she could see what they couldn't. They sought her out and paid her in goods or pot for her visions, but the general consensus was that she was a charlatan drug addict. At this point, he didn't care. He'd consider anything to get TJ's eyes off him.

"I can read your mind, Trufaaante. You better watch what you think." She leaned in and said something to Pamela. "I will speak to her only."

Shit, here we go, he thought, surprised it had taken her this long to go off the deep end. He looked down at Pamela.

"She wants us to go to the where the water's blue," Pamela called up.

"What the hell, Tru? This isn't getting us anywhere," TJ said. "Maybe I should try some of Alicia's contacts at the Agency."

"We got no phones, remember?" Trufante said. "Lost in the explosion. Maybe she's not far off. They're looking for a wreck, right? Let's head out to the ocean side and have a look around. We know the radar signature of Hawk's ship. It's a long shot, but I got nothing else."

"Better than just sitting here," TJ said and started the engine.

Trufante went down the ladder to the deck to help clear the anchor and secure Cheqea's boat with a large weight he pulled from a storage locker. TJ cut the wheel and they backtracked toward the Bahia Honda Bridge.

* * *

Mac sat up slowly, trying to get his bearings. He felt his head, discovering a large knot where Ironhead had butted him. "Where's Alicia?" he asked Wallace, who was standing in the shade of the cabin with a rifle by his side.

"Hawk's got her locked up. Haven't seen him this mad in a long time," he snickered.

"Go tell him I want to talk," Mac said, shuffling his body to the gunwale and sitting up.

Wallace nodded and stuck his head in the cabin. A minute later, Hawk appeared.

"That was stupid," he said.

"Let's have it," Mac said.

"What are you talking about?" Hawk stared at him. "Did Mike knock the rest of the sense out of you?"

Mac's anger supplanted his injury and fatigue. "You're holding out."

Hawk didn't respond.

"There's got to be something more. You wouldn't risk a search like this expecting to get lucky on one dive without some other information." Coincidences were uncommon, in his experience. "Why don't you let me take a look at that coin? Maybe Alicia can figure something out."

He still needed to buy some time. His head was spinning, and the only way he saw to get out of this was to find whatever Hawk was looking for and hope an opportunity presented itself.

Hawk reached into his pocket, withdrew the coin, flipped it, and tossed it in his direction. "Don't guess you can spend it here."

Mac grabbed the piece of silver and slowly rose to his feet, using the gunwale for support.

"You don't look so good, Travis. And Mike is out of pills, so you might want to steer clear of him," Hawk said and went inside.

Mac sat back on the deck, studying the coin. A minute later, he was surprised when Alicia came out the door. She went right to him.

"Are you okay?" she asked.

"I'll be fine, but we need to get out of this, and the only way I can figure right now is to find whatever he's looking for." He handed her the coin.

"What's this?"

"I don't know how it ties in, but I expect it does," he said.

She rubbed the silver piece between her thumb and forefinger and then held it to the light. "It's old and Spanish, but that's all I know."

"Old? That's it. Maybe we can date it and use that for the declination."

"If you're right, it might get us closer, but it's still not the key," she said. "I thought this had something to do with the Mayans."

"I'm thinking I was looking for the wrong thing all these years. I assumed the clues led to Mayan gold, but thinking about it, they had an early presence here and were certainly wreckers. Maybe they just used their tattoos as a way of passing down information. If this coin is connected, I'd bet it's a Spanish wreck he's looking for. Help me up," he said, reaching out for her.

She leaned in, placing an arm under his. Together they got him to his feet and went to the cabin. Side by side, they sat in front of the computer screens comparing images of Spanish coins to the one sitting on the table between them. Holding it up to the camera mounted on the screen, she took a picture of it and was about to start running her recognition program when Hawk appeared behind them.

"We're going to be on the next set of numbers shortly."

Mac looked at him. His head was pounding from the blow he had taken, and he doubted they'd had enough of a surface interval to get any kind of bottom time without an extremely lengthy decompression schedule. Without thinking through the consequence, he blurted out, "I'm done for the day."

Chapter 24

Mac heard the lock engage. He knew he had set Hawk off, but didn't expect this reaction. Now, locked in the hold, he was starting to get desperate for a way out of this. He looked for anything on the inside of the steel door that would free them, but it was a watertight hatch—the only lock was outside. Alicia lay on the floor where she had landed when they pushed her in. In the corner were a single laptop, a pencil, a pad of paper, and a chart.

"You okay?" Mac asked.

She nodded and pulled herself up, resting her back against the cold steel bulkhead. "What are we going to do now?"

"Sorry. It was worth a shot," Mac said, the guilt of his unsuccessful attack eating at him.

"Hand me the computer," she said.

"You're not really going to help them," he asked.

"Of course not. I'm going to help us. I was hesitant to try anything before, thinking he'd check the computer, but we've got nothing to lose now. If he was going to kill us, we'd be dead. He needs us."

Mac knew she was right. "You could have reached out before?"

She nodded. "But the risk was not worth it." She paused. "I have to admit to being sucked in by the puzzle. If we can solve it, it could make us all rich."

"But if we solve it and don't have a plan, we'll be dead."

They sat in silence for a minute. "Okay. So back to the beginning."

Mac had an idea. "You keep on the puzzle. I've got some thinking to do." He slid the laptop toward her.

"The coin should give us a date range. That'll narrow things down, but it's still going to be plus or minus a mile or so. That's a lot of ocean," she said.

"We need to keep on it. While the recognition program is running, can you search for wrecks around the time of the coin?" Mac asked.

She turned back to the computer and started typing. "I'm going to try and get a message to TJ."

"Worth a shot." Even if Hawk was monitoring her, things couldn't get much worse.

* * *

Mel read the article beginning to end. She pulled out her phone, reluctantly scrolled to Mac's contact info, and tried to call, but the phone went to voicemail. That was not at all unusual for him, and she wasn't worried, but the headlines had sucked her in. First there was an article about the chase through the backcountry. His name wasn't mentioned, but she knew the area, and it was very close to her father's island. Hawk was involved, and that was never good, but though a coincidence, it didn't directly involve Mac. She remembered several run-ins her dad had with the antiquities dealer that left a bad taste in her mouth.

A smaller article had a picture of a wrecked boat run into a bridge near Flamingo Key. The top-billed article was more disturbing. Two days earlier, a boat had blown up after several witnesses reported a chase and gunshots. The wreck had just been recovered. Boats blowing up and crashing into bridges was not the norm here, the trail usually leading to Trufante and then to Mac.

Her curiosity got the better of her. She put down the paper and paid the bill, asking the waitress if she knew anything about who owned the boat that had blown up.

The answer tightened the circle, and adding in the stop-work order on the house, there was enough circumstantial evidence for her lawyer brain to kick in. Whether through reason or paranoia, the answer came back the same—the incidents were related and all had something to do with Mac.

With some time on her hands before her flight back and her curiosity piqued, she drove to The Keys Fisheries, where the waitress had told her she could find the owner of the boat that had exploded. Parking by the retail store, she got out and walked over to the dock. Not really knowing why she was here, she gazed at the marina. Leaning against the same well-worn spot on the rail where the tourists would watch the tarpon feed later tonight, she checked out the remaining boats. The marina was only half-full, many out on charters, but several caught her attention. One had five outboards hanging from the transom, and she laughed to herself about the ridiculousness of the setup.

Though she had distanced herself from the Keys, she still knew her boats, and the display of power amused her. She moved her gaze to the boat next to it, a small center-console, similar to one her dad had owned, and realized it was damaged. Walking toward it, she could see the top had been removed and walked closer to get a better look. It meant nothing by itself, but this was starting to look like another in a growing list of coincidences. She was about to leave when she heard someone call her name.

"Woodson, is that you?"

Walking toward her was a heavyset woman with sleeve tattoos on both arms and a streak of blond running through her auburn hair. On first sight, Mel didn't recognize her and was about to ignore her and walk past.

"It's Celia, Monica's sister," the woman said.

Mel recognized her now, though she was considerably

different than the young girl she remembered.

"Hey," Mel said, not knowing what else to do.

"You look the freaking same. Heard you had a bad go of it with the wreck," she said.

Mel didn't want to go into the details of her life with the sister of someone she would rather forget. "Doing okay," she said. To sound social, she added, "How's your sister?"

"Shit. That old cow's married three times and has a tribe of kids. Didn't turn out too well for her."

Mel couldn't help but laugh. She'd always thought it would go that way for her.

"So, what brings you back here? Hope you're not looking for Mac," she said.

"Had a legal matter I had to deal with. And, yeah, I guess I am."

Celia cocked her hip and her expression changed. "Me too."

* * *

They had just passed under the Seven Mile Bridge. Pamela and Cheqea were below on the deck, and TJ was at the wheel, with Trufante beside him.

"Which way you want to start?" TJ asked.

"What about the radar?"

"This one doesn't have nearly the definition of the unit on the other boat. I can't tell what's what out there." He pointed to the green screen.

"If it was me, I'd head southeast. The reef's hard coral, shallow and longer there. Most of the wrecks happened on that side of the light," Trufante said.

TJ cut the wheel and headed toward the small light marking East Washerwoman Shoal. He steered toward the outside of the marker, avoiding the rock piles surrounding it, where the charters caught their baitfish, when he saw a boat rolling with the seas. It was its aspect that first caught his attention, abeam to the direction of the waves. It wasn't anchored, and from his vantage point on the bridge, it seemed there was no one aboard.

"What do you make of that?" he asked Trufante.

The Cajun put his hand to his brow and squinted. "Ain't no one on her, if that's what you're asking."

"I'm going to have a look," TJ said, cutting the wheel toward the drifting boat. "Hand me those binoculars."

"What about Alicia?" Trufante asked, grabbing the glasses from the compartment running over their heads.

"This'll just take a minute. Go on down and grab the boat hook. I'll take you to seaward and let 'er drift in," TJ said, adjusting the course to move parallel and windward of the boat. Before he approached, he scanned the drifting vessel with the binoculars, not seeing anything except the logo for what looked like a turtle hospital on the bow. He dropped speed and started to come alongside, gently correcting his course as the boats moved together. "Now," he yelled to the deck.

Trufante was on the port gunwale. Leaning over, he extended his lanky frame over the side, using his long arms to reach for the drifting boat. The hook grabbed its bow rail, and he pulled the boat toward him. With one hand on the bow rail of the drifting boat, he took the dock line in his other hand and slung it over the rail. Quickly, before the boats could move apart, he released the boat and pulled the loop on the line toward him, threading the end through it. When it was snug, he tied it around the midship cleat. "There you go, cowboy," he called up to TJ. The two boats were secured together.

TJ climbed down the ladder, tossing two fenders over the side. He went past the women, who were deep in conversation about something he didn't quite catch, and went to the line. "Come on."

Together they pulled the line in and brought the boat alongside. When it was secure, Trufante hopped gingerly between the boats, landing on the open bow of the center-console. He looked around and went to the helm.

"Blood," he called to TJ.

"Where?"

Trufante held up a T-shirt, its original white, now a deep crimson.

"That's the guy from Hawk's boat," TJ called back. "Hey, Pamela, do you remember what that guy was wearing?"

She left Cheqea and came to his side. "Yup, fashion first," she said.

"How far's this turtle hospital?" TJ asked.

"Just 'round the bend on the other side," Trufante said.

"Can you start it?" TJ asked.

Trufante went to the helm and shook his head. "No keys."

TJ went to a storage locker and pulled several lines out. "I'm going to make a bridle. Tie it off to both bow cleats." He started tying lines together and handed the loop to Trufante, then went to the transom of the sportfisher and secured the ends to the port and starboard cleats.

"Come on back," he said, climbing back to the bridge. He waited until Trufante was back aboard before pushing the throttle gently forward. Slowly he turned into the waves to gain control of the other boat. The line came tight, and he accelerated slowly, trying to find the sweet spot where the sportfisher could pull its tow efficiently.

Trufante climbed back to the bridge. "Change of plans?"

"It's better than running blind out there, looking for a needle in a haystack. They could be in the Bahamas by now." The following sea made the procedure difficult, with the different-size boats accelerating at different speeds as they surfed down the backs of the three-foot waves. They had several close calls where the smaller boat almost reached the transom of the sportfisher, but TJ fell into the rhythm and manipulated the controls, keeping the boats apart. The boats were running well together now, keeping the same speed.

They reached the Seven Mile Bridge, crossed underneath, and entered the channel on the Gulf side. Trufante pointed to the chart plotter. "You can take her through here. Plenty of water, just watch out for the bank out there." He pointed to an area just to the north of the bridge.

The water was calmer on this side, and TJ pushed the throttle down, gaining a little speed. In fifteen minutes, they found the cove where the hospital was located.

"You know this place?" TJ asked Trufante, looking for information about the small cove.

"Knew a girl that used to work here," he said.

TJ just shook his head and started slowly into the cove. Once inside, he docked the boat alongside a narrow dock and hopped down to the deck.

"Turtles," Cheqea said like a little girl. "Come on, Bama, let's check 'em out."

The two women were on the dock, heading toward the large black tanks.

"Best if I wait here," Trufante said. "Not sure if that girl is still here or not."

TJ shook his head again and walked to the office. Inside he went to the counter and asked for the manager. A few minutes later, a woman came out, and he pointed to where they had docked the boat.

"Thank you," she said.

"Not a problem, but I'm thinking something went on here last night," TJ said gently. "Is there anyone I can talk to?"

"We talked to the sheriff already," she said.

"Just a few questions," TJ pleaded.

The woman thought for a second. "Okay. One of our doctors can help you," she said, walking through a door.

TJ looked around the shop while he waited, paying special attention to a metal cutout of two turtles on the wall, thinking it might make a nice gift for Alicia.

The manager came back with another woman. "This is Jen. She can help you."

"Do you know who the man was that took the boat?" TJ asked, after taking her to a quiet corner.

"Mean guy. Had a big gash on his side that I stitched up. He took some drugs and ran out of here. The next thing we knew, the boat was gone."

His head fell at the dead end.

"But, I put a chip in him," she said.

Chapter 25

"I think I have it," Alicia said.

Mac was leaning against the wall in the hold, nodding off. "What?" he asked, trying to gather himself. Fighting through the headache and grogginess, he listened.

"The coin is Spanish and dates back to the late sixteen hundreds."

"That leaves a lot of ships," he said.

"Not as bad as it sounds," she said. "Once a year the Spanish put together a flotilla to bring the riches of the Americas back to Spain. The convoys were well armed, often numbering into the twenties, to avoid privateers and pirates. There are records of individual ships being lost during the years after the coin was minted, but the 1715 and 1733 fleets both sank near here."

"It's not from either of those groups," Mac said, moving towards her. "Those wrecks are too well documented. I think we're looking for one of those single ships, either lost at sea or sunk in a battle."

"I disagree. From everything that I've read, they would never send a solo ship. It's more likely it was attached to one of the other flotillas at the last minute and not documented."

Mac thought about what she said. "You might be right."

"So, should I put together a trail of evidence from one of those fleets?" she asked.

"The 1715 was the most famous. Let's steer him toward the 1733 flotilla."

"You sure?" she asked.

"Look at it this way. If it's either of those, the date and time are well known. That should keep him happy and narrow down the search area significantly," he said. "Just hope Trufante gets here before he finds out we don't know anything."

"Got it." She started typing.

Mac looked around the hold, trying to think if there was any way out or anything to use as a weapon. Alicia was working on the laptop, which in itself could knock a man unconscious, but it might also damage the computer in the process. Besides that, there was only the chart, the pad of paper and pencil. He remembered a movie where the hero had used common objects like these to make weapons and pulled them towards him.

Pulling a page off the pad, he experimented with different methods of creating a weapon from the paper. The pencil could do some damage, but he would have to be in close quarters. He put both items down, not getting the results he was after.

"What are you doing?" she asked.

"I saw somewhere that you could make deadly weapons from this kind of stuff," he said.

"Gimme that." She reached for the pad. Tearing off a few pages, she started making tubes, one long one and one short one that fit around the longer one. Taking the elastic tie from her hair, she attached it to a slit in the longer tube. With the shorter section between her fingers, she slid the long piece through and while holding it, pulled back the hair tie. The smaller tube shot through.

"Nice, where'd you learn that trick?" he asked.

"What do you think we did all day at the CIA? Sit around and stare at data?" She put the sling down and started making what looked like little bullets. When she finished, she pulled back the smaller tube enough to allow one of the projectiles to sit in the end of the larger tube and released the trigger. The bullet flew out and hit the wall across the room.

"You could take someone's eye out with that," Mac said.

"Exactly. I've got a few more tricks just like it." She grabbed the chart and started making a spear that, when completed, was hard enough to do some damage.

He was skeptical, but they had no choice. "Before we make a break for it, we need a plan," Mac said. Just as he said it, they heard a boat cruise by. "Hear that?"

"Yeah, it's a boat."

"That's our best shot. We are sitting over some prime yellowtail bottom. Sooner or later a fishing boat is going to anchor near here. All we have to do is wait until we hear a boat circling and we bang on the door, just like Hawk said," Mac said.

"So far, so good. What happens then? I shoot their eyes out with this?" Alicia held up the paper gun.

"Honestly, I would scrap that one and just make a couple of blow guns. But, yeah," Mac said, moving closer to the exterior bulkhead so he could hear if the boat was near.

A few minutes later, Alicia had two blow tubes and a dozen projectiles. Mac looked at the sword. It looked a little flimsy. "What if we reinforced that with the pencil?"

Alicia took it from him and started to rework it. She handed it back and tugged at the choker around her neck. "What about this?"

Mac moved toward her and examined the device. He would need tools to remove the collar, but the inside was what he was interested in. If he could insulate her from the shock, it would render the unit harmless. Working one finger around the inside of the collar, he felt for the probes. There were two—one on either side of her neck located by the carotid arteries. "I think this'll work," he said, taking a sheet of paper and folding it over and over until he had a one-inch strip several folds thick. He took this and wrapped it perpendicular to the collar, circling it several times before tearing a slit in either end and sticking them together.

She moved her neck around, clearly more uncomfortable than she had been before. "Would it be bad if I told you I was scared?"

Mac looked at her. "You know how far you've come since we first met. Running around the everglades in high heels, clutching a life preserver."

She laughed. They were ready now, and just as he thought it, they heard a boat.

* * *

"What do you mean, you put a chip in him?" TJ asked.

"It's a GPS device. We use them to track the turtles we release. Come on." She led them through a door and into the hospital area. Around the corner there was a workroom with several computer stations. She sat at one and started typing.

TJ watched over her shoulder. She pulled a tag out of her lab coat and entered the number into a box on the screen. A long minute later, a flashing dot appeared, showing the location of the tag.

"Just past Coffins Patch," TJ said after she zoomed in.

"Does that help?" she asked.

"It's a place to start," he said and then thought for a second, wondering what Alicia would do with this information. "Is there any way to track it in the field?"

"There's an app for that," she said.

He looked up, realizing he had no phone. "That's going to be a problem," he said and explained what happened. They both stared at the screen, watching the blinking dot. "They must be anchored out there." He peered at the screen. "Looks like a couple of hundred feet of water."

"Tell you what. Keep your VHF on sixteen and I'll check on it every so often and let you know if the position changes." She took a pad and wrote down the coordinates of the chip.

TJ thanked her, then left the hospital and ran to the boat. He called out on the way to Pamela and Cheqea, who were leaning over one of the turtle tanks, to meet them aboard. Climbing the stairs to the bridge, he shoved a sleeping Trufante to the side and started the engine. He was about to ask Trufante to get the lines, but he was still half-asleep, so TJ called down to Pamela. She helped Cheqea aboard, untied the lines, tossed them on deck, and stepped over the gunwale. As soon as her feet hit the fiberglass, he pulled away from the dock.

"Wha's up, my man?" Trufante mumbled.

"You get into the old chief's weed?" TJ asked.

"Mmmm. Maybe," he said, laying his head against the bolster.

TJ ignored him. For the first time in days, he had some tangible information that might lead to Alicia. Restraining himself from pushing the throttle down until he was clear of the breakwater, he moved into open water at a fast idle and, once clear, accelerated toward the bridge.

"Turtle Hospital, Turtle Hospital, do you read? This is *Alicia's Dream*, over," he called out on channel sixteen, repeating it several times before he got a response.

"Roger. Go to seventy-two," came the response.

He switched channels and confirmed that the chip was still in place. Pulling the coordinates from his pocket, he engaged the autopilot, entered them into the chart plotter, then hit the GOTO button. The path showed a straight line over land, the most direct route, but he ignored it, knowing it would adjust once he cleared the bridge. Once on the ocean side, they would be there in twenty minutes.

* * *

"So are we going to stand here or go do something about it?" Mel asked.

"Effin' right, girlfriend. Give me a second, and let me get the keys to that bad boy," Celia said, walking toward a small shack on the corner of the dock.

"That's yours?" Mel asked when she returned.

"Shit, yeah. You think these freakin' fools can run a business? It's bad enough they think they're captains because they can put a piece of dead fish on a hook. No, no, no." She shook her finger in the air. "They work for me." She jumped aboard the boat, and a minute later, one at a time the five engines started. "Think you could get the lines?" she called to Mel.

Working a boat was in Mel's blood, and she untied the boat, instinctively knowing what effect the tide and wind would have on it. With one line slipped over the outside pile to keep the wind from blowing the boat into its neighbor and the other lines free, she called to Celia that they were ready. The boat started moving backwards into the lagoon, and Mel sensed when it had enough momentum to overcome the wind and released one end of the line. They were clear now, and she pulled the line towards her, leaving it in a neat coil on the deck. She went back to the cockpit, where Celia was juggling the throttles, reversing the port engine and using the forward momentum of the starboard engine to turn the boat.

"Looks like your old man taught you a thing or two," Celia yelled over the scream of the five 200-hp engines.

"Something like that," Mel said. "Where we going?"

"Thought we'd check out that old place of your dad's. Word is, that's where Mac's been hanging out," she said, pushing the throttles to their stops.

Instantly the boat pulled out of the water and was up on plane, running fifty knots, cutting easily through the backwater chop. Mel leaned against the padded rocket launcher behind them, having to admit it was exhilarating riding on a boat again—especially one this fast. She watched the familiar landmarks go by, and before she knew it, they were in the channel leading to Wood's island.

"Watch that rock there and take her straight in," Mel warned her as they approached. Celia pulled up, and the memories flooded back the minute her feet hit the sandy bottom. Taking a line to the single pile, she tied off the boat and waded to shore. "You coming?" she called back to Celia.

"Just got a pedi yesterday, and I freakin' hate sand. You check it out. I'll be here," she called back. She turned on the VHF and called out over the static, "Going to listen in on my idiots. Always talkin' trash to each other, bragging about what they're catching and lying about where they are."

Mel walked down the path, not knowing what to expect. She called out Mac's name several times as she approached the house, but there was no answer. Her emotions got the better of her when she saw the burned-out remains, and tears welled in her eyes, but at the same time, she felt a tightening in the pit of her stomach that she knew was resolve. Collecting herself, she turned to the shed and opened the door. Hoping to find some kind of clue, she looked around. She saw his phone and picked it up. Holding it, she felt something—it was as if she was connected to him.

On the off chance that there were any recent calls or texts, she powered it up and scrolled through the screens. Nothing looked useful, just Trufante's number and someone named Alicia. She set it down and left, finding nothing else that might help.

Without looking back, she walked toward the small beach, waded out, and pulled the line off the pile. "Nothing," she said to Celia once she was back aboard. "Unless you know someone named Alicia."

She was silent for a second. "*Alicia's Dream*?"

Mel looked blankly at her.

"I just heard a boat called *Alicia's Dream* hail the Turtle Hospital," she said.

Mel picked up the mike. "*Alicia's Dream, Alicia's Dream,* this is ... " She looked at Celia for the name of their boat.

"*Horsepower from Hell*," she said.

"*Alicia's Dream*, this is *Horsepower from Hell*—over."

Chapter 26

Mac heard an engine and moved closer to the bulkhead, placing his ear against the cold steel. The vibrations of the generator transferred through the hull, causing too much disturbance to hear, so he backed away. From the rumble of the motors, he could tell the boat he had heard had slowed, and he waited patiently to see if they were going to anchor. He sensed that time was becoming critical. Hawk was becoming impatient and volatile. Add in Ironhead's apparent addiction, and he was looking at a recipe for disaster. They needed to get out of here before something set off one or both of the men.

A few minutes later, he could still hear the engine, but it sounded like the boat was sitting in one place, probably anchoring. They needed to act fast, before the fishermen could drop the hook, if they were to use them in the escape. Whether they would be willing or not was another matter, but at least they would be off the boat and hopefully out of range of the shock controller.

"Ready?"

She nodded, and he moved to the hinge side of the door, clutching the pen sword in his right hand. Alicia stood in the middle of the room with the laptop in front of her, carefully held in front of her body to conceal the blowgun. Everything was staged to look as if she was ready to share some new information with Hawk.

Mac took a breath and banged on the door. The sound of the boat outside was still there, and he heard footsteps coming toward them. It was time. A loud click sounded and the mechanism locking the door moved. He looked one more time at Alicia and caught her eye, trying to reassure her. On their last escapade, she had grown admirably, working through several fears and phobias on their trip through the Everglades to Cuba, but this would be one-on-one.

The hinges creaked as the door opened. "This better be good," Wallace said.

Mac frowned, slightly disappointed that it wasn't Ironhead. He had hoped to get revenge, but that would have to wait. Wallace would be easier to overpower. He clutched the weapon and moved backwards behind the door as it opened.

"Well? What do you have?"

Mac peered around the door, watching her.

Alicia stood her ground. "I will show it to Hawk," she said.

"Then it better be real good," Wallace said, scanning the room, looking for the other occupant. "He's a bit on edge."

Before he recognized the ambush, Alicia dropped the laptop to her side with her left hand, and with her right, she raised the blow gun to her mouth, inhaled, and blew the preloaded projectile at Wallace. Mac didn't wait to see if it hit. Springing from behind the door, he grabbed the man around the neck, placing his left hand over his mouth. He aimed for Wallace's shoulder but, not trusting the homemade knife, he wound up, and in that second, Wallace squirmed. The sword point went through his eye. The man screamed, the sound of his agony increasing as it echoed off the steel walls. He dropped to the floor and Mac quickly checked him for a weapon.

"Go," Mac called to Alicia, who appeared frozen in place, the blowgun still in her hand, staring at the blood spurting from the man's face. "Now," Mac ordered, cursing that the plan was going sideways already. He took her arm, pushing her out of the doorway and into the small companionway. He had not intended to kill the man, but in case he was still alive, he paused to lock the door.

Forcing himself to slow down, he climbed the short flight of stairs to the main deck. The original plan had been to take down whoever came to get them and take their weapon. Unfortunately, Wallace had been unarmed.

Mac heard activity above. Hawk and Ironhead must have heard the scream. Their cover blown, Mac had a choice between retreating or facing two armed men. Climbing to the top step, he decided that forward was better than backward.

The water was their only chance to escape. "We're going over the side. Just put your head down and go." He knew Alicia had become a proficient diver in the time since he had met her. Starting to breathe deeply, he purged the carbon dioxide from his lungs, preparing to submerge. Catching her eye, he encouraged her to follow the same breathing pattern.

He heard someone coming toward them and took one last breath. Backing down one step, he extended his arm to move Alicia behind him and waited. Just as the man took the first tread, he reached out and pulled him down the stairs, using the man's own force against him. Ironhead tripped and fell past them to the bottom of the stairs, but Mac knew a short fall was not enough to put him out of commission. A glance down the stairs told him that Ironhead was already gaining his feet. They would have only seconds before he attacked. Peering around the bulkhead, he saw that they would be exposed for several steps before they reached the side and could jump.

Signaling Alicia, he took the last two steps as one and entered the cabin. Hawk faced them, but he was caught off guard, and in the time it took him to raise his gun, Mac bull-rushed him, knocking him over. The gun flew from his hand, but Mac kept going. Hawk was back on his feet, faster than Mac had expected, and had a hold of Alicia, trying to take the computer.

"Let it go," Mac yelled.

She released the laptop, sending Hawk reeling backwards and giving her the precious seconds she needed to escape. Checking that Alicia was still behind him, they ran through the cabin and emerged on deck. A gunshot came from the cabin, and he risked a quick look around. The boat he had heard was still there. Grabbing her arm, he took her over the port side with him.

He swam underwater, hoping she was still with him. Just as his lungs were about to burst, he surfaced, blinked the saltwater from his eyes, and quickly scanned the surface. A large center-console was fifty feet away, but he had to stop. Alicia was struggling about ten feet behind him. He went back to help her and they gained some ground, but were still only halfway to safety when he heard another gunshot.

Forcing himself ahead, he sidestroked toward the boat. More shots were fired, but he was only ten feet away now, staring at the bow of the thirty-plus-foot fishing boat. Alicia was coming up beside him. Still not knowing if they would offer help, he called out.

"Effin' Travis. If they shoot up this boat, I'm out of business," Celia yelled over the bow rail, shaking her hand at him. Someone came beside her and he blinked, not trusting his eyes as Mel extended a boat hook. He reached for it, and with his other arm extended, he tried to reach Alicia, but just as he was about to grab her, she screamed.

Spinning in the water, he faced Hawk's boat and saw him standing on deck with the controller for the shock collar in his hand. Ironhead stood next to him, and even from this distance he could see the smile on his face as Hawk hit the button again.

Mel brought him back to the present. She pulled the boathook, using it to drag him through the water to where Alicia lay motionless. "Come on. She looks like she's unconscious."

More gunshots came from Hawk's boat, but by the sound of Celia's cursing, he didn't think they had connected. Just as he was about to grab her, Alicia's body convulsed again, and he pulled his arm back. The paper insulators they had made were worthless in the water, and if he made contact with her, any shock would be transferred to him as well. Instead of grabbing her around the neck in a lifeguard hold, he took her shirt collar and started hauling her toward the boat.

As they approached the transom, or what fiberglass he could see around the five outboards, he heard Celia yell, "Throw them a line. We gotta get out of effin' range."

She was at the wheel, but Mac clearly saw her look back at him.

"One scratch on this effin' boat and you're a dead man, Travis. Two boats in one freakin' week." She cocked her hip, shook her head, and engaged the throttles.

Mel tossed a line from the stern, but the forward momentum of the boat took it just out of his reach. "Slow down," she yelled to Celia.

"Swim, Travis. Insurance'll cover one boat, but two losses in an effin' week ain't gonna work for me," Celia yelled over her shoulder.

Mac looked up at Mel.

"Swing to port. I'll have a better angle," she called to Celia.

A second later, she threw the line again. Celia cut the wheel, and this time the momentum of the boat brought the line to them. He grabbed the end, wrapping the cordage twice around his wrist. As she picked up speed, Alicia slipped away, being dragged facedown through the water. If he didn't do something quickly, she would drown. Disregarding the risk of shock, he pulled her closer, rolled her on her back, and wrapped his arm around her neck.

When Celia finally stopped, his arm was numb, and he couldn't stop coughing out the seawater forced into his mouth.

"Me and you gotta talk," Celia said, coming toward the transom. Mel stepped aside and Celia grabbed his shirt, hauling him aboard with one hand. "Freakin' insurance dude wants to meet you."

Mac stared up at her, trying to catch his breath. He ignored the rant and looked over at Alicia. Mel was hovering over her, but there was no sign of life.

* * *

The sportfisher ran through the opening in the Seven Mile Bridge, leaving the bay waters. They crossed into the Atlantic with the throttles all the way down and the tachometer redlining. Immediately, the seas changed and he had to correct his course to fight the wind and current. With one eye ahead and the other watching their path on the chart plotter, tunnel vision took over, and he ignored everyone else aboard, focusing only on the line on the screen that showed the most direct course to Alicia. They covered the eight miles to the site quickly, slowing when he saw two boats sitting a couple of hundred yards apart.

Trufante came up beside him. "I'm thinking that big one there's Hawk." He shielded his brow and squinted in the sunlight.

"Here," TJ said, handing him the binoculars. "Tell me for sure—not what you think."

Trufante put the glasses to his eyes and fumbled with the focus. "Uh-oh.... "

"What?" TJ asked, slamming his palm into the wheel.

"Celia and some other woman're in the other boat. Look at that son of a bitch—that one's got five engines on 'er."

"Who is Celia and how does that matter? Is the other boat Hawk's or not?" TJ asked.

"Yeah, it is. And for Celia, she can be more dangerous than a gator with a nail in its tail. You tangle with that cat, you're gonna get scratched."

TJ steered wide of the woman's boat and closed on the trawler.

"Maybe not so fast. He's got guns," Trufante reminded him.

TJ slowed, knowing he had run out of plan.

"Wait!" Trufante yelled, putting the binoculars back to his eyes and facing "Celia's boat. Hot damn. That's Mel, and it looks like two bodies in the water."

Without asking for any further information, TJ sped towards the smaller boat. Running outside of both boats to provide some cover, he eased alongside Celia's boat and saw Alicia on the deck. "Tie her off," he called to Trufante. With a half dozen steps, the big man was down the ladder, over the gunwale, and by Alicia's side.

"Well, if this ain't the misfits' freakin' reunion," Celia said loud enough that they all could hear. "Even my idiots can't get in trouble like y'all."

"No time for niceties, girl," Trufante said. "Hawk's pulling anchor."

"That means it's time to take my five babies and get the frick outta here," Celia said. "Y'all get her on the other boat, and I'm gonna haul ass before I got no children left."

Mac and TJ transferred Alicia to the deck of the sportfisher. Pamela and Cheqea hovered around her, softly singing something no one understood. Once they were all aboard, Mac looked over at Mel. They hadn't exchanged more than a glance since he had come aboard, and now he couldn't take his eyes off her. She must have seen the pleading in his eyes.

"If you've got room for one more," she said and climbed over the gunwale to TJ's boat without waiting for an answer.

Before they could look up, Celia was gone, the five rooster tails and churning white water showing her trail.

Chapter 27

Hawk stormed back into the cabin with the laptop under his arm. Mike was behind him, neither man speaking. "What happened to the other idiot?" Hawk asked.

Mike looked at him and went below without answering.

A few minutes later, he emerged alone. "Dead. Stabbed in the eye," Mike said.

"Shit," Hawk said, looking at the wake of the sportfisher in the distance. "Get the anchor. They're heading to Boot Key."

He went inside and started the engines, hitting the power button for the windlass and waiting impatiently while the anchor came aboard. Mike came back in the cabin, and he gave him the wheel.

Mike would pay for letting Travis and the woman escape, but at least he had the laptop. Though not an expert, he knew his way around computers. Going to the desk, he opened the lid and started searching for the data Alicia had been working on. Checking the file history, he glimpsed several articles on the 1715 and 1733 shipwrecks. He had suspected that it was one of the flotillas, but from what he saw, the woman hadn't found out any more than he already knew. The last file opened was a chart. Clicking the icon, he waited for it to open. The screen flashed and several lines of code suddenly ran across the screen just before it went dark.

He tried rebooting it, but nothing worked—he still needed her.

* * *

TJ had the sportfisher running at full speed toward Marathon. Trufante was on the bridge with him, pointing the fastest course to Boot Key Harbor, the closest anchorage to get Alicia to the hospital. He left the controls to the Cajun and climbed down to check on her. Pamela and Cheqea were off to the side, chanting something he didn't understand. Mac and Mel hovered over Alicia.

"Her vitals seem okay," Mac said, removing the final bolt that held the collar on her neck. He tossed it aside and looked at the bruises where the electric shock had entered her body.

"What can we do for her?" TJ asked.

"I don't know. I'm just hoping she comes to before we reach the harbor and have to decide whether to take her to the hospital or not. That could cause some problems," Mac said.

"You need to think about her and not you," Mel scolded him. "Forget the whole business. Let Hawk do whatever he wants with the damn treasure."

He thought for a minute. He knew she was right, but if he relented, he was giving up his best chance at getting his boat back and rebuilding Wood's house. This was not the time to argue, though. "I'm going up to see where we are," he said, leaving TJ and Mel with Alicia. He slid the door open and passed by the two women sitting on the bench. Without a word, he climbed the ladder to the bridge.

"Cheqea has some magic. She can help the woman," the old chief called up to him.

He stopped halfway up. Doubting it, but not thinking there would be any harm, he nodded to her and watched both women go into the cabin.

He climbed the rest of the way to the bridge and scanned the horizon. The first markers were approaching and he needed to decide what to do.

"How is she?" Trufante asked, breaking the silence.

"Appears stable, but she's still out," Mac said. He could see the look on his face, knowing how rare it was for Trufante to show emotion.

"Kinda become attached to that one," he said. "We still heading to the hospital?"

Mac nodded. He moved to the aft bench to think. He had no hard reason to avoid the hospital, just a gut feeling that it would be bad news—and then he realized what it was.

TJ climbed back up and sat next to him.

"Hawk still needs us, right?" He didn't wait for an answer. "He knows there's something missing."

"How can you even think like that when Alicia is down there unconscious?" TJ asked. The boat slowed down at the first marker.

Mac had little time to convince him, now that they were entering the harbor, but he was certain he was right. "He's not going to let this go," he said and played his ace. "The sheriff is in his pocket."

This got TJ's attention. "What's that got to do with anything?"

"He knows she's hurt and would expect us to get help. I'm guessing he called his buddy and has a deputy sitting in front of Fishermen's just waiting for us. If nothing else, they're still looking for answers about Celia's boat."

He could tell TJ wasn't convinced, but before he could speak, Mel yelled up from below.

"She's conscious."

TJ went down to the deck.

"Just hang in the channel and let's see what happens," Mac told Trufante and followed TJ down.

They were all around her now, but it was Cheqea by her side.

"How is she?" TJ asked.

"Just opened her eyes. Let's give her some space," Mel said, pushing the men away.

Mac and TJ stood on the back deck, staring at the mangroves on the side of the channel. "Let's get that bastard," TJ said. "Take the treasure and hang him out to dry for what he did to her. We're really close to solving this, and now that we have Cheqea--"

He didn't finish his sentence. While they were talking, Hawk's boat had pulled up alongside. Mac turned to TJ. "Don't tell him she's alive," he whispered.

Hawk was at the rail, facing them as both boats held their positions, Trufante and Ironhead skillfully manipulating the controls to hold the boats together. "What do you want? We need to get to the hospital," Mac called across to the other boat.

"Shame, Travis. It didn't have to go like this," Hawk said. "And I'd be careful about that. You see, the authorities are already alerted and looking for you."

Mac got little satisfaction from having correctly deduced his intentions. "You're the one that did this to her. They should be after you."

"You know the sheriff's got it out for you," Hawk said. "The building department too. There's even a mechanic I know over at Bill's place," he threatened. "Why don't we work together here? I'll help her and you help me."

Mac stared at the man, wondering how anyone could be so greedy that he would trade a life for some information. "What do you want?"

"Whatever you're hiding on that laptop. And then it'd be good to know what that crazy Indian woman's doing aboard."

Mac had no bluff to call now. "Call off your dogs, and I'll work with you," he conceded. "But we're partners." He had to say it, even if he didn't trust him.

"Mac. I have it," Alicia yelled from the cabin.

Both men stared at each other. Mac spoke first, trying to

evaluate how to play this. "Seems we are at a standoff now, if she's figured it out and you have the computer."

Hawk stared at him. It was a long time before he spoke. "We can work something out. Why don't we pull over to the side dock at Burdines?"

"That's fine, but first I want to hear you make a call to the sheriff. Call him off and we'll talk," Mac said, having no intention of setting foot on land, and then he realized that even sitting here, they were vulnerable.

Hawk took his phone from his pocket and pressed several buttons. Before he could put it to his ear, Mac stopped him.

"On the speaker. I want to hear both sides of this."

Hawk laid the phone flat in his palm. Mac could barely hear it ring, but Hawk didn't know that. On the fourth ring, a gruff voice answered. Hawk went back and forth with the voice that Mac immediately recognized as the sheriff's. He couldn't really make out what the sheriff was saying, but Hawk was clear—he would get his cut if he cooperated.

"Just a second," Mac called to Hawk and then looked up at Trufante at the helm. "Watch him." He gave one last glance at Hawk and went inside.

Alicia was sitting up on the bench. Her short wet hair, unrestrained after she'd sacrificed her elastic tie for the paper gun, was plastered against her face and she looked pale.

"You okay?" he asked.

"Yeah. That was quite the shock," she answered and moved her gaze to Cheqea. "Show him." Cheqea laid her forearm out on the table. "I saw it when she helped me," Alicia said.

"Hello, Mac Travis," the woman said. "Always in trouble. You and Trufaaante."

Wondering if Cheqea really had helped, he answered respectfully, "Old mother."

"See. Mac Travis asks for help and here is Cheqea," she said.

Mac knew this could go on for hours and thanked her, then

looked at Alicia.

"The tattoo is a star chart. This is it," she said.

Mac could see the excitement on her face; the paleness he had seen just a minute ago had faded, and her color returned. He looked at Cheqea's arm and saw what looked like constellations, and he knew she was right. Ancient mariners had used the relationship of stars to each other and the horizon to navigate—this was the key.

"Do you want to see this through?" he asked Alicia. He could feel his adrenaline kick in now that the answer was close, but after what she had been through, it would be her call.

"To the end. I want him to pay for this," she said, rubbing her neck. "We need the computer. He shut off the Wi-Fi when he locked us in the hold. I never backed up the data."

Mac went back on deck and called to Hawk. He agreed to meet, and the two boats separated. They crossed the channel, swung around, and pulled up to the side of the gas dock. Mac hopped over the gunwale and went to one of the groups of tables and chairs on a concrete patio. Trufante was about to follow, but Mac called him off. He was little protection, and the beer cooler inside the store was too close.

Sitting across from each other, the two men were silent for a few minutes, each calculating how to make the best deal for themselves. Mac wanted to say something, but after a few years around Mel, he had learned a few things. Better to let your opponent open. He didn't have long to wait.

"Come on, Mac. Let's help each other out here," Hawk started.

"There's no reason to help you," Mac said.

"The sheriff was already looking for you before the unfortunate incident with Wallace," he said, rubbing his head as if he had remorse. "Your fingerprints are all over that room."

Hawk looked to the left at the parking lot. Mac followed his gaze and saw the sheriff's car. Two uniformed men leaned against the hood: the deputy from the other day and the sheriff himself. The sheriff caught his glance and tipped his hat.

Mac turned back to Hawk. It was either work with him or go to jail. "Go on," he said, knowing it would be better to let him state his offer and then counter.

"Fifty-fifty partners. Whatever we find, we split. Each of our costs are our own," Hawk said.

The split was fair, but he had Alicia. "You cover all the expenses. We bring the coordinates."

Hawk rubbed his head and appeared to think for a minute, but Mac knew he had him. He had no options.

"We work off my boat, then," Hawk said.

"No. You work off your boat and we'll use the sportfisher. Lend me a rebreather setup and pay the gas." They were close now.

"Done. Tomorrow morning. We meet at five thirty a.m. by the last marker leading out of Sister Creek. If the seas cooperate, we stay out for several nights. If not, we will come in and anchor together. At all times, the boats stay in sight."

Mac extended his hand, skeptical about making any kind of deal with Hawk, even though he knew that both men didn't intend to honor it. They did have a better chance of finding the treasure with his help and equipment than without it. The problems would arise when it was found. He knew that if they found it, Mel would insist on documenting the recovery and doing things legally. Especially with the permit in his name, he was leaning that way as well. There were no illusions as to what Hawk would do when they found it—they would need to be prepared.

"I need the laptop back, then," Mac said.

"No tricks, or the sheriff'll be all over you," Hawk said.

They each walked to their own boats. Ironhead approached the sportfisher a few minutes later with the laptop, the rebreather and a tank of nitrox mix. Alicia took the computer and gave the case a cursory examination before heading into the cabin. Mac gave the gear a brief inspection before handing it to TJ. Hawk's engines were already running and he departed immediately, heading back into the harbor.

Mac called up to Trufante to start their engines and went to get the dock lines. He tossed them aboard and hopped over the gunwale, indicating a narrow channel where they would anchor tonight. The spot would give them a clear view of the exit to Sister Creek and the main harbor. With their manpower, they could set up a watch schedule and make sure Hawk remained in the harbor.

Chapter 28

As they headed toward the anchorage, Mac realized that provisions could be a problem. With a crew of five, and facing the possibility of being out for several days, they needed to replenish their food and water. Even in the Keys, there were no grocery stores with docks, and without a dinghy, they would have to improvise. Expecting Hawk would dock at his ex's house tonight, Mac guided Trufante to the interior of the harbor. Where the channel split, instead of bearing right toward Sister Creek, he pointed to the smaller arm on the left. They passed several condos, and he heard Trufante remark that Dockside, a favorite haunt of his, had lost their lease and been forced to close.

Passing the closed restaurant, they followed the canal to its end by a deserted marina. TJ guided the sportfisher into one of the slips, and the group huddled on the deck. There was no way that Mac was going to let Trufante, Pamela, or Cheqea off the boat—that was a sure recipe for trouble, so he assigned TJ to watch them. Alicia went back into the cabin to resume her work. Mel stepped onto the dock in front of him and they started the five-minute walk to Publix, the local grocery store.

Inside, they cruised the aisles, loading a cart, bantering over what to buy and what not to. At least there was no discussion when Mac passed the beer aisle without stopping. It was heartwarming being with Mel. Even doing a mundane task like shopping with her brought a smile to his face. There was so much he wanted to tell her, but he knew better than to bring it up now. The watch schedule he had drawn had purposely placed them together. The midnight shift would have a few long and hopefully quiet hours for them to catch up.

Each hauling four heavy bags, they walked back to the marina and loaded the food into the galley. As soon as everything was stored, Mac cast the lines and called up to TJ to start the engine. He wanted to secure their station for the night. After several maneuvers, TJ had the large boat turned, and they headed back out the channel. Back at the fork, Mac climbed up to the bridge to check the depth finder, and after determining how the current and tidal swing would affect them, he gave the order to drop anchor.

The boat swung, facing bow to the current, and after checking that the line was taut, Mac tied it off to the bow cleat. The holding here was good, maybe too good, making a quick exit difficult. He thought about the problem for a minute before walking across the foredeck to the bridge. "Have you got a quick release ball?" he asked TJ.

"In the port cabin," TJ called down from the bridge, giving Mac a thumbs-up signal to ask if the anchor held. Mac returned the signal, and he cut the engine. "Stay there, I'll grab it."

A minute later, the two men were on the bow. Mac was pulling the extra line from the locker.

"No need," TJ said, taking a section of line downstream of the cleat. Doubling the line on itself, he tied a simple overhand knot and pulled, leaving a small loop to which he clipped the ball. "Drop out some more line so this is in the water and retie it. If we have to make a run for it, we've got two options: either we cut the line, or if we have time, we can pull the rest out and release it. Either way, the buoy in the water will mark the gear."

Mac nodded at the simple trick, having used it tarpon fishing. With the red ball floating next to the bow and the line tied off, Mac pulled the remaining line from the locker and coiled it on the deck. "Be a shame to lose that much line if we have to make a run."

They shared a meal together and split into shifts. Mac set the schedule by couples, leaving Cheqea out of the roster. First up were Trufante and Pamela. She seemed excited about the adventure, but soon became bored. "I'm going down to get some sleep. Wake me at midnight," he told Trufante and climbed down from the bridge, having assigned them the early shift as a preventive measure. He was pretty sure there was no alcohol on board, but Trufante had a nose for it, and he preferred to have others awake during their shift.

On the way to the forward berth, he passed the bench and table. Alicia and Mel were hovering around Cheqea.

"You see, Mac Travis, I am helping you. Now what are you going to do for me?" she asked with a snort.

He ignored her, thinking they should take pictures of her arm and dump her somewhere. Her true craziness was still there; it just hadn't reared its ugly face yet.

"Making headway?" he asked Alicia.

"It's slow," she said, looking up from her work. "If I blow the scale, it's going to be way off."

"Okay. Let me know. I'm going to try and get a few hours of sleep," he said, moving forward to the berth.

The boat was still, with only a rare passing wake upsetting the peace, and he started to nod off, but TJ was on the port bunk snoring, making sleep difficult. Just as he was about to give up and go back to the cabin, he heard Alicia call out.

"We have it!" she said excitedly. Mac climbed out of the bunk and went to them. He was standing over the group, trying to figure out what was going on. "You were right—it's the stars."

Mac looked closer. On the screen was the night sky, but the date in the corner was 1733. "What am I looking at?" he asked.

"The answer. I already have the other tattoos scaled and

marked here as coordinates." She showed him the same chart she had been working with on Hawk's boat. "Assuming it's the 1733 wreck, it was probably sometime the next day—July sixteenth—that the wreckers were on the site."

"We know all that already," Mac said, wondering how this was going to tie together.

"If you were out there in a boat, with no navigation aids—no GPS or compass—how would you mark your location?" she asked.

Mac wasn't in the mood for any more riddles, but he thought it through. "The stars, and maybe the depth. Depth would be easy—just drop a lead line. The stars, though… " He thought for a minute and it came to him. "I would orient myself north to south using Polaris and then look for a star rising over the site."

"Exactly. We find that star and we know where the site is," she said, opening the window with the star chart. "That's Canopus, the second-brightest star in the night sky, but mainly visible in the Southern Hemisphere. Look at it hovering over the surface like it is marking something."

"Canopus is the key?" Mac asked.

"It appears so," Alicia said. "Watch."

Mac stared at the screen as she moved a day at a time. Every day, the stars moved slightly, each at their own angle. "So, how do we know when?"

"I'm having to guess here. Assuming they had no instruments, I would figure the stars' positions were recorded just after sunset, when they became visible," Alicia said.

"I'd agree," Mac said.

"On the night of July sixteenth, 1733, Canopus was here, at one hundred and sixty degrees." The star chart disappeared from the screen and was replaced by the chart with the compass roses. "I'm going to add that line and—"

"X marks the spot." Mac squeezed her shoulder. "What are the coordinates?"

She wrote something down on a pad of paper and left the

cabin. The entire group, less TJ, who was still asleep, climbed to the bridge and huddled around the chart plotter, watching her enter the numbers. "Here we go."

A symbol appeared marking the waypoint.

"Not too far from where we were," Mac said.

"Far enough that you never would have found it," Alicia said.

Mac knew she was right. A typical dive covered a very small area, and this was almost a half mile away. "One hundred sixty feet," he said.

* * *

They were here together, but Mac felt they were worlds apart. Sitting on the bridge, under a waning moon, with just enough clear sky to make out a few constellations, Mac searched for an icebreaker. Conversation had never been his strong suit. Throw in a relationship and he didn't know what to say.

"That dive's pretty deep. What's your plan?" she asked.

Thankful that she had started the conversation, he explained the rebreather and side-mount tanks they would be using. "Dark and cold, mostly," he said, describing the previous dive.

"What about Hawk's man?" Mel asked.

"He's a good diver, but underwater would be the place to take him out if I had to," Mac answered. He had been thinking about Ironhead, knowing that it would be up to him to deal with the man. Underwater was the logical venue—but that might go both ways.

"Just be careful down there," she said.

"Not going to try and talk me out of it?" he asked.

"I've learned some things over the last year, Mac. One of them is that there's no changing people. I always thought that if I could tame you just a little, things could work out between us, but I know if you're going to be happy, you need to be you."

He was quiet for a minute. "To tell you the truth, I haven't been happy since you left."

She looked at him with a tear in her eye. "But, I just don't see—"

He reached in and kissed her. It wasn't that romantic, and it didn't last that long. The moment was more like the signing of a peace treaty, an agreement that somehow they could find a way to be together without changing each other.

They sat with their bodies pressed together, and the night passed quickly, the slight chill to the air pushing them closer. TJ came up to take the four a.m. shift with Alicia dragging behind him, but Mac waved them off. There was only an hour left until they needed to get up anyway, and he was too content to sleep.

"Might as well get some breakfast going," TJ said, leaving the bridge.

Alicia remained behind for a minute. "Nice to see a smile on your face, Mac," she said and climbed back down to help TJ. Soon after, he smelled coffee brewing and bacon frying. The sky began to lighten, and they brought their breakfast back to the bridge to watch the sunrise. The group was quiet, only a few of them having slept, and though he was one of those who had, Trufante was never a morning person.

"I think we should ditch the research," Mac said to Alicia. TJ was up on the bridge, and the rest of the group was cleaning up from breakfast.

"Why?" she asked.

"It's caused enough trouble already. I think we drop on this site and if it's there, great. If not, we put this to bed and move on. I don't want Hawk as a partner forever, and without the data he has no leverage."

She looked at him. "There's a spot in the cloud where I can stash and protect it."

Mac wasn't sure what the cloud was, but he knew what she meant. "No, I mean double-delete it, or whatever you do so no one can ever reconstruct it."

Reluctantly, she went to the computer and executed the hot key sequence she had installed earlier. The computer screen went black, and she looked at Mac. "Done."

It was five thirty now and they radioed Hawk, confirming the meet at the mouth of Sister Creek. TJ started the engine and Trufante handled the anchor, clipping the ball to the bow rail in case they needed it again. Slowly, TJ pushed the throttles down and the boat moved forward. At idle speed, they followed the mangrove-lined channel, emerging in the main waterway that led to the ocean. He added a few rpms to the engines, and the boat coasted at a fast idle behind several fishing boats heading out for the day. At the mouth of the inlet, they saw Hawk's trawler, sitting by the last green marker.

Following his signal, they approached his starboard side, where he passed across a two-way radio to allow them a private means of communication. The boats separated, and Mac took the radio up to the bridge, where he keyed the mic and gave Hawk the coordinates.

Chapter 29

Once Hawk confirmed he had the coordinates, Mac nodded to TJ. The sportfisher jumped forward, plowing through the waves driven by the fifteen-knot southerly wind, causing the heavy boat to take a long minute before it planed out and was able to reach cruising speed. TJ headed toward the outside of East Sister Rock, a small island with a private residence, then cut the wheel to port and lined up their heading with the course on the GPS screen.

"We should beat them there by a good ten minutes," TJ said.

"Best slow it down. Let him think he's in charge," Mac said, looking behind them at the slower boat. "I'll get everything ready." They had carefully altered the coordinates they had given Hawk to allow him to anchor slightly away from where they estimated the wreck to be. If they arrived first and anchored away from those numbers, he might get suspicious.

TJ dropped his rpms to match Hawk's speed, and together the two boats headed for the reef. They passed over the shallow water and slowed when they reached the one-hundred-foot line. Mac stood by the transom holding a watermelon-sized buoy with a weight and line attached to it. Trufante was on the bow waiting to work the anchor.

TJ allowed Hawk's boat to circle and zero in on the coordinates they had given him. A few minutes later, a similar marker buoy was thrown from Hawk's boat, and a second later they heard the chain click through the windlass as he dropped anchor.

"Okay," Mac called.

It took TJ several quick corrections before he was satisfied and yelled for Mac to throw the buoy. Mac dropped it over the transom, and TJ worked the boat. Sensing the current, he positioned the boat so the bow was just upstream of the buoy and called out to Trufante to drop anchor. After a few adjustments, he shut off the engine and they looked across the hundred feet separating the boats. Hawk was also anchored, and Mac could see Ironhead on the back deck gearing up to dive.

He went to the transom and started to spread out his gear on the deck. Trufante pulled two tanks from the hold while he pulled on the heavy wetsuit and side-mount harness. The suit was suffocating, and he started to sweat. "Come on," he called to Trufante, impatient to get in the water. Looking across to Hawk's boat, he saw Ironhead pull the mask around to the front of his head and look back over at him.

Mac slid into the straps of the rebreather and fastened the buckles, making a few quick adjustments. Out of habit, he pulled the retractable cable to check the compass, holding it straight out in the direction of Hawk's boat to see which direction he needed to head to meet the other diver. Once underwater, there would be no landmarks and he would need the help of the device.

With the tanks clipped to his side, he took the mask, placed it over his head, checked his hoses, and moved through the transom door. On the swim platform, he leaned against the transom and put his fins on, and with a quick glance at Mel, he gave a thumbs-up sign, followed by a classic giant step entry into the water. After a quick adjustment to his buoyancy, he checked his gauges, then with the compass held out in front of him, he finned toward Hawk's boat, where Ironhead waited.

The men exchanged a quick look, and Mac thought he saw pain in Ironhead's eyes. He followed Ironhead down the water column, surprised that he was descending much more slowly than on the last dive. Mac cleared his ears and checked his gauges, adjusting his buoyancy to hold him a few feet from the bottom. Ironhead turned and gave him the okay sign, which Mac returned and together the men set off, following the same search pattern as yesterday.

Mac ignored the schools of yellowtail, focusing all his attention on the bottom, and the man a few feet in front of him. They worked their way through the first two legs of the pattern, and Mac checked his gauges. Their prearranged bottom time was forty-five minutes, and at a hundred sixty feet, they were already past their no-decompression limit. Just finishing the pattern would leave them with at least an hour of decompression time.

The third leg took them past Hawk's boat and closer to the true coordinates. As they approached the next leg, Mac increased his vigilance, wondering if Alicia was really capable of getting this close on the first try. She'd seemed confident, but he had been at the salvage game too long to trust data that was hundreds of years old and passed down from generation to generation by body art. Ironhead was still in front, but moving very slowly, veering from side to side, and having trouble controlling his buoyancy. Mac took his eyes off the bottom and studied the man. After his years here, and his training as a commercial diver on the oil rigs in the Gulf, Mac was well aware of the symptoms of a distressed diver—and Ironhead was showing several.

The third leg revealed nothing, and already an hour into the dive, they started the final turn. Mac scanned the bottom, his LED light flashing against small fish scampering above the sand, but revealing nothing else. With every minute that went by and every patch of sand he passed, he became more pessimistic about finding anything and started thinking about what would happen when they surfaced. Hawk would be livid, especially when he found out that they had deleted the data. Realizing he should have gone back to Celia's and gotten the gun from the center-console, he tried to think what weapons were available to counteract the arsenal he already knew was aboard Hawk's trawler.

A quick check of his gauges confirmed what he'd already guessed—the dive was over. They had found nothing. He glanced at Ironhead, who still looked slightly disoriented, and finned toward him. Mac looked at his eyes, but they were glazed over. He reached out to grab the back of his vest in order to help him to the surface when the man struck back. Whether it was instinctual or planned, Mac had to act, and when he saw the knife in Ironhead's hand, he knew he had been played.

Ironhead slashed out for him, but with the weight of the tanks, Mac was too slow and a second later he saw blood, rising green through the water. Turning quickly, he finned backwards, trying to put some space between them so he could figure out how to counter the attack. The blood was still rising, and he chanced a glance at his arm. The wetsuit was cut through, revealing a deep gash. In that instant, Ironhead lunged again, but Mac was able to fin to the side, the blade barely missing him. He turned, trying to locate Ironhead, but realized the other man had anticipated his move, and just as he spun around to locate him, he felt a tug on his vest and inhaled seawater.

Ironhead must have cut the hoses behind him. A huge cloud of bubbles escaped from the rebreather now that the closed circuit was broken, and he slid back into the disturbance, using it as cover while he reached for the regulator attached to his right tank. He was in a bad spot now, and his first thought was air, but before he could put the mouthpiece in, he felt a hand jerk it away. There was no time to reach for the other regulator on his left side. Holding his breath, he pulled away, staying with the bubble stream. Ironhead released the hose, and Mac struggled against the heavier man, but felt his arm reach around his neck. Feeling the cold steel of the knife against his throat, he lashed out one last time. Not expecting the reaction, Ironhead was pushed off balance and reached his free hand around Mac's chest to stabilize himself, hoping to gain enough leverage to pull the knife across his throat.

Mac knocked the hand away, struggling to hold on to the air in his lungs and knowing he had no time left. Ironhead reached for him again, but Mac swatted his arm away. He pulled back to prepare for the next attack when his hand brushed against the compass attached to his vest. Instinctively, from years of using the device, he pulled the retractable cable. Ironhead had him again, and just as he felt the pressure of the knife, he saw the thin-coated wire holding the compass. In a desperate move, he wrapped the cable around his adversary's forearm and pulled.

Ironhead dropped the knife and started to hammer Mac with his free hand, but Mac pulled harder, knowing this was his only chance. He was getting light-headed and started to loosen his grip on the cable when all of a sudden there was no more resistance. Not sure what had happened, he backed away and saw Ironhead's forearm drifting toward the bottom and a cloud of blood floating toward the surface. Immediately, before he could ascertain the condition of his opponent, he grabbed the regulator.

Disoriented and breathing deeply, he looked around, but the silt kicked up from the fight hid the bottom. Finally, his breath evened out and the water cleared. Ironhead was on the bottom, facedown. From the blood loss, he assumed he was dead. Moving toward him, Mac went to retrieve the knife from the sand. He picked it up, and just as he was about to turn away, he saw an irregular shape in the sand. Despite his condition, he wanted a look and quickly took stock. His arm had stopped bleeding, either from the cold water or the compression from the wetsuit; otherwise, he was uninjured. His biggest problem was the long decompression he was faced with, and after checking the gauge on the tank he had been breathing from, he realized it was almost empty; the exertion and depth had quickly depleted it. Knowing the full tank strapped to his right side was more than enough for at least the ascent and probably the first decompression stop, he sank to his knees and fanned his hand back and forth, moving the sand away from the object.

After a few minutes, he had the surface of the object uncovered and saw the roughly cylindrical shape of a stone ballast. Excited now, he scooped sand away from it and found another by its side. There was little else he could do except get safely to the surface. Reluctantly, knowing the ocean bottom could swallow his find in a second, he checked the compass, now swinging by his side, and finned west toward TJ's boat.

Several times during the ascent, he had to control his excitement and slow himself, the risk of surfacing too fast vastly outweighing the importance of delivering the news of the discovery. At thirty feet, he checked the computer and his air supply. He would hang here until his tank was near empty and then surface. Looking up, he saw the hull of the sportfisher fifty feet away. Carefully maintaining his depth, he swam to the far side of the boat so it would conceal him when he surfaced. Unless he had seen the blood come to the surface, Hawk would not be expecting the divers for at least another hour before he became concerned. A few minutes later, he was below the boat and took another breath. Feeling just a bit of resistance, he knew there were only a few lungfuls remaining in the tank, and he surfaced amidships.

TJ was not expecting him either, and he had to call out quietly to get their attention, scolding them when they all rushed to the side. "Slide me a couple of tanks and take these," he called out quietly, unclipping the first tank from his side. "Don't let Hawk see."

"You're hurt," Mel said.

"I'm good. Don't let Hawk see you all over here. He'll get suspicious," he said, handing the first empty to TJ and taking a full one, which he clipped to the harness.

"Where's Hawk's man?" TJ asked.

"Shark bait," Mac responded, switching the other tank out. "And I think I found it."

Chapter 30

Mac had time to think now—a lot of time. According to the computer, he had an hour and ten minutes of decompression stops starting at thirty feet. To make it easier for him to maintain his depth, he held on to the weighted line TJ had dropped from the transom. Finally, the adrenaline started to wear off, his breathing settled, and he tried to get comfortable. He floated horizontal in the water, sipping air from the tank on his right side, holding the line with his left hand and checking the computer on his right wrist every few minutes. The time passed slowly, but there were some things he needed to work out.

First was Hawk. Without his two henchmen, he was partially neutralized, but he still had a least one gun aboard. Given the chance to get to shore, he would quickly hire more muscle and get the sheriff involved. A short-term solution came to him after he had been down for ten minutes. With another twenty minutes at thirty feet, he could easily slip over to Hawk's boat and cut the anchor line. It wouldn't do much except give the man something to think about, but it was a start.

Holding his depth, he remembered the heading he had taken before he got in the water. He left the line, and with the compass extended in front of him, he swam to the boat, careful to maintain his depth to continue his decompression. He looked up at the surface as he approached. The seas were two to three feet, high enough that the waves would conceal his bubble trail—unless someone was specifically looking for him.

A few minutes later, the hull of the trawler was visible above him and he swam toward the bow. At the anchor line, he reached into the rebreather vest and retrieved Ironhead's knife. Slowly, he started sawing through the thick nylon line. It parted, and he held on to the section floating from the anchor and watched as the current took the boat.

The tide was outgoing, and with the wind from the northeast, the boat slowly turned abeam to the seas and started drifting toward open water. Soon, it disappeared, and he swam back to the line hanging from TJ's boat to resume his decompression.

The next problem was the treasure. Provided he could take Hawk out of the picture, what should he do with it? He'd been in enough trouble with the authorities not to risk salvaging anything without a permit. He thought about diving at night, but as soon as the same boat was spotted on the same spot for more than a few nights, the locals would get suspicious. Any vessel anchored in one location for too long drew the attention of both the local fishermen, thinking it was a hot spot, or the authorities.

His time at thirty feet was up, and he moved up to twenty. As he got shallower, the swells above made holding depth more difficult and he was glad for the line. Something about the depth triggered his memory and he remembered the silver being cached in the canal by Flamingo Key. That might be his answer.

Before he could formulate a plan, he heard the distinctive sound of a boat's propeller. It was impossible to tell direction underwater, but he could tell it was coming toward him. Clinging to the line, he waited as the sound got louder, and a minute later he was staring at Hawk's boat, the distinctive hull and color visible under the water. The boat stopped and idled above him.

His computer showed he still had thirty minutes of total decompression time left—ten more minutes at his current depth and the final twenty minutes at ten feet. Every dive computer had a safety factor built into their algorithms, but they were brand-specific, and he was not familiar enough with the rebreather equipment to know its limits. But, in the end, it didn't matter as he looked up at the two hulls within a few feet of each other. He had to know what was transpiring on the surface.

Releasing the line at the transom, he swam past Hawk's propellers, wondering if he could sabotage the boat, but he decided the risks were greater than the reward. He might be able to disable one of the trawler's engines, but with only the dive knife, he doubted he could do both. And that didn't solve the problem of what was happening on the surface. Finning to the bow of Hawk's boat, he saw the cut anchor line still attached and swaying in the swells. There were still five minutes left in his twenty-minute stop, but he had to act now.

One at a time, he discarded his fins and started to pull himself up the line. Just before he reached the surface, he released the clips on the side-mount harness and attached the tanks to the anchor line. Next he undid the clasps on the rebreather and wiggled out of the unit. Removing the knife, he slid it under the wetsuit on top of his wrist and worked his way up the line.

Things got interesting as soon as he was out of the water. The bow was rocking with the seas, taking the loose line with it as it bobbed up and down, throwing his body against the steel hull. In addition to the force of the waves, he was tired, and looking up, he saw the crux of the climb, where the line entered a small opening just below the deck. He would have to lift himself over that and onto the deck, almost impossible with his wounded arm and his current level of fatigue. He thought for a second, then gathered his breath and in one motion swung his legs over his head, grabbing the line between them.

With the added power of his legs, he was able to climb the line, but the swing of the ship threw him against the hull three more times before his feet finally reached the deck. With everything he had left, he tightened his core, lifted his torso, grabbed the bow rail, and hauled himself onto the deck. Breathing heavily, he stayed flat, inching his way back, past the wheelhouse and close to the aft deck, where he could see Hawk. He was standing by the rail, yelling something at TJ across the water, but more troubling was the pistol in his hand.

Mac moved back to the wheelhouse, crossed to the starboard side, opposite of where the action was taking place. Staying close to the bulkhead, he drew a breath and stepped lightly onto the deck. Hawk was fifteen feet away, only the beam of the ship separating the two men, but he was still unaware that Mac was there. The man was ranting, clearly out of his mind, waving the gun over his head. Across on the sportfisher, all heads were down except Cheqea, who was standing across from him ranting back.

Pulling the knife from his sleeve, Mac held it in his right hand and crossed the deck. His dive booties silenced his steps, and Hawk had no idea he was behind him until Cheqea called out.

"Mac Travis, you come to save me."

Hawk must have seen her eyes move and turned to face Mac. Only three steps away, he saw the gun barrel come up. Mac lunged forward, grabbing Hawk around the waist, his momentum taking them over the side. They spun in midair, and before they hit the water, Mac heard a shot fire. The two men were in the water now, grasping at each other, but Mac had the advantage of the wetsuit, its buoyancy allowing him to concentrate on the other man, while Hawk was fully clothed and had to expend most of his energy to keep his head above the water.

Mac had him in a headlock, trying to subdue him. He didn't want to kill him, just disable him enough to figure out what to do with him. But someone on the boat had other ideas, and he saw the reflection of the sun on a dive tank as it came slamming down on Hawk's head. Immediately, the struggle ended.

"Who—" Mac started.

"Evil man," he heard Cheqea screaming on deck.

Hawk was facedown in the water now, and carefully, Mac

went to him. There was nothing he could do. The man was dead.

"Why did you have to do that?" he screamed up to the boat.

"Evil man," Cheqea screamed back.

Mac knew he was fighting a losing battle. He needed to figure things out before another boat came over to investigate. Swimming the few feet to TJ's boat, where Mel helped him aboard, he sat on the swim platform with his back against the transom, trying to catch his breath.

All three were dead. Ironhead's body was over a hundred feet below the surface and would probably never be found. He suspected Wallace was still in the hold where he had left him.

"We have to get rid of this." He looked at Hawk's body, floating not five feet from him. He turned when he heard someone wailing behind him. "What's that?"

"Cheqea got grazed by that shot. No real damage, but she's carrying on about some kind of evil," TJ said.

Mac was out of patience. He stood, walked through the transom door, and called to Trufante, "Give her whatever she's got in that bag of hers. Have Pamela take her into the cabin. She seems to be able to communicate with her."

Trufante took the women and went inside. It was quiet on deck now, with Alicia, TJ, Mel, and Mac staring at each other, wondering what to do.

TJ was first. "If Cheqea is all right, I say we tow his boat out a ways and scuttle it."

Mac nodded, looking at Mel.

"He may be right. There's no explaining our way out of this. Better to go missing. It'll be dark in a couple of hours. I agree with TJ," Mel said.

Alicia nodded her ascent. Mac turned and grabbed the boat hook from under the gunwale, extended it, and reached over the side for Hawk's body.

"I'll take it and his boat. You guys just follow," he said.

Mel looked at him. "I'm coming with you."

Mac gave the hook to TJ and jumped back in the water. "Hold on. I'll get him aboard," he called to Mel. TJ released the hook, and Mac grabbed the body, sidestroking to the trawler. He reached the transom, climbed out of the water, and dragged Hawk's lifeless form aboard. Leaving the body on the deck, he went to the wheelhouse and started the engine. He looked back, then dropped the engine into reverse and backed down on TJ's boat. When he was a few feet away, he called over for Mel to climb onto the gunwale and jump. She landed on the deck and came beside him, giving the dead body a wide berth.

Together, the boats ran out to the three-hundred-foot line, deep enough that Mac had no worries about the wreck being discovered. Mel had run the boat while he prepared to scuttle it. He dragged Hawk's body down the stairs and stashed it in the same hold as Wallace. Then, he weighted the bodies, left the door open, and started to locate the thru-hull fittings, opening each one as he went. Water started to flood the lower deck, but he knew it would take an hour or so before it was high enough to endanger them.

The trawler was starting to list to starboard, drifting beam to the waves. TJ steered alongside, allowing Mac and Mel to hop off the sinking boat. He moved a few hundred feet away, far enough that his boat would be free of the inevitable whirlpool created when the trawler sank.

A cloud of smoke floated from the cabin when Trufante, Pamela, and Cheqea finally emerged to join them at the rail and watch Hawk's ship take the first wave over her port side. The ship rolled, taking more waves. It wasn't long after sunset that it finally disappeared below the surface.

Chapter 31

Despite having Mel next to him in the forward berth, Mac slept little after their watch. He had reversed the shifts from last night to mitigate any effects from the shortened decompression stop, but rest eluded him. Trufante and Pamela had taken the first watch, with TJ and Alicia on now. He couldn't get comfortable after the beating his body had taken, and the knife wound throbbed incessantly, the ibuprofen he had taken earlier doing nothing to help the pain.

In the brief periods that the pain abated, thoughts of the three dead bodies they had left behind took its place. He didn't take violence lightly, and although there had been no alternative, he regretted the killings. Slowly, he eased himself out of the bunk, trying not to wake Mel, and moved silently through the cabin, where Trufante, Pamela, and Cheqea were asleep. He climbed the ladder to the bridge and sat on the aft bench.

"No sleep?" TJ asked, turning to face him from the helm seats.

Alicia was typing something on the laptop, but looked up. "You okay, Mac?"

"Yeah. You'd think it would have been easy, but no," Mac said.

"Want to talk about the dive?"

Mac looked out over the ripples on the water visible in the

moonlight. They were back in Sister Creek, but instead of the main channel, they had taken a side canal and were surrounded by mangroves. The privacy was reassuring, but with it came the mosquitoes and black flies. He swatted at something on his forehead and tried to find the flaw in their plan.

"Sure. Pretty simple, really. No depth concerns, the deepest canals I've seen in here are twenty feet. With the scooter, we should be able to cover the two miles pretty easily," Mac said.

"I've got a full charge on it," TJ said. "Daylight's in about an hour. We should gear up soon."

Mac looked toward the east, willing the sun to rise. There was nothing dangerous about what they were about to do—he was just ready for this whole affair to end. "I'll go down in a few and get the gear organized."

They sat together in silence for a few minutes, the only noise the buzzing of the bugs and Alicia on the computer.

"What're you so busy with?" Mac asked her.

She looked up, and he could see the shadow of the rings under her eyes in the reflection of the screen. "Filing the claim for the wreck. I want to get this in before there are any questions."

Mac nodded. As he had expected, Mel had convinced everyone to do this legally. He had no expectations of getting rich even if it did yield. The silver he was hoping to recover this morning was going to be his payback. The sky lightened slightly, giving the first indication of dawn. "Ready?" he asked TJ.

They climbed down to the deck and worked in the dark, setting up their tanks. Mac was grateful for the simplicity of the standard BC and regulator setups that TJ had aboard as backups for his charter customers. After the last few days of technical diving, it was a welcome relief. Their plan was to get in the water just as the sun broke the horizon. They would be in the dark for the first section, but it would be easy to navigate the main channel with the phosphorescent light of the compass. They knew it would be a challenge without lights, but both preferred stealth to convenience, and once they reached the side canals, there should be enough sunlight penetrating the murky water.

Mac and TJ sat side by side on the swim platform, with Alicia behind them, waiting to hand off the scooter and a backboard they had rigged with inflatable floats. The first rays of sunlight were visible now, and Mac gave the thumbs-up sign. Together they slid into the water and looked back to Alicia. She handed TJ the scooter and Mac the backboard.

It was awkward navigating the dark canal, but after several near misses with the bottom, they finally got the hang of the setup. With the backboard tied to a short line directly behind the scooter, they each grabbed a handle. Without being able to communicate, Mac navigated with the compass, steering the unit with his handle, and TJ held the other, working the throttle. The buzz of several motors passed overhead as they crossed the main channel, probably fishermen out to get the morning bite. But they were plenty deep to avoid the propellers. Finally the sun gained sufficient altitude to cast enough light on the water for them to see, and they entered the side canals. Mac worked through the canals by memory, finally making the last right turn and entering the canal where he had seen Hawk stash the treasure.

The scooter pulled them down the dark canal, until the bridge pilings were just visible in front of them. They had passed the spot where he remembered seeing Ironhead dive, but the bridge was the only landmark. They would backtrack from there. The visibility was bad, his hand barely visible at arm's length, but that was to be expected—the benefit being they would be invisible. Even if someone saw their bubble trail, it could easily be explained as an underwater spring or manatee.

Reversing course, he tapped TJ on the shoulder and motioned to the bottom. He set the scooter down, and together, remaining only an arm's length apart, they started combing the rocky floor. The first pass yielded nothing, but the sun was higher now and, along with the incoming tide, improved the visibility. His air gauge read two thousand pounds, enough to recover whatever was here and make it back to the boat—if they found it quickly.

Able to work farther apart now, they went back over the same ground. Mac noticed something off to the side and, at first thinking it was a shark, saw TJ signaling to him. His heart sank when he saw it was only an old lower unit from a discarded engine. Faced with the reality that there was nothing here, he checked his gauges and signaled TJ that the dive was over. The silence of the water was overwhelming as he tried to figure out what had happened to the packages he had seen Hawk place just the other night and how to tell the crew they were not there. They reached the main channel, and he navigated across until they turned left. With the poor visibility, they had to surface before reaching the boat.

Alicia, Trufante, and Mel were all standing on the swim platform, eagerly waiting for them, and he saw the disappointed look on their faces when he handed up the empty backboard.

"It's not there," he said, stripping off his gear.

"What could have happened to it?" Mel asked.

"I got a good mind it was his ex. She's in everyone's business," Trufante said.

They all turned to look at him. "Makes sense. She could have seen him put it down there the other night."

"I know her," Mel said. "Maybe we should pay her a visit."

* * *

Mac and Mel walked to the front door. TJ was waiting with the boat at the dock of a vacant house, in the canal across the street. The house had all its windows covered with hurricane shutters, a sure sign it was vacant. They had decided against taking the boat, preferring to walk, thinking it was the better, less alarming option.

Mel knocked on the door, and together they waited. A few

minutes later, a woman whose hair was died a vibrant orange opened the door, a glass of wine in her hand. Her bloodshot eyes indicated it wasn't her first.

"Mrs. Hawk?" Mel asked.

"Yes?"

"It's Melanie Woodson. You were my English teacher in middle school," Mel said.

"Oh dear—Mel?"

"It's me. This is Mac," she introduced him.

"What can I do for you, dear? It's been a long time."

"I was wondering if we could come in and talk to you," Mel said.

"I suppose," she said, opening the door wider and moving inside. "If it's about my ex-husband, I'm afraid I can't help you, though."

If this was not going to yield any information, Mac wanted out fast. The house looked like his grandparents': dimly lit, with plastic covering the aged furniture, and the place smelled of cats. "Come on, Mel. This is a dead end."

"Wasn't that you here the other night?" the woman asked Mac.

She must have been watching. "Yes, ma'am," he said, sensing there was no love lost when it came to her ex. "He has something of mine," he probed. If she had seen him, she might have seen them place the cache in the canal.

"If it's what they put in the canal, he took it before they pulled out of here a few days ago," she said. "Would you like some tea?"

Mac looked at Mel, telling her with his eyes to decline.

"No, thanks, but I'll take a rain check," Mel said.

They said goodbye and left the house.

"It's on the boat," Mac said.

* * *

The weather could have been better, but it could have been worse. With the wind from the northeast, the sportfisher battled the chop that quickly grew into five-foot swells as they moved away from land. Mac was playing the odds, not wanting to wait in case someone had seen them scuttle the boat. He also had another problem: he didn't know the exact location.

"Once we hit the three-hundred-foot line, we'll start watching the depth finder," he said to TJ, who was at the wheel.

"Coming up on it. This is the ballpark, but it might take a while," TJ said. "You sure this dive plan is going to work?"

"Let's find it first," Mac said. Turning to the deck below, he called to Trufante, "Throw some baits out there. Make it look like we're trolling."

"Right on," Trufante said and disappeared into the cabin.

Several hours later, Mac looked up from the depth finder, his eyes tired from staring at the screen. Fortunately, at this depth, the bottom was sandy, with very little in the way of features, making a wreck the size of Hawk's trawler easy to spot. They had loaded a half dozen dolphin into the fish box, and every so often, he heard Trufante call "Fish on" and help Mel and Pamela, who manned the rods. Cheqea must have been in the cabin. It was a good thing they had a diversion, because although treasure hunting was glamorized in movies, in real life it required hours and hours of drudgery.

"Is that it?" TJ asked.

Mac looked back at the screen. There was definitely something there. "Throw the buoy," he called down to Trufante.

"Got to pull this fish in."

"Now! The fish can wait," Mac yelled back. Trufante tossed the yellow float they had rigged with a twenty-pound weight and four hundred feet of line. Mac turned to TJ. "Let's circle back and get a better look."

Mac zoomed in on the bottom, carefully watching the screen as they passed over the wreck again. There was no scale for the length, but the numbers on the side showed it rising forty feet from the ocean floor—just about right.

"I'm going down to rig everything," he said to TJ.

He would circle the site while Mac prepared for the dive. The plan was problematic before it started, the first issue being that they had nowhere close to enough anchor line. It would take close to six hundred feet of rode to safely anchor in this depth. The second problem was the depth. Three hundred feet usually required mixed gasses that they did not have. Instead, Mac would use the rebreather and limit his bottom time to ten minutes. Even with that short of a dive, he would have over two hours of decompression stops. To facilitate entering the wreck, they had rigged tanks to several lines. Dropping one at a hundred feet and the other at sixty would eliminate the need for him to carry them. In addition, TJ would hang at the hundred-foot depth, and Alicia would relieve him when he ascended for his sixty-foot stop. The plan was sound, except it would leave Trufante at the helm.

"Ready," he called up to Trufante. He turned the mask around on his head, checked his gauges, and did a giant stride into the water. Dropping ten feet to avoid the surface chop, he waited for TJ, who met him a minute later. Together they slowly descended to the bottom of the hundred-foot line, where they gave each other the okay sign.

Mac dropped further into the dark water, running the dive profile through his head again. At two hundred feet, he shivered when he hit a thermocline, but soon the top of the trawler came into view. Swimming toward the buoy line that lay alongside it, he unclipped the weight and took the free end of the line with him. In just the few hours it had been in the water, the ship had already attracted fish, but he ignored them and moved to the cabin door. Switching on his dive light, he checked his gauges and started counting in his head. He had five minutes to find the coins.

After securing the line to the door handle, he entered the dark cabin. He moved to the stairs and started to descend, but thought twice about it. If he knew Hawk, the treasure would be in his cabin. Thankful that he knew the deck layout already, he spun around, following the companionway to the door at the far end.

The contents of the room were spread over the floor, and some of the artifacts Hawk had kept were visible, but Mac was looking for something bigger. Moving to the locker, he struggled against the weight of the water to pull the door open, then was pulled inside by the force of the water entering the cavity. Slowly he regained his equilibrium and checked his watch. Two minutes remained, but when he looked up he saw four canvas bags.

There was no way to navigate back through the ship with his fins, so he removed them and slid them under one of the bags. Grabbing one bag in each hand, he walked through the ship, the extra weight helping to keep him on the deck. He reached the line and pulled in twenty feet, where he tied on the first bag. A few feet away, he tied on the next one. He had less than a minute left, but his decision was easy. There was no way he was repeating this or leaving anything behind. Without the weight of the coins, he floated back, grabbing on to anything he could to help pull him along. By the time he reached the bags, he was already almost a minute over his time limit. Hoping there was a safety factor in the decompression schedule, he grabbed the remaining two bags and trudged back through the ship. Tying them both to the line, he released it and pulled himself toward the surface.

The decompression stops had been painfully boring, especially not knowing if the bags really contained the coins. Hawk was surely capable of a ruse. Finally, he was at sixty feet and Alicia met him with a fresh tank. TJ gave the okay sign and finned towards the surface. After another hour, he looked at Alicia and gave the thumbs-up to surface.

Although he was worn out from the dive, he couldn't wait. Dropping his gear, he yelled for Trufante to steer to the buoy and reached over the gunwale with a gaff, snagging the line when he passed. "Drop her into neutral," he called to the bridge and waited for Trufante and TJ to help. With Mel, Pamela, and Cheqea hovering over them, the three men started to pull in the line. Mac could feel it stretch with the weight of the bags, but he willed it to stay intact. Finally, they could see the first bag in the water, and a few minutes later, they were on the deck of the boat.

"Go for it, Mel," Mac said.

She looked at them and went to the first bag. Opening the clasp, she unrolled the watertight seal and stuck her hand deep inside. They stared at her, waiting. Then a whoop soon came from Trufante, and they saw the coins in her hand.

Chapter 32

The group gathered in the cabin surrounding the bags of silver, no one knowing what to say, until Cheqea broke the silence.

"Mac Travis pays Cheqea for favor," she said.

Mac looked at her. "Yes. You'll get a cut, but there's one more thing." They all looked at him. "We're going to file the papers for the salvage rights where the ballast stones are. We'll do it right, and don't expect much profit, but after expenses, whatever we profit will be yours. It is your heritage and legacy."

Cheqea grinned and went to him. He wanted to push her away, but Mel caught his eye and he allowed the old woman to embrace him. "Okay. We better get out of here," he said, turning away.

"Where to?" Mel asked.

"I've got a debt to pay, and then we can figure things out," Mac said, giving directions for TJ to head back to land. They passed through the center span of the bridge, where they turned and followed it back to the entrance to the cove at Keys Fisheries.

They backed into the slip next to the center-console, and Mac left the others on the boat, but it wasn't necessary. Celia was already coming for them, building a head of steam as she approached.

"Effin' Travis. What now? You think you can just come and take your boat after wrecking mine, you got another effin' thing coming," she said, shaking her phone at him.

Mac ignored her and walked back to the sportfisher. He climbed aboard, motioning for her to follow. They went inside the cabin and he handed her two bags. "I think this covers it."

She smiled, grabbing the bags. "Effin' does, and the insurance company doesn't have to know. I'm putting six on the back of the next one."

He laughed and watched her go, swinging her hips as she walked down the dock to the shed.

* * *

After sharing a quick meal together, they stood on the deck. With each group holding their share, they said their goodbyes. Celia had given TJ and Alicia a slip for the night. Tomorrow they would head back to Key Largo.

"What about me, Mac Travis?" asked Cheqea, holding her bag tightly.

"I'll drop you back on the island," Mac said.

She shook her head. "I gotta go see somebody. You wait here."

He nodded and they watched her haul herself to the dock and walk to the shed, where Celia was probably counting her take. There was no doubt that Cheqea would be coming back without the bag, but with enough of her medicine to last a while. That left only Trufante and Pamela.

"What are you going to do with your share?" Mac asked him.

"We have a house to decorate," Pamela said, pulling the Cajun to her.

They shared a laugh at the thought of Trufante being domesticated and watched the two walk upstairs to the bar. TJ and Alicia went up to the bridge, leaving him alone with Mel in the cabin. He started to tense, not knowing where this was going, but desperately not wanting to lose her again.

She came up beside him and put an arm around him. "You going to pay me back too?" she asked.

He pulled her close and kissed her. "And how would you like it?"

"I want to go back to my dad's place," she said, kissing him back.

Thanks For Reading

For more information please check out my web page:
https://stevenbeckerauthor.com/

Or follow me on Facebook:
https://www.facebook.com/stevenbecker.books/

Sign up for my newsletter
Click or enter the address below
Get Wood's Ledge for FREE!
mactravisbooks.com

[Image: view.jpg]

While tarpon fishing in the backcountry of the Florida Keys, Mac Travis discovers a plot to drill for oil in the pristine waters.

Also by Steven Becker

Mac Travis Adventures

Wood's Relic

Wood's Reef

Wood's Wall

Wood's Wreck

Wood's Harbor

Wood's Reach

Tides of Fortune

Pirate

The Wreck of the Ten Sail

Haitian Gold

Will Service Thrillers

Bonefish Blues

Tuna Tango

Storm Series

Storm Rising

CPSIA information can be obtained
at www.ICGtesting.com
Printed in the USA
JSHW032323050420
4986JS00002BA/661